HOODIE

Carl Snyder

Copyright © Year 2026.

All Rights Reserved by **Carl Snyder.**

No part of this publication may be reproduced in any form, or by any means, electronic or mechanical, including photocopying, recording, or any information browsing, storage, or retrieval system, without permission in writing from Carl Snyder.

ISBN

Hardcover: 979-8-90190-187-8

Paperback: 979-8-90190-186-1

Table of Contents

Trouble Trouble 1

Ephemeral Green 9

Invincible 15

Forming Alliances 21

Rude Awakenings 27

Pressure 35

Stand 4 Something 41

Zero to a Hundred 48

The Sun Don*t Shine Forever 55

Full Court Press 61

Point of No Return 67

Stick to the Script 75

Shifting Gears 81

RIDEALONG 85

Low-Hanging Fruit 91

Grass Roots 96

See No Evil 102

Trouble Trouble

The last bullet slipped through the front of the man's oversized skull, then exploded out the back of his head, releasing human confetti into the air, descending all over a girl's pigtails, and finally splattering all over the blood thirsty concrete streets. While he lay there on the ground, I could see the warm liquid oozing out of the back of his busted skull. As the asphalt got moist by gulping the sanguine liquid, I wondered if a beautiful red rose would someday grow through its cracks.

My mother yelled, or rather screamed, my name out of our sixth-floor apartment window, and I hurried over to her beckoning call. As soon as I reached our apartment door, my mother flung the door open and grabbed me by the collar.

"Boy, if you don't get your butt in here," she grunts. "Didn't I tell you if those idiots start shooting out there, you get your behind up these stairs?" Frowning, she continued without giving me the chance to reply, "You run, idiot—like you in a god damn race. Now go wash your face and hands, so you can eat."

It was dinner time. I didn't want to catch HIV, so I washed my face and hands thoroughly before placing myself at the sometimes breakfast but mainly dinner table. As I struggled to eat the last of my veggies, I could hear sirens in the distance, and I sat there thinking, inwardly hoping they were for my mom. No sooner had I finished eating than my mother gave me a grimace look and violently grabbed me, and started tearing the clothes off my body. I could hear the sirens closing in. They were right downstairs! It won't be long now. There was banging on the door. Finally, they arrived to rescue me.

The next morning, I got up, washed my face, brushed my teeth, got dressed, and scrubbed the black stains off my white Nike. As I scrubbed the J's clean, I realized what Billy's older brother Chemistry said was true: all colors do come from black. Smiling, I quickly wiped off the remaining red streaks, then headed downstairs. *Ah!* The air was fresh as I opened the front door. It no longer smelled like the Fourth of July as it did last night. *Oh!* On my way to school, I found a fresh piece of barely used chalk. I knew it was going to be a good day. There was a drawing or a sketch of a person on the ground. I stood looking at it, wondering if I would ever be able to make a drawing as good as this. I did not know, but I knew it was Selfie time! I pulled out my iPhone and snapped a picture next to the sketch. I believe that artists get paid a lot of money. He had to be someone famous because I've seen these drawings all over the world, especially on the streets where I come from.

The strange thing was that they never signed their name, and I used to wonder why they always drew on the ground or floors – never on the walls. Or why it was always people's bodies and not flowers or something else. I might never know. Either way, he was the best! For hours or sometimes days, the work was corded off with beautiful yellow ribbons, so no one walked on it. To make sure no one did, he even has his own police security —I mean detail. That's what they called it, police detail. Just as I finished my thought, Marisol snuck up behind me and started joking.

"Well, well, well, look whose skipping to school like Toto down the yellow brick road," she said jokingly. She was then giggling.

"Ha Ha, real funny, Dorothy from Hades with your red bottoms, oops, I mean bottomless shoes. Is that your pinky toe touching the ground? EELL," I barked back.

Just as I finished my statement, I saw Marisol's pinky toe retracting back into the sole of her green and white Shell-Toe Adidas like a turtle pulling its head back. Now on a roll, I'm animated, bobbing my head like "you're gonna wish you never messed with me." She started it, and I was sure to finish it.

"Now, we know who doesn't wear socks, unless those have holes in 'em too," I shouted, "Holy-Molly! I hope you're wearing underpants—probably those granny panties," I finished, bursting into laughter.

"Okay, I'm tapping out—shut up," she warned before giving me a buggy on the arm.

"Owe?" I yelped.

"Gee, I barely even touched you," she said.

We walked together to school, and as we approached the red and white stop sign, her eyes widened. She glanced at me and lifted up my short sleeve, revealing a rainbow of just reds, blues, and purples. As her eyes became crystal clear, I imagined her singing, "Somewhere over the rainbow where skies are blue." She massaged my shoulder and imagined a new, brighter rainbow minus those colors.

"All right already. I'm not dying. Billy's brother, Chemistry, always says, "What doesn't kill you will only make you stronger, and I woke up feeling like Black Panther!" I exclaimed. I showed off my dynamite moves like Jay-Jay on a Good Times rerun, so I did the Rerun too and shouted "What's happening," and raised my hand in the air to receive a high five.

"Yeah, whatever," Marisol said in a small voice, clearly frustrated, leaving me hanging. After a second passed, she prodded, "Tell me what happened."

"I don't know," I said, looking away, "I can't remember, but I must have had a good dream last night because the last thing I remember is being body slammed into a tub of scolding hot water by Mancho-Man Randy Savage. Mean Gean and even those little Hulka Maniacs were there too," I blabbered in my wrestler's voice as my words tumbled out one after another.

"You're lying! You got another beating. You have to tell," she pleaded with me.

As usual, I dodged her interrogation and searched for a reason to change the topic. Thinking on my feet, I dug in my pocket and pulled out the piece of chalk that I found.

"Look what my favorite artist left me," I boasted proudly, flashing the bright-orange chalk.

"You're just trying to switch the topic, and I don't care what Billy's brother says. There are some things that can kill you, and your mother is no different than that lady in the movie 'Misery.' What does Chemistry know anyway? He doesn't even have a job," she responded, mocking their names.

"Yes, he does. He's a scientist coming into his own," I fired back.

"Yeah, in his own mind," she retorted, and we both started laughing. You see, I knew Chemistry was no scientist, but he sure knew a lot about science. He told me that the 'Father' — whoever that is — taught him everything he knew.

"Hey, what are those black spots on your Js?" she inquired with a suspicious look on her face.

"You mean my LBJs," I corrected her. Whenever she mentioned my shoes, I always had to do my very own rendition of James Brown's Footloose while remixing Miley Cyrus and Juicy J's song, *"James on my feet, James on my feet, James on my feet, uh huh so get like me."* Marisol hated this and always used this big word uh, pro-, pre-, appropriation, yeah, that's it! She claimed that I'm appropriating Michael Jordan's legacy. She was mad because her father wanted to be like Mike, but he couldn't fly like him, so he ended up working in a candy factory. I always asked her how she could say that Jordan is better than the King when we never ever saw Jordan play. Coming back to earth, I said in a quiet voice, "Oh, I thought I got it all." I located the spots, licked my thumb, and bent down to remove the black spots. The black dots immediately liquefied and smudged into red streaks. Before I could bring my thumb back to my mouth to get rid of the red smudges, Marisol grabbed my thumb and began to shout.

"What are you crazy, that's blood!" she began shouting in disbelief, but I interrupted her mid-sentence.

"That's not my blood," I informed her, and then frantically wiped the cherry-red streaks off my thumb.

"Really," she remarked, looking at me with a doubtful expression.

"See, I told you Billy's brother Chemistry knows a lot because that proves that all colors do come from black," I said, defending one of my idols.

"No, it doesn't. It just means that blood turns into a really dark red color when it dries. So, if it isn't your blood, then where did it come from and whose is it?" she prodded.

I sighed and thought to myself, my brain speaking on its own, *"She thinks she's so smart. She likes to ask these three-part questions to trip me up. When she grows up, she should be an investigator or a district attorney because she's really good at interrogations. If I let her, she would probably waterboard me for answers. She might make a good dentist, too."* I was really just buying time because she was tryna get me to snitch. I said to myself, *"I may be a lot of things, but I'm nobody's snitch. You'll never take me alive, copper!"*

"Hey, snap out of it," she snapped her fingers. We had already arrived at the front of the school building. Woo, saved by the bell, literally.

"I'll see you later, Dorothy from Hades," I hurriedly said, and took off running into the school building, feeling like I dodged a bullet. Unfortunately, for me, I didn't look in the direction that I was running, and of all the people to run into – out of the gazillion students bustling through the hall – I ran right into Ms. Mitcheck, the school dean. I bounced off of her round belly, practically knocked her over, and broke my chalk into two pieces. It turned to dust the moment it came in contact with her number twelve men-sized shoes. To make matters worse, I forgot to wipe the blood off my sneakers, and just like a hawk hovering over its prey, Ms. Mitcheck zoomed in on the blood. It seemed that she could smell it as she lifted her nose and moved closer to get a better look. I was in big trouble now. What would I tell her?

"Mr. Hoodie, now you know there is absolutely no running in these halls. Never!" she emphasized, waiting for me to fill in the rest of the line she stole, or rather uh, pro-pre-ated from Smoky.

"Ever-ever-ever-ever run around these halls no more, never ever," I said, dragging the last syllables.

"Now, get up because you have some explaining to do, young man," she said, tilting her glasses, squinting at the red streaks on my Js—that's LBJs.

My head and shoulders slump down as we walk to the dean's office. I can hear a chorus of whispers and giggles in the background. Just great! No support from my peers when I needed them. They even have the audacity to murmur, "ooh, ooh, somebody's in trouble-trouble." Uh! Pro-pre-ating the late great Bernie Mack's line in Player's Club, "Trouble-trouble, gonna be some trouble," he was hilarious. A wide grin spread across my face as the thought occurred to me.

"Is something funny, Mr. Hoodie?" Ms. Mitcheck asked.

"No, no, absolutely nothing funny, man. I mean, ma'am," I shook my head.

"Excuse me. Oh, you think this is a joke. We'll see how funny it is when the police officer gets here," she responded.

"THE POLICE," I shouted in my head.

Whenever a black child got into the slightest trouble in school, the white lady always had to call the police. I didn't shoot anybody. It was always about racial profiling, and I was a victim of it today.

Yeah, she's racial profiling me, I think to myself.

"Ms. Mitcheck, please do not call the cops on me. I won't run in the halls anymore. I promise! Ms. Mitcheck, please, you don't understand. My mother's gonna kill me," I ranted, pleading for my life. I tried to pull her in the opposite direction, but she dragged me along like a lifeless doll. Her office was getting closer and closer. I knew I couldn't survive another beating right after the one I received last night. Trust me, my mom thought of herself as the rapper Drake. She doesn't have a problem with Meek Milling Me, back-to-back, or three-peating like Jordan. My mother would beat me so badly that I couldn't tell if it was real or a nightmare. I remembered someone telling me, "You got knocked the fuck out." She always beats the memory out of me. I never went into the details or recalled them, as Chemistry called it the devil's lair.

"Well, you should have thought about that before you ran through these halls knocking people over, attempted to start a school riot, and you're obviously involved in a crime. Hoodie, you're a no-good criminal. You're going to jail," she bragged.

Criminal—going to jail—I'm no criminal. You knocked me over and broke my chalk. I never incited a riot. She's trumping up charges on me—I'm being framed. My mind was racing as I retorted to comebacks. I went back to pleading.

"I can't go to jail. I'm too young for prison. Do you know what they'll do to me? They'll eat me alive in there. Ms. Mitcheck, please reconsider!" I was begging her now.

She smirked, "Reconsider. Where do you get these fancy words from, Hoodie?"

"IDK. I mean, I don't know. CSI, I guess," I answered her. I was no fool. I could tell she was fishing again. We finally reached her office. I was nervous and sweaty from trying to pull her in the other direction. It was like pulling a freight train, or maybe it looked more or less like waterskiing – like being pulled by a speedboat. I collapsed on the floor as we entered her office.

"Hoodie, if you don't get up off that floor right this instant, I will call your mother," she warned me, resting her clenched fist on her hip. I was lying on the floor thinking, what if I just lay down here until the cops arrived? Yeah, I bet the tables would turn. I could easily tell them that she balled up her fist, and the next thing I knew, I was on the ground, or maybe I would just tell them she touched my doggie, and she would really be in trouble. Nah, I couldn't do that because even I knew that was wrong—that was no white lie. I guess that's a black lie because the punishment was extremely severe for wee-wee touchers. Grudgingly, I sprang up off the ground like Black Panther. I'm used to being knocked down, so I'm experienced in getting back up or playing possum if I even get a whiff of an extension cord. I'd rather be shot with an AR-15 than be hit with an extension cord. They killed dreams and birthed nightmares. Just the thought of an extension cord brought me to tears, and I dropped to my knees as if I were praying—palms pressed together.

"Please, Ms. Mitcheck, look in your heart—you gotta look in your heart," I begged her, shaking my prayer hands, as I did my best impression of the Irish gangster in the movie "Miller's Crossing"—he plays the bullying-older brother in Spike Lee's "Do The Right Thing." I could tell by the look on her face that she wasn't going for it. She couldn't care less if my mother succeeded in beating the shit out of me. She had not been successful yet. I would never let her make me shit my pants. What was she thinking anyway? Who made someone shit on themselves and thought that's okay? Was I adopted?

Raising her voice, she screamed, "Get up off the ground right this instant." No sooner than the words left her mouth, the school resource officer entered the office. The tension around the room changed as she collected herself and appeared composed. Two-faced? I just looked extra frightened as I got up from the floor, trembling.

"Please don't hit me anymore, Ms. Mitcheck," I yelped and ran behind the school resource officer.

"What! I never—I would never," she stuttered, looking at the school resource officer. She emphasized never as she tried to convince him. I clenched his pants and from behind him, I smirked at her., I stuck my tongue out at her, and that really pissed her off. She lunged forward, but before she could reach me, the school resource officer shielded me.

"Ms. Mitcheck, I'll have to report you," he warned. She looked at him, stunned.

"He's lying, and he just stuck his tongue out at me. I won't have any of this—I called you to this office because the little credent has blood on his shoes. Let's see you con your way out of that, you little…" Before she could finish her statement, the resource officer cut her off.

"Ms. Mitcheck," he said firmly before looking down at me. I thought he would point out that "Hoodie was just a child." You gotta love these children's rights. Once we got gay rights, I knew kids' rights weren't far behind. But, unexpectedly, he bent down to get a better look at my sneaker, and without any second thought, I attempted to hide one foot behind the other. He caught me red-handed and looked up to find me looking in the other direction.

"Mr. Hoodie," Ms. Mitcheck said, dragging out the syllables in my name, realizing that I lost my cool, "Please explain to us why you have blood on your shoe? Where did it come from, and whose blood is it? You're obviously not bleeding anywhere that I can see," she questioned.

Oh no! I think to myself, hoping that she isn't contemplating searching my body.

"Yes, Mr. Hoodie, where did this blood come from?" the officer demanded, standing up and towering over me. Boy! How soon the tables have turned.

I thought of a response quickly. I hurriedly explained, "I kicked a cat—a dead cat—and the blood got all over my shoe. I tried to wipe it off. I thought I got it all. I couldn't really see that well because it was at night, and I had to get up early for school. That's all I know," I finish my statement, trying to catch my breath. I was a mess. I began to fidget. Not knowing what to do with my hands, I tucked them in my pockets.

"Hmmm," the resource officer exclaimed and reached for his radio. He turned to Ms. Mitcheck and said in a firm voice, "Ms. Mitcheck, I think I'm going to have to call this in. The police are looking for a five-foot-nine suspect responsible for a recent murder."

Five-foot-nine, I'm only four-foot-nine; the real suspect was at least a foot taller than me. I immediately started yanking on the resource officer's arm, who suddenly had an ignorant case of 'I'm not looking at you.'

"I'm just over four feet tall. I didn't kill anybody. I didn't see anything, I don't know anything. Please, you gotta believe me." I pleaded with him. But, he wouldn't even look at me, and Ms. Mitcheck was grinning from ear to ear.

"No, Mr. Hoodie, you're going to jail," he said bluntly, still refraining from looking at me.

"Why am I going to jail? I didn't do anything," I pleaded.

"You're going to jail for the murder of…" he paused and looked like he was choking on his words or something. Then he blurted out, "The murder of an innocent feline."

Before it registered to me that they were pulling my chain, they burst into laughter. I started laughing with them, or rather at them. They didn't even suspect a thing. It was obvious that he didn't make it through the police academy, and that's why he was just playing school cop. So pathetic, I thought to myself, slapping my knee and getting a real laugh in.

"Why are you laughing?" Ms. Mitcheck questioned and turned her full attention to me. "Ya'll is funny. Ya'll crack me up," I said with my amusement. Though it faded away as I noticed neither of them was laughing anymore.

"It seems to me that you are laughing at us, as if we've forgotten about that blood on your sneaker," The resource officer commented suspiciously on my behavior. "You didn't actually think I fell for that, Mr. Hoodie, did you? For crying out loud, I used to be a mall cop. Do you know how many young punks—I mean—young-criminal-shop lifters have tried to pull a fast one on me, do you?" He screamed. I took a step back as it screamed 'bad cop' all over. Oh! I was so scared now, was I?

"The cat was already dead when I got there. I didn't kill it," I spoke firmly..

"I thought you said it was a dead dog," he responded, and before I could challenge him, Ms.Mitcheck chimed in.

"Yeah, I thought you said it was a dead dog."

"I did?" I responded, baffled by this turn of events.

"Yes, you did," She claimed.

"That's what I heard," the resource officer said.

"Man, I'm tripping," I mistakenly thought out loud.

"You what?" He asked.

"I meant, I mean, I don't know. I want to speak to a lawyer." I blurted out.

"A lawyer!" They say simultaneously with their eyebrows raised. I suddenly realize that I'm not too good at this cop-and-robber stuff.

"Why would you need a lawyer? I'm going to ask you one more time, Mr. Hoodie, where did the blood come from?" He demanded in a stern voice. I chose to stay quiet and did not utter a damn thing. *'Shoot, I can play hardball too,'* I thought to myself.

"Okay, so you want to play it like that," He shook his head up and down. He looked towards Ms. Mitcheck and asked her, "May I use your phone, Ms. Mitcheck? I'm going to have to call this in, department policy." She didn't even think twice about helping him call the boys on me, one of her own students.

I looked at her and shook my head, thinking, *'She's a snitch.'*

I couldn't believe she would drop a dime on me right in my face. Once I told all the popular kids about this, her street credibility would be forever ruined. I smirked to myself.

"We'll see if you have that smirk on your face when the real cops get here. Oh, I'm sorry," she retorted, realizing that the resource officer was staring at her.

I was not about to stand there and take it anymore. I blurted out, "Yeah, we'll see if you have that smirk on your face when I tell everyone you're a snitch."

"Mr. Hoodie, Ms. Mitcheck is not a snitch. Didn't anyone ever teach you the difference between a law-abiding citizen and a snitch?" the resource officer asked.

"I know a snitch when I see one, and she's a snitch," I snapped at him while I squinted my eyes in her direction.

"No, she's not. Let me help you out. The term snitch is exclusively used for individuals who commit crimes, and in the event that they are caught, they give up other people in exchange for a get out of jail free card. Now, law-abiding citizens are only doing their civic duties when they cooperate with law enforcement. Do you see the difference?" the resource officer asks.

"I guess," I responded.

"Now the question you have to resolve with yourself is, are you a law-abiding citizen or are you Huggie Bear?" he questioned.

"Huggie Bear?" I repeated inquisitively.

"Oh, that may be a bit before your time. Are you a snitch?" he asks.

"Hell no. I mean no—no way," Hoodie replies, shaking his head.

"Then you shouldn't have any problem explaining to us about the blood on your sneakers because you're a law-abiding citizen doing your civic duties," Ms. Mitcheck chimes in.

"That's right, Mr. Hoodie, so what do you say?" the resource officer remarked, bending down to look me in the eyes. He had this big smile on his face -just looking silly.

"What do I say—you'll never take me alive, copper, is what I say. I want a lawyer—tu comprende?" I responded using a little bit of my Spanish to them. Yeah, they thought they had me with that entire citizens' duty bull-sugar. I got their citizens' duty all right. What about a citizen's duty when it comes to Rodney King, Trayvon Martin, Michael Brown, Sandra Bland, or Emmett Till—I was screaming inside. Then the sound of someone knocking on the office door interrupted my thoughts. *'Oh no! It just got real—it's the cops,'* I squirmed inwardly.

"Good afternoon, officer," Ms. Mitcheck greeted the black officer as he entered the room.

"Good afternoon, I'm Officer Day. You called about some suspicious blood on one of the students?" He enquired, looking from Ms. Mitcheck to the resource officer.

"Yes, our student Mr. Hoodie here has some blood on his sneaker, and he has not been straightforward about how it got there," the resource officer informed him. Then, the real cop looked at me, and all I could think of was KRS One's song Black Cop. As I played the song in my head, all I could think was, *'Officer Day, you look more like officer night—midnight.'*

"Mr. Hoodie," he extended his hand out in a handshake gesture. I looked at his big, crusty paw and back at his face and repeated it twice before finally giving him a closed fist bump. He noticed my reluctance to shake his hand. Shoot, I was hoping he got the picture and pulled it back. What was he thinking by coming in here with hands that looked like he threw powder in the air before a basketball game?

"Officer Night, I mean Day," I responded, and while Ms. Mitcheck couldn't hold back her laughter, the school resource officer had an embarrassing grin on his face, holding back his tears.

"That's okay. I get that a lot, but where did the blood come from, young man?" he questioned.

"I already explained to them that I kicked a dead cat last night. I thought I got all the blood off my sneaker," I responded firmly.

"Well, I guess there's no crime in kicking a dead cat. Now, where exactly did this take place?" he poked with a follow-up question.

And not able to think of an answer quickly on my feet, I blurted out: "Uh, IDK, I mean I don't know—I can't remember." Man, I was horrible, tripping over my own words. Even a blind woman could tell I was lying through my teeth.

"Okay, I see. Have you contacted his parents yet?" he asked, addressing Ms. Mitcheck.

"We were just about to do that before you arrived," she responded.

"Mr. Hoodie, what is your home phone number or a number where I can reach your mother?" she asks. Now, I knew she didn't really expect me to give her my mother's number.

Shoot, she'd better look through her files—her lazy ass.

"Oh, it's 555-2555," I gave her one of those movie numbers. Officer Midnight just looked at me and smirked as he noticed Ms. Mitcheck dialing the number to Hollywood Boulevard.

"It's a fake number," the school resource officer blabbered, obviously still trying to prove himself eligible for the police academy. Ms. Micheck lost her cool, slammed the phone receiver down, and caught the attention of both officers. *'This is it."* I knew I was done for and jumped back to curl up behind Officer Midnight. He looked down at me and then back at Ms. Mitcheck. And sure enough, the look on the school resource officer's face showed his concern about not getting credit for a bust. *Let's see how fast his citizen's duty kicks in.* My mind made a snarky comment.

"Excuse me, Officer Night, I mean Day, I think there is something you need to know," The officer stuttered. Boy, the look on Ms. Mitcheck's face was priceless. She knew he was about to throw her under the bus.

"Mr. Halsey," she blurted out and tilted her head in a gesture that said - *if you're even thinking about doing what I think you're about to do, don't.* Unfortunately for her, the black cop picked up on it, and it just made her look guilty for what Mr. Halsey was about to reveal.

"Well, you see when I, when I came in here, the boy was sprawled out on the ground. When he got up, he yelled out, 'Ms. Mitcheck, don't hit me anymore.' She immediately denied it, but she has made several aggressive actions like we've both just witnessed that corroborate the kid's statement," he finished, really adding on the Law and Order language.

"Wait, no. He's lying. I can explain," she raised her voice an octave or two.

"Ma'am, I'm going to have to ask you to calm down," Officer Midnight said firmly.

"No, I will not. This is bullshit and you know it!" she yelled, pointing her finger at Mr. Halsey. He gave her one of those I-didn't-know-what-else-to-do shrugs.

"Don't you give me that, you black bastard," she barks, infuriated.

Oh no, she didn't' and right on cue, I looked at the black cop, and the next thing I knew, Ms. Mitcheck was in handcuffs being hauled off to jail. Now that's what I called the school-to-prison pipeline finally working for the people. It was epic, all of the students who were laughing at me were now laughing at Ms. Mitcheck shouting.

"Trouble-trouble gonna be some trouble," they even chanted, "lock her up, lock her up."

Word on the street was that on the way to the precinct, Ms. Mitcheck turned into Taylor Swift, trying to save her own tail. She gave up the whole administration at breakneck speed. She even gave up the innocent school secretary for concocting marijuana laced Christmas cookies for the annual employee holiday party.

Ephemeral Green

Just when I thought I had escaped a bullet, I came back to the reality that I would have to face my mom when I got home. The school resource officer coordinated with the arresting officer and placed a call to my mother, requesting her to report to the precinct. I was allowed to remain at school for the remainder of the day. They may as well have sent me home because the only thing I could think about was the ass whooping I was sure to get when I got home.

I could hear my mother now, *"Didn't I tell you if the school calls me, I was gonna whoop yo ass."* I counted about sixteen lashes, give or take a few, that I was destined to receive.

'You see, in black households, you get a lash for every syllable spoken. I'm no speech-ologist, but I think an ass whooping in Chinese would be much worse.' As I finished my thought, Marisol came sneaking up behind me again. I really believed this girl could be an assassin.

"Everyone's saying you snitched on Ms. Mitcheck," she said in a snooping way.

"What. This can't be happening. I'm screwed at lunch time," I responded.

"If you're sticking to that story, then you're definitely screwed," She remarked.

"Sticking to what story? I haven't even told you anything yet. See, there you go again, being an interrogator rather than a friend," I reminded her for the thousandth time.

"I'm sorry. I can't help it. It's in my blood. I'm a certified snooper, and I'm darn proud of it. Do you know how many followers I can generate with the latest gossip? Boy, my IG is gonna be lit!" She finally admitted, getting all excited like a kid in a candy store. Wait, let me rephrase that because I get excited in candy stores. She got all excited like a baby eating a cheese doodle. Yeah, she drooled with orange cheese powder all over her face, looking like an orangutan with ponytails.

"And to talk about snitching, huh. You wanna be a certified dry snitch, a no-good-dime-dropper," I replied.

"And a good one too. I don't have any shame in my game. I plan to speak truth to power. So, if you wanna come to school with doo doo on your sneakers, then don't get mad at me for telling it like it is. Like the rapper Yella Beezy would say, 'that's on you, baby,'" she said in such a proud way and started doing the Nay-Nay, sticking her tongue out.

I had nothing, so I gave her the finger. Well, I actually gave her the index finger, but it looked like the middle finger. She got all roweled up, acting like she wanted some smoke. I just swerved all that hate. *"She won't get to You too me,"* I thought to myself.

"Listen, if you sing like a canary all over social media, it's the same thing as snitching, and on your friends, that's the worst," I said. My voice rose an octave or two. She immediately became conscious of the other students roaming the halls.

Now raising her voice, she uttered, "Wait a minute, you're not gonna turn this on me. The word on the street is that you're a snitch, not me."

"I'm not gonna be too many snitches," I warned her because now I'm roweled up, stepping towards her. She just looked at me, rolled her greenish-brown eyes, snapped her fingers, did one of those model spins, and headed in the other direction, mouthing off: "Save your breath, fat boy, you couldn't beat a flight of steps."

I just looked at her. I was now conscious of everyone roaming around, and she just body shamed me in front of all my peers. Usually, this would mean war, but I'm a marked man and in no position to be creating frenemies. According to the rapper Fabolous, a frenemy was a supposed friend who was more like an enemy. Besides, Marisol knew too much. She knew my whole itinerary, and that could put me in real danger.

"I'm not fat. I'm chubby," I yelled at her back as she faded into the very crowd that became an audience, bursting into laughter at my remarks. I ducked my head and took off running in the other direction, and I swear I noticed a whole bunch of kids pointing fingers at me. The word was out. I had about ten minutes before lunchtime, and just like that, Marisol gave me an out.

I started reasoning that it was an opportune time to go on a diet, so there was no need to go to the school cafeteria. I remember the last snitch who got crucified at lunchtime. Kids actually mocked the poor kid Marvin in effigy. I had no plans of suffering the Trump effect. I'm not giving my fellow democrats a chance to throw me out with the bathwater. I had to clear my name, and I knew just what to do. It was time to get down and dirty and tell it like it is.

Within minutes, I was at my locker retrieving supplies to carry out my plan. Once I pulled this off, no one would ever think to call me a snitch ever again. Rumbling through my locker, I finally found what I was looking for – stink bombs! In order for this to work, I needed at least three to make things, *"Smokey,"* I said in my best Jim Carry impression of the Mask.

I had about a minute until the cafeteria would be filled to maximum capacity. I kneeled down outside the school's PA system room. I took two deep breaths, lit all three stink bombs, snatched the door open, and launched them into three different corners of the room. The smoke filled the air immediately with the foul order in hot pursuit. The school announcer flew out of there, gasping for air and at the same time holding his nose. He looked like he was about to throw up. I flew in there and, like a rapper in the Stu, I went in.

"Listen up, all you chicken-eating mother suckers. Yeah, you sucked up that titty milk too."

I could see all of them now shaking their heads in denial. I heard later that quite a few kids actually spit out the container milk they were drinking at the moment they heard my accusation, as if they had flashbacks.

Now back to what I was laying down on the people. "I'm here to set the record straight. Hoodie will never be nobody's snitch or bitch – mic drop," I announced and flew out the door just in the nick of time.

The school resource officer was right on my tail. Lucky for me, the smoke clouded the hallway, so he could barely see me as I darted down the hall. There was no way he was catching me in my J's. That business earlier with Ms. Mitcheck was a fluke. Just imagine running full speed into an airbag being deployed, I bet you'd be knocked clean on your ass too.

No sooner than I entered the cafeteria, I heard Marisol in the distance shouting, "That's my boy!" with a chorus of *"Hoodie, Hoodie, Hoodie"* following her statement. The next thing I knew, I was being bum rushed by a crowd of students chanting my name, and I was instantly thrust on top of a future lineman's shoulders and paraded around the cafeteria. Then it felt like the hand of Almighty himself snatched me by the collar, clean off the baby bear's shoulders. Feet dangling in the air, I struggled to turn around and saw none other than the mall cop.

Looking down at the ground, I realized how high he had me in the air. We were eye-to-eye. I started yelling, "I'm not fat, I'm not fat," and all at once the whole cafeteria started chanting, "He's not fat, he's not fat." It was epic, at least until my shirt gave way, tearing off my body and dumping me to the ground shirtless, revealing my chubby belly.

The entire cafeteria went silent, and then suddenly I heard a really faint chant start picking up steam, and now everyone chanted, "he is fat, he is fat, he is fat." The room erupted into chants and laughter, but the school resource officer was not laughing at all. Instead, his eyes were nearly bulging out of his head as he looked down at me. He immediately draped what was left of my torn shirt over me and whisked me out of there like I was POTUS.

I got one last glimpse of Marisol with her mouth wide open. I even read her lips as she silently mouthed, "uh-oh." The cat was out of the bag, or rather out of the shirt, and all I could hear in my head was the tune, "Somewhere over the rainbow."

As soon as we entered the hall, Mr. Halsey stopped me dead in my tracks and started interrogating me.

"Did Ms. Mitcheck cause these bruises to your body? If she did, then I need you to tell me because this is actually much worse than I thought. You won't get in any trouble for telling who did this to you," he tried to assure me.

I just exercised my right to remain silent because, of all people, I knew he would use anything I said against me. He couldn't seriously think that I would confide in him after I witnessed him drop a dime on Ms. Mitcheck. Nope, I wasn't adding any more fuel to the fire that was already raging. I just hoped he didn't take my silence as an admission to anything that I didn't actually say.

And right on that cue, he warned, "Well, I'm going to have to inform your mom about the new intel."

"The new what?" I asked, knowing exactly what he said, I just wanted him to say it out loud.

"The new intel, you know, intelligence," he retorted. I just shook my head in disbelief.

Obviously, he thought things had heightened to the level of an FBI investigation. I didn't trust him either way, but the moment he said, *'inform your mom* rather than *'call your mom,'* it just reinforced what I already knew. He was an unconscionable snitch. He would turn his own mother over to the judge, jury, and executioner. Where I'm from, like 50 Cent once said, "we don't play that."

"Listen, I don't know what you're talking about. I didn't have any bruises on my body until, until you had a Bruce Banner moment and rend me of my clothing, you dig," I said accusingly.

"What, wait, you're not trying to imply that I did that to you, are you?" he demanded, shaking me by the arm. And right at that moment, the school secretary and it seemed like half of the student body walked out of the cafeteria. Boy, he almost shit himself when the secretary called his name out in an alarming manner. And on cue, students started chanting, *"Hands up! Don't shoot! Hands up! Don't shoot!"* He immediately released his grip on me and tried to recover my bruised body.

"I was just trying to get him to tell me who did this to him," he whispered to the secretary who was now approaching us. One of the students yelled out, "We all can hear you, why are you whispering?" Clearly angered, Mr. Halsey looked up and shouted, "Lunchtime is over; all of you need to get to class as of this moment."

"As of this moment," a student mocked him, shouting back from within the crowd, sending the group into roaring laughter.

"Mr. Halsey, please calm down and just take him to the principal's office. I'll handle the students," she says, extending her hand out, gesturing for us to leave in the opposite direction of the crowd that swelled to a mob, reflecting standing room only.

"Okay, students, I need you all to disperse that way and find your classrooms. Today has been an exciting day to say the least, and we could all use some time to reflect on making this school environment a safe and happy place." Before she could finish her sentence, students were scrambling up the hall in the other direction.

I guess it was the soft-Sesame Street language that acted like a mob repellent. Student mobs don't hold up too well without a challenge. If only Mr. Halsey had kept talking a little bit longer, then they would have had to focus on something other than me. Now I had to deal with the school principal. I guess Billy's brother was right – new level, new devil.

Before we reached the principal's office, Mr. Halsey attempted to deter me from implying that he was responsible for the bruises on my body.

He started off, "Now, Mr. Hoodie, there has never been any bad blood between us. I never cited you for running in the halls. I have always been very respectful towards you. Now, prior to you implying that I caused those bruises. I had no reason to discredit what you said about Ms. Mitcheck, and I do recall her claiming that you were making things up. By you falsely accusing me, I have to wonder – are you telling the truth about Ms. Mitcheck? That is, as long as you're making these claims about me," he pleaded, trying to clear his name.

He didn't care about Ms. Mitcheck at all. But, in so many words, he was telling me that as long as I left him out of it, he wouldn't set off any alarms. This guy was really despicable. *"We never really know who is around us,"* I thought to myself.

"No one else even saw these bruises. I have another shirt in my locker. Why don't you just let me get it and cover up?" I suggested. I could see that he was thinking really hard, and then a little smirk appeared on his face. I think I lost my leverage. That's why rule number one is to keep your mouth shut.

"No, Mr. Hoodie, we're going to the principal's office, so you can begin telling us how you got those bruises," he said, as if he had an edge up on me.

"Well, I'll just tell him you tore up my shirt, and the next thing I know, I had bruises," I warned him.

"Listen, kid, I'm not going to risk my job helping you cover up for someone who's abusing you. Wait a minute, are you being abused at home?" he suspected.

"How dare you. My father is a war veteran, and my mother feeds the homeless, works in soup kitchens, rescues abandoned animals, and feeds the homeless – wait – did I say that already? Well, you get the picture. Unlike you, who is a sinner, my parents are saints. Now tell the principal that," I ranted.

"That's exactly what I plan to do," he said and opened the door to the principal's office.

I was doomed. Two calls to my mother in one day and a trip to the precinct, my body was sure to come up missing. I just stood there picturing myself on the back of a milk carton. These people obviously didn't know what my mother was capable of. Marisol was not lying because my mother is ten times worse than the antagonist in the movie *Misery*. There was nothing I could do now.

As I sat in the waiting area to the principal's office, the hall cop was inside ratting me out. Within seconds, the principal stormed out of his office and inspected my body. I didn't even bother to try and implicate Mr. Halsey. I realized that I talked too much, and the information I gave him about the extra shirt in my locker would have been damaging evidence against me.

I reached a reasonable conclusion that it was this very reason he smirked. He would have told the principal about my proposal to allow me to get the extra shirt and cover the whole mess up.

"Mr. Hoodie, you're going to remain in my office until the bell rings. Your mom said that you usually walk home with Marisol Combs. Is that correct?" The principal asked.

I just nodded my head in the affirmative. "Mr. Halsey, would you please go to room 112 and inform Ms. Parker that her student Marisol Combs should immediately report to my office when the bell rings," he asked in a suggestive way.

"Yes, sir, right away," Mr. Halsey responded.

In my head, I was screaming *"just like a good old neggra-yessa"* because he damn sure didn't break those syllables up. At least that's what it sounded like to me, *yessa boss*. Oh, you should've seen this Negra dashing out of the office like he was on strict orders from the President of the United States. Chemistry said that it's Negras like him who keep us stagnated as a people.

I believed him, too, because this fool was bowing his head like he was Japanese and doing all kinds of gestures that a Negro butler would do in a black and white film. I wish I could have slapped his ass. As I sat there waiting for the bell to ring, I started to wonder what exactly the principal told my mom. I had no idea. I was completely in the dark, and that was bad.

"I am for the GI Joe motto: knowing is half the battle. Like my mom would say, I ain't know jack shit! I'm doomed. I'm clearly a jack ass." No sooner than I finished my thought, the bell rang, and Marisol came busting into the office, stormed by me, and went straight to see the principal. She was moving so fast that she didn't even notice me.

I could tell that she was scared to death. I could see her working for the man, and that she could easily sell her own people out. You already knew how she interrogated me. Nah, I was just kidding, Marisol meant well, and she was a down ass sista if I ever knew one. I just wished she would stop using me as a crash-test dummy for her future aspirations of becoming a DA.

Marisol returned with the news, and somehow, she was entrusted with chaperoning me home. I can't believe this. They chose her to ensure my safety. This was downright disrespectful. She was only eleven months older than me, not even a full year. We were the same age for a whole month. I won't hear the last of this. They had officially made her think she's my big homie.

"So I know you're gonna tell me everything," she insisted as soon as she walked out of the office. She couldn't even wait until we cleared the premises.

"There's nothing to tell," I said, rising to my feet.

"Come on, don't be like that, we've known each other since kindergarten," she reminded me. She had a point. We were sixth graders now, and that's a long time. On the way home, I told her everything – well, not everything. Some things were on a need-to-know basis. She tried to convince me that she needed to know, but I wasn't going for it. She needed to respect my privacy and the fact that I lived by the code of the street.

I wasn't telling her or anyone else about the red streaks on my sneakers. *'Boy, I'm really beginning to understand why Chemistry says that colors can get you in a lot of trouble.'* Another thought appeared in my mind.

As a matter of fact, just the other day, some of the older kids suggested that if I wanted to hang out with them, then I should change my favorite color to red. But my favorite color was purple. Those guys were really serious about their favorite color because they beat the shit out of this kid whose favorite color was blue. If my mother heard me say that, I'd get a George Foreman blow straight to the mouth.

Back to the older kids, I think the reason they beat the guy whose favorite color was blue is that he thought blue was better than red. I know who else likes blue, and I'd like to see them try that on. I figured the only reason that they didn't beat me up was because I like purple, and if you mix red and blue together, you get purple. I guess that made me neutral in the matter. I snapped out of the daze I was in, gave Marisol a hug, and headed towards my block.

My block looked like a ghost town, with yellow ribbons flapping in the wind and dusty white pavement tracking each of my steps. I rushed up the stoop's steps in front of my building and entered the lobby. As the door was closing behind me, I heard someone yell out, "Hey, hold up, Lil man."

I don't know where he came from because there was absolutely no one outside. It was him. I thought to myself, he looked rather calm for someone who had just committed a murder. He even had the nerve to smile at me, showing off his gold and diamond-encrusted teeth.

"You know what the word on the street is?" he asks. But before he could get another word out, I blurted out:

"I didn't snitch. Ms. Mitcheck had it coming for her anyway. She allowed the police to arrest Dae Dae, Vernon, Mel Mel, and even little Jimmy for minor infractions. They never killed anybody – oops – I mean harmed anyone," I rambled with the last words leaving my mouth in slow motion.

"Nah, Lil Man, the word is that last night that fool got what he deserved, and ain't nobody missing him, you feel me," he pretty much demands, sticking his fist out, awaiting mine.

"Yeah, I feel you. I never liked him. He robbed Ki Ki's grandmother," I told him as we fist bumped.

"Lil Man, you alright!" he said and exited the building.

I wiped the sweat off my brow and darted into the elevator. My heart was trying to escape from my chest. All I could think about was the fat kid in the movie Juice. You know the one that Bishop shot – the one that starred in the movie 'Lean *On Me.*'

"They used to call me Joe, but now they call me Batman," I said aloud, quoting the famous actor Morgan Freeman's line, trying to calm my nerves, feeling much better that the elevator door finally shut.

'Man, it has never taken that long for the elevator door to shut,' I contemplated with my interlocutor. If you let me tell it, the door even seemed like it jammed for a second, making this slow screeching noise and thunderously slamming shut. It sounded like the gates of Hell slammed behind its new, unenthusiastic resident. For a moment, instead of ascending, the elevator descended. I mean that shit dropped like I was at Great Adventures on the infamous Free Fall ride. As my heart shot to my brain, I came back to my senses, and the door opened to my floor. You would think I would be relieved, but the irony of getting off an ascending elevator reinforced an earlier thought: *New level, new devil.*

I didn't even have a chance to stick my key in the keyhole. The door flung open and, as I remember it, my mother was still standing at least ten feet away in the middle of the living room as the door slammed shut behind me. You guessed it. I was the unenthusiastic resident of hell on earth, and the late Prodigy wasn't rapping – this was not a drill. Shit was about to hit the fan and fly everywhere!

Invincible

The next morning, I got up and raced to the bathroom to brush my teeth and get ready for school. Although I stayed up late last night and made sure I got the remainder of the red streaks off my sneakers, I put on my LeBron Soldier 2 throwbacks. Now, I thought I would have had the day off, but yesterday my mom received a call informing her that I would be allowed to attend school even after all the ruckus I caused. The acting dean said that the circumstances could likely have caused any child to act out. In addition, the school noted that students have due process rights that need to be recognized. So, until a full investigation is conducted, I have permission to resume my normal school schedule. *"I think it's all a bunch of boloney. They are just trying to play nice, hoping that we don't sue and get that big body Benz. Where's the zero tolerance when a kid needs a day off?"* I finished my thought and rushed out the door, flew down the steps, and within seconds exited my building.

It hadn't rained yet, so my favorite artist's piece was still pretty much intact. However, the yellow ribbons were now strewn about, flapping in the wind, up against the black gates, wrapped around tree branches, and plastered against a metal garbage bin. Until today, I had never paid attention to the black letters running the length of the yellow ribbons. Today, they were screaming at me, piercing the firewall I'd created to block out inner city madness. *'Marisol did this to me,'* I thought to myself, and speaking of the devil, she darted out from behind a moving car, practically scaring me to death.

"I didn't think I would be seeing you this morning," she said, apparently looking all over my body for any new wounds.

"What did you think I'd be dead? And before you begin interrogating me, I didn't get the usual floor mopping treatment. I think it's a result of what Billy's brother Chemistry says about being hot. My mom is just waiting for the heat to cool off, and once it does, I am sure to be on the Eye Witness News," I grudgingly informed her.

"Maybe this will be a wakeup call for her because it could be her in jail instead of Ms. Mitcheck. Oh! I heard that Ms. Mitcheck made bail last night," she bragged.

"Really, I can't believe she made bail overnight. I figured she'd at least spend two nights in jail for abusing someone else's child. Oh, I forgot white privilege dictates who gets bail and who remains imprisoned," I complained.

"What! Ms. Mitcheck didn't abuse you. That's a lie, and to make it even worse, you're protecting the real child abuser," she reminded me.

"Well, she verbally abused me, calling me a no-good criminal. Who's the criminal now? I bet she'll think twice before she messes with me again," I fired back.

"What if she retaliates against you? I mean, did you see the True Crime Story episode about the principal who killed some of her former students? They lied on her and she came back with a vengeance," she said, obviously trying to scare me.

"I see you're not wearing your turtle-toe Adidas," I said, changing the topic.

"All of her victims were male students—not one girl," she replied, ignoring my attempts to dodge her efforts to rattle my cage.

"It really is a nice morning," I shot back.

I guess she couldn't take it anymore because the next moment, she blurted out, "Ms. Mitcheck is going to kill you. She is definitely a woman scorned, and you are the reason for her labor pains."

"Ms. Mitcheck isn't pregnant," I blabbered and immediately tried to snatch my words back, realizing that I lost the verbal stare-down battle.

"Ah-ha, I knew you would cave in sooner or later," she boasted, and just as the words left her mouth, we had reached the school steps. My heart skipped a beat, realizing that we were finally here. I dreaded entering the building and possibly running into my attacker. Okay, I have to adrrüt that I began to lie to myself, justifying my false accusations.

'Hey, they do it to us all the time,' I told myself. Besides, she sent five of my boys to jail for minor school infractions. It was karma for her! She turned us into super predators, erased our humanity, and then had the nerve to complain that we were wilding.

"Now she knows how it feels," I unconsciously voice aloud.

Right on cue, Marisol chimed in, "There you go, talking in your head again and unintentionally revealing your true feelings. I feel sorry for you if you choose a life of crime because you are certain to eventually give yourself up and then complain that somebody ratted you out."

"No, I wouldn't," I replied, slowly ascending the steps. Everything was moving in slow motion. I was hoping for a hero's welcome. Shoot, I got rid of the mean dean, but now, I have the whole faculty walking on eggshells.

'Not even one person cared to thank me,' I thought to myself as I walked by, student after student, classmate after classmate. Marisol annoyingly waved her hand in my face, trying to gain my attention. Then she started pointing frantically in the direction directly behind me, warning me to turn around. When I told you, I almost shit myself when I turned around to see a woman who looked just like Ms. Mitcheck standing behind me; it was no understatement. Not even my momma could do it, and that damn Marisol almost got me.

"Boy, you should have seen the look on your face," Marisol got out before she started laughing uncontrollably. I even let out a nervous laugh. All that talk about the True Crime Story must have gotten to me because I started questioning my lies. Some part of me knew that my lies would eventually catch up with me, but I reassured myself that until I had my Jack Nicholson "you can't handle the truth" moment, I would stand on my tiptoes. This country was built on lies. I was not the only bad guy here.

"What that makes you good. No, you not good, you just know how to hide. Me, I don't have that problem," I blurted out, doing my Scarface impression, revealing my true thoughts once again.

"No, buddy, in this instance, you are the only bad guy. I have to admit that Ms. Micheck is really, really mean, and she may even struggle with unconscious bias, but she is the farthest thing from a child abuser. You have to come clean and restore her reputation," she pleaded with me.

I dropped my head in the opposite direction and mumbled, "I have to go to class."

Marisol was right, and the truth was starting to eat me alive. Billy's brother, Chemistry, would have said, "That's your blackness showing because the white man is the father of lies."

"I guess that's why black people always said the devil was a liar. They were referring to the white man." I mumbled slowly, as if having an epiphany. When I reached the classroom and opened the door, all eyes were focused on me. Then the chants of "Hoodie" came flooding into my eardrums, and it sounded like sweet music to my ears, drowning out my conscience. I am a hero! I hesitantly reminded myself. *"They like me, they really like me,"* I said to myself, doing my Jim Carry impression. I don't know why I ever doubted myself in the first place. *'Marisol is just mad that she's not the one who took down Ms. Mitcheck,'* I reassure myself.

Now that I was officially a ghetto-super star, I figured it was the perfect time to start laying down my Mack on the ladies. As soon as I got up the nerve to strut over to the group of girls who were whispering and giggling, obviously about me, our first-period teacher abruptly entered the room, commanding silence by her mere presence. You see, in elementary school, the first-period teacher was no-nonsense because their job was to set the tone for the day. At least, that was what Billy's brother Chemistry claimed. However, all of my first-period teachers since first grade had been really nice. It wasn't until I got to the sixth grade that teachers, during all periods, dramatically changed overnight. I think it was a conspiracy to derail us before we made it to junior high school. I could easily name ten boys who were doing well in school, and then all of a sudden came sixth grade, and the faculty's unquenchable thirst to land them and any other kid that looked like us in detention.

Once a guy started going to detention, eventually the school would call the Boys on you. One kid was even fingerprinted for taking extra chocolate milk at lunchtime! It's a good thing they don't serve strawberry milk because I would have been in a police lineup. And lord knows you don't want them with your picture because they could easily mark you for dead. According to Billy's brother, Chemistry, *'the cops who harass and arrest us also use our photos for target practice at the shooting range.'* He claimed that the proof was in the number of kids being shot in Chi-town. He kinda had me lost on that one, but I still wondered why all of the target pictures were black—why not white?

"May I have everyone's attention now that you all have settled in nice and comfortable?" Ms. Peterson said, hunched over her desk with her glasses hanging from the tip of her long nose. Everyone was completely silent with their eyes fixed on her, and just as always, Billy was glued to the front row. He had a rule to never talk to me during class, claiming that I was too much of a distraction and didn't know when to quit. Whatever the hell that meant. I told him he sounded like somebody's momma. He told me he always gets all A's. He had a point, but I was no slouch myself.

Even through all the inner-city madness and my low-income status, I aimed to be a high achiever. I bet he didn't know anything about landing a ninety-six on a science exam while sitting for an hour straight on black and blue butt cheeks. He lived with his grandparents and had a much older brother. Everyone knew that grandparents don't beat their grandkids because most grandparents are tired of whipping their kids' asses years ago. Now they played like they were all sweet and nice when the real truth was, they were the ones who created the monsters that were giving butt whippings. Although people claimed that the apple doesn't fall far from the tree, our family tree was on a hill, and I promised myself to break the cycle of abuse when I have kids.

"Mr. Hoodie," Ms. Peterson called my name right on cue as if she knew I was in my head and far removed from the classroom.

"Yes, Ms. Peterson," I responded.

"You have to report to the principal's office immediately," she said in a warning tone.

"Ooh," sounded the chorus of student instigators.

'In hopes of laughing at someone else's pain, just like that, unity goes out the window. I can't trust any of these fools as far as I can throw 'em — they're all venomous snakes! I snatch my books up like a G, and I don't even dignify their attempts to see me down.' I thought to myself. With my head held high and chest puffed up, I exited the room. I couldn't help but think the worst. Why did they want me in the principal's office? Somebody must have snitched on me. *'Marisol,'* I thought for a second, *'Wait, I didn't tell her anything. If she said something, she's lying.'* Nobody knew about the cherry-red streaks but me and only me, I reassured myself as I reached the principal's office. When I reached for the door, I noticed the flicker of a badge, and it wasn't no mall cop badge either. It was the real deal. 'Shit!' I called myself, easing my hand off the doorknob to head in the other direction, and bounced right off the mall cop's belly.

"Oh shit, oh shoot, I mean Mr. Halsey. Yeah, I was just about to go get my other, uh, other book out of my locker. I'll be right back," I blurted out and tried to walk around him.

"Where do you think you're going?" he demanded.

"I'll be right back. I just have to get my…," before I could finish my sentence, he opened the office door.

Oddly, he was smiling when he said, "Look who I found about to head in the other direction. It seems to me that he got a good look through the glass of the office door and something spooked him," he said, tapping the badge on his chest.

My thoughts made a snide remark, *"Here he goes again, tryna make it into the academy. He thinks someone is stupid. He's obviously signaling to Officer Day that I was trying to duck him.'*

"No, not true, as I was just telling this mall cop," I said before smirking. Continuing, I informed them that I was only trying to retrieve my book because I did not know how long I would be in the principal's office.

"Well, there's no crime in trying to catch up on your reading, is there?" Officer Day responded. Before I could say a word, he asked, 'By the way, what's the title of the book you're reading?' *'Not this time,'* I think to myself. *'You fool me once, that's on you, you fool me, well, once you get fooled once, it means you can't get fooled again.'*

"Moby Dick," I said flatly.

"Oh, the story about the big fish," he said. Oh, I wanted so badly to say 'no, the story about the big dick,' grab my doggy, bend my knees and rise to my tiptoes, and give him a 'heehee.'

'Shoot,' I figured, he set himself up for that one.

I settled for a safe, "uh-huh."

"Well, I'll walk you over to get it," he offered, putting me on the spot.

"No, that's okay," I hurriedly answered him, giving myself up.

"No, I insist. Besides, it will give me a chance to speak with you one-on-one," he contended.

"One on one," I thought to myself aloud.

"Yes, one-on-one. Just me and you," he confirmed.

Immediately, I realized I had done it again. I slumped my head and headed in the other direction, attempting to take him the long route, and right on cue, I could hear the high pitch of the smallest American coin hitting the ground.

"The lockers are in the other direction," Mr. Halsey yelled out.

"That's fine," Officer Day said, waving him off.

'This guy was good,' I thought to myself.

I guessed there was no more use in trying to get over like a fat rat on him.

"So, I guess you knew that, huh?" I asked him.

"Uh-huh. It's part of my job description to pay close attention to my surroundings. In some instances, knowing where you are can be a matter of life and death, and nobody wants to die," he remarked. His words stung like a bee. I was no dummy either. I don't think this has anything to do with Ms. Mitcheck. From that moment on, I thought it was in my best interest to remain silent and keep my mouth shut.

Picking up on my silence, he restarts the discussion, "As I was saying about paying attention to details, I noticed that you live in the Brown Housing Projects. You wouldn't have happened to be outside the other night when that shooting took place?" I gulped back dry spit, and my Adam's apple revealed my anxiety. But before I could say a word, he warned me, "Now you don't have to answer anything if you don't want to, because technically your parents have a right to be present."

'Woo,' I damn near wiped the sweat off my brow at that news. I guess he really did not know who he was dealing with because my mom would never agree to questioning me about any crimes. I didn't have a thing to worry about.

Confidently, I told him, "Well, in that case, this discussion is over." I finished my sentence, grinning from ear to ear. When he grinned back, I knew I was completely doomed. You see, all along he was gauging my reactions—my body language and my responses. He had me by the you-know-whats.

"Oh, I'm sorry, you didn't let me finish. Your mom gave me permission to question you, She waived her right to be present," he said, grinning from left-back skull to right-back skull. 'There goes my damn Adam's apple again, giving me up.' I thought to myself as the Adam's apple did its thing again.

"You can talk to me, Hoodie," he looked down at me, trying to sound convincing.

"There's nothing to talk about. I wasn't outside that night," I lied.

"Well, the problem with that story, unlike your dead cat story, is that your mom says the opposite."

"Why would she?" I blurt out, not realizing that I was revealing my thoughts again. However, this time I was mad, and when I get mad, I'm nobody's pushover. "What do you have on my momma?" I demanded.

"Why would you think I have something on your mother?" he patronized me.

"Look, Officer Day, I'm not stupid. I know my mother would not willingly allow you to question me out of her presence. She's too noisy," I added to throw a little misdirection, drawing a laugh from him. The truth was that my mother would be terrified of what I might tell them about her whooping my ass unless he knew that my mother was the real culprit and not Ms. Mitcheck. Where the hell was Marisol when you needed her? I was a firm believer in the idea that two heads are better than one.

Officer Day seemed to notice what I was thinking and he responded gently, "Listen kid, I don't think you're stupid. In fact, I know that you are rather intelligent for your age. You kind of remind me of myself when I was younger. You're certainly smarter than that mall cop," he said, drawing a chuckle out of me. No sooner than I let the chuckle escape me, I realized that he was just tryna get me to let my guard down. It was time for me to form Voltron and call on the Black Lion. I could hear the phrase "and the Black Lion forms the head" ringing out in my mind. But before I could say a word, we'd reached my locker. I don't know if the expression on my face gave me away or what, but I didn't want to open my locker. I haven't had a book in my locker all semester. You see, I never make a habit of leaving my books in the locker because you could make an easy target if you always looked prepared. "Oh, he's a good boy," I could recall older students saying before they'd knocked all the books belonging to some poor kid to the ground, and him along with them.

Pulling me back out of my third-grade memory, Officer Day said, "Well, here we are," slapping his crusty hand on my locker—my exact locker! As I slowly raised my hand to the combination locker, I could feel his stare piercing my soul. My hand started to shake as I thought of some way to stall the inevitable of being revealed as a liar. This was crucial because in law enforcement circles, credibility is crucial. If Officer Day knew that I was telling incredible stories, it would lead to more questions, and more questions would require more answers. I was not prepared to tell a thousand lies. Billy's brother Chemistry always said, *"It's harder to keep up with your lies the more lies you tell them."*

Thinking fast, I mumbled, "Could you back up a little? I can't concentrate with you right over my shoulders. Sheesh, I feel like I'm in one of those movies where the bank robber says, 'you have three seconds to open the safe before I blow your…'" Immediately, Officer Day cut me off.

"Woe, woe, kid, it's not that serious. I'll be seeing you around. Enjoy the rest of your day and stay out of trouble, he said as he walked away without even looking in my locker. Although I felt a bit relieved, I didn't like the idea that he would be seeing me around. As his frame disappeared around the corner, I had the sudden urge to shout out, "Not if I see you first." Unfortunately, he was completely gone, and I was left mumbling the words under my breath.

"Boo," Marisol shouted in my ear. She was so loud that it caused me to jump out of my skin. She spun around and pinned my back against my locker, nearly losing my footing.

"Sheesh, what are you crazy? You nearly scared me half to death. What's wrong with you?" I shouted, sounding like I wanted to cry.

"Aw, poor baby," she responded while doing a clown gesture of wiping the imaginary tears from her eyes with her lips puckered up in a sad face. She was the worst, trying to rub my humiliation in—talk about adding insult to injury.

"I see you're not going to be happy until you give me a heart attack."

"What? You're too young to go into cardiac arrest. Of course, that is, minus you subjecting yourself to an unnatural cause like a drug overdose. You're not doing drugs without me, are you?" She inquisitively asked, playing around.

"I just smoked a pound about a week ago," I fired back instantly, remixing Bobby Smurda's 'Caught a Body' song. Continuing, I complained, "Where were you when I needed you? When the man is breathing down my neck, you find a way never to be around—typical Marisol. What are you afraid that being linked to the hood might ruin your chances of ever becoming a D.A.? " I questioned, flinging a number of insinuations at her.

"Boy, please. If anything, my association with the Hood should add to my qualifications. I have what they call 'insight,' but you wouldn't know anything about that," she shot back and placed her fist on her hip like girls do when they are either telling you off or have already told you off. In this case, she was signaling that she had just told me off and was anxiously waiting for my response. I guess she had her hand close to her hip, so she could be ready to fire.

Not knowing any better, I couldn't resist. So, I engaged her naivety. "Have you ever heard of mass incarceration?" Before she could respond, I went on, "I guess not because if you did, you might not be so proud of joining the system that has kept black youth in bonds and chains from slavery and slave codes to black codes and Jim Crow, culminating in Hyper Incarceration." Mocking her, I placed my hand on my hip only to find myself being made a laughing stock as a group of students happened to walk by just in time.

One of the boys shouts out, "Hoodie's coming out of the closet," causing the whole group, Marisol included, to burst into laughter. I didn't waste any time removing my hand from my hip.

"I, I," I spluttered, but man, they didn't even let me give them an explanation as they waved me off. Students love drama, and for them, the version of my coming out was far more interesting than the truthful version about me mocking Marisol.

"Whatever, whatever," the group responded on cue, appropriating the rapper Remy Martin's song. They didn't happen to mind the fact that, in heckling me, they changed their cadence to sound like female rappers. I could even swear down because I saw at least two of them switching and snapping their fingers, obviously, taking the opportunity to come out themselves. But they were gone, and my anger instantly turned on Marisol. However, just like a sista not wasting an opportunity, she jumped all over me.

"You Negroes kill me tryna be all anti-the man, but in all actuality, you are doing absolutely nothing to up end the system. Idiot! Part of changing the system is becoming a part of it so that you or we can have a say so. Just like Langston, I want my place at the cable and my slave code-black code-Jim Crow resisting ancestors don't expect anything less from me and you, brother. The only way to get the man's foot off our necks is to become the man, and anyone, including Billy's brother Chemistry, who tells you different is a damn liar and a fool," she dismissed me. As she turned to walk off, all I could do was smile because that's exactly what Billy's brother Chemistry said.

"Hey, Marisol, wait up!" I yelled out, running to catch up to my sister from another mother!

Forming Alliances

I finally reached my building to find Mr. Easy Street waiting in the lobby. He was draped in all black with the brim of his hat pulled nearly to the rim of his nose, concealing half of his face. It immediately became obvious to me that he was here for me. And right on cue, all of his attention zoomed in on me.

"Hey, Lil man, I heard you had a visitor today," he said, awaiting my response. I could tell by the look on his face that he was dead serious and in no mood for games. All I could think of was going to church with Ga-Ga on Sundays, and I could almost hear her preacher always saying, "The truth shall set you free."

"Yeah, man. It was just a beat cop snooping around about Ms. Mitcheck," I responded, noticing that he didn't follow. I continued, "The school dean that I let Grey Hound run over, the one that got Ray-Ray and them locked up."

"Right, right, Lil man, you all right," he said as he pushed himself off the wall that he was leaning on and walked to exit the building. He must have sensed Billy's brother Chemistry coming up the steps to enter the building. The men brushed shoulders as they went through the door in opposite directions. Chemistry was the much bigger man, standing at least a foot higher than Mr. Easy Street. With his chest sitting directly under his chin, Chemistry turned to look down at the much smaller man, who revealed a sly smile.

"My bad," he said and kept heading in the opposite direction until he vanished.

"What's up, Hoodie? You all right? That fool wasn't messing with you, was he?" He hit me with a series of questions before I could even respond to one of them. Then he just stood there and awaited my response.

"Nah, I was coming in and he was on his way out. That's all, nothing serious," I lied. I could tell by the look on his face that he wasn't buying it for one minute.

"Hoodie, you know I got your back, right?" He questioned, expecting me to answer in the affirmative.

"Hell yeah, I know you got my back," I said, all excited, trying to break up the serious mood that fell over the lobby.

"Listen, man, I know what's going on. You don't have to lie to me. Shit, the whole hood knows what's going on. It's only a matter of time before the cops come knocking at your door if they haven't already. Word on the street is that the boy blew that lowlife's brains out all over your J's and all over some poor little girl's pigtails. Now I know you're struggling with the whole idea about keeping your mouth shut or the whole idea about snitching, but if you ask me, you should have never been put in that position in the first place. I mean, what if one of those bullets would have hit you or that little girl? Bullets don't have names on them, but these fools don't seem to realize that fact," he lamented.

"I gotta go upstairs," is all I could come up with, and then I reached for the elevator door. It was a good thing that he lived on the first floor, so I didn't have to worry about any further interrogation on my way up. Chemistry just nodded his head like he understood. I have to admit that I felt relieved that he had my back. But how the hell did anyone find out about my J's?

'Marisol,' I whispered to myself. *'Nah, she wouldn't have. I mean, she couldn't have because I never told her anything. There were only a few people who even knew about the red streaks on my J's.'* I began to go over them in my head: Marisol, Ms. Mitcheck, the Mall Cop, Officer Midnight, and me. I'm betting Officer Midnight had something to do with this new set of events. He was applying pressure, or rather trying to smoke me out. He was playing a dirty

game that gonna end up getting my head blown off, and I was too young to die. *'I can't let that happen,'* I voiced to myself as I exited the elevator.

The smell of peining hit my nose the moment I stepped off the elevator. Okay, so if you didn't know what that was, I was talking about roasted pork shoulder. If you ask me, Latinos made it the best. For some reason, I started to feel like I was being served up and set to roast on a stake like a poor defenseless animal. But if I was certain about one thing, it was the fact that I would not go out without a fight. When I opened the door, my mom stood hovering over the stove, checking on a pot of rice and beans. She was making my favorite, and that immediately drummed up cause for concern. I hadn't done anything worthy of this kind of treatment.

Something was up, but I just couldn't put my finger on it just yet.

"Hey, there goes my little man," she said, smiling. Now I knew something was wrong. I hadn't been her little man since I don't know, perhaps when I was fresh out of diapers.

"Hi Mom, it smells like you're making my favorite. To what do I owe this honor?" I questioned.

"Well, I just thought with everything going on that you could use a nice home-cooked meal," she said in a soft tone of voice. I couldn't get the image of Hansel sticking his hand out of a cage, as the witch checked to see if his fingers were fattening up. The witch had every intention of eating him and Gretel the moment that they showed signs of fattening. They were sure to end up in the human-sized pot that the witch anxiously stirred with a paddle, adding other ingredients. As my mother stirred, she looked more and more like that witch. Snapping me out of my daze, my mother urged me to go and wash my face and hands. "Supper will be ready in a little bit," she informed me.

On the way to my room, I fumbled through my pocket to retrieve my cellphone. I quickly thumbed a text message to Marisol that read,

'My mother's acting really strange, making my favorite meal!'

Marisol responded with, *'yeah, I think she's up to something. Go and play your video game and see what she says.'*

I didn't think I was using my better judgment, but I took her advice, scrapped freshening up, and instead played the video game, 'God of War.' An hour must have passed before my mom abruptly entered my room.

"Oh, you're in here playing video games. Well, your dinner is ready. Hurry up and finish the game, so you can eat your food while it's hot," she said, smiling. Then quietly exited the room. I was flabbergasted. If I didn't know any better, I would have lost my mind that very instant. I picked up my phone and called Marisol. This was no time for the limits of a text. I needed full responses in real time. Marisol picked up the phone immediately, not even the least bit ashamed of revealing her itching ears.

"Hello," she answered before I could even say hello. Continuing, she asked, "Let me know what the scoop is. Did she whip you for playing the video game, or did she ignore it?"

I thought to myself, *'Damn, this girl is good. How the hell did she know that my mom would even think of ignoring the fact that I played a video game after she distinctly told me to wash up for supper? In my house, that was cause for an automatic Mike Tyson Punch Out session, and my mother would relish being Iron Mike. I had to be about eight years old the first time that I didn't rise after a ten-count. All I could remember was waking up the next morning with a screaming headache and a swollen lip. My mom claimed that I was doing about ninety when I ran into a wall. However, I have a clear memory of bobbing and weaving three of Ball-Bull-type blows before I hit the canvas.'*

After about thirty seconds, Marisol clearly got annoyed with my exiting into the world of my thoughts.

"Hello," she said again with emphasis, dragging out the "o" sound.

"Oh, she didn't even make a big deal about me distinctly ignoring her instructions. Shoot, now she has me going crazy, speaking in her terms," I mumbled a bit overwhelmed at the chain of events that just took place in apartment 6C. I wondered if I was in the right apartment.

Was that really my mom, or was she abducted by aliens?

"Well, unless your mom was kidnapped or abducted by aliens, something is definitely up."

"I know. I was just thinking the same thing. You must have read my mind. Stay out of my head, Marisol. Seriously, stay out of my head," I warned her.

"What do you mean? I'm not in your head. I just know your mom, and I know the way she's acting is way out of character for her. Do you think your mother had another conversation with the cops? I mean, she did start acting strange after the police interviewed her," she said, sounding off all types of alarms in my head.

"I know. I was just thinking the same thing. You must have, wait, you just did it again. Stay out of my head. I'm warning you. As a matter of fact, do you know my man Tone?" I asked, eagerly waiting for her response.

"Tone who?" she asked.

"Dial Tone," I replied as I dialed George Bush, the call-cancel app. Boy, I wish I could see the look on Marisol's face when she realized I got her. Shoot, she deserved it. She was all up in my business. I mean, she did provide some valuable insight, but it was shit I already thought about. She was like one of those rap producers who "wanna be all up in your videos." *'I'm tired of her. I'm taking my talents to Death Row.'* I thought to myself, as images of Suge Knight, P. Diddy, and Bron Bron flash through my mind.

The next thing I heard loud and clear was: "Boy, if you don't get your butt in here and eat this damn food, I'm gonna put my foot up your ass!" It was my real mother yelling at the top of her lungs.

"She's back," I grumbled. And sensing I did not want to be turned into a "rootie tootie candy ass," I acted like I knew better and pictured my Barney-Ruble feet driving a Flintstone mobile to the kitchen. The truth was, before my mom finished her last syllable, I was seated at the kitchen table. You see, in my home, the combination of the words "Boy, if you don't" was tantamount to the combination of words "On your ready, set, go!" Yes, you guessed it. There was an inherent head start embedded in the former. In other words, if you knew better, you wouldn't wait around for the word "go," unless you wanna experience a five to ten. Trust me, you do not want to experience five to ten minutes of my mother whooping yo ass. She was in heavy-weight condition, and if you really pissed her off, she would go the distance on that ass. I was talking twelve rounds of heavyweight boxing, Forman style, grilled, cause your ass gonna feel like it was on a George Forman grill after she's done.

"Yes, mother, I am here," I announced, not even startling her.

She just remarked, "Oh."

"You see, the trick was to make her think she's crazy, so you race to get to or do whatever your mom said before she finished the sentence. That meant you had to have the skill of a ninja and stealth, silence, to convince her that you were there all along. To put it another way, this was my chance to say, "What the hell are you yelling for? I'm right here." That's what she would say, "Now of course, I did that tacitly if not internally. And I mean in my innermost being, because if you think Marisol can read minds, then you haven't seen anything when it comes to my mother. She can read my mind before I even think what I was going to think. How is that even possible?" I wonder to myself.

Continuing, she bragged, "I made your favorite," finishing with a bright-sunny smile. I couldn't help but think to myself, *'Imagine a cigarette brand using her smile in a TV ad to get people to smoke. It would have to go something like the following in a Chris Rock voice: "if you like the taste of butter, try these."*

'"No, I'll pass," I reasonably could see anyone saying, turning down her offer immediately. They would use my mom's butter-yellow teeth to deter people from smoking, if not quit smoking altogether.' I quietly chuckled to myself before nearly jumping out of my seat at the sight of my mother hovering over me, David Blaine style. Yes. Her feet were elevated off the ground. That was my story, and I was sticking to it.

"Boy, get out of your got damn head. I see you have something really funny on your mind. How about sharing it with everybody?" she said. *'Everybody,'* I think to myself, *'it's only me and her in here. My mom must be talking about her alter ego or split personality. Trust me, someone else is living inside her. She is not alone!'*

"Hoodie, I have something really important to talk to you about. You hear me?" I nodded my head up and down in agreement as I chomped down on the mouthful of food. She continued, "You like the food?" I nodded again.

"Okay, so the cops were by here today questioning me about the poor decisions you made. Now, you have to tell the cops what happened out there the other night because I'm not gonna have all this heat being brought down on me about the way I'm raising my child. Shit, they always want to blame the parent. But when a Bitch put foot to ass, they wanna lock a mother fucker up," clearly angry, she vented out.

I was now chomping in slow motion, and I could literally hear every chomp as I tried to slow down in fear of her hearing me chew the food. I could see a vein the size of an extension cord swelling up in her neck. I nervously gulped down the food that now seemed like dry cotton as it went down. I was nearly choking. Hand shaking, I slowly reached for the cold glass of Pineapple Sunkist soda. Okay, it was C&C pineapple soda, but it tasted like Sunkist made it. No disrespect to C&C, though. Just as I picked the glass up, my mother slammed her fist down on the sometimes breakfast, sometimes dinner table.

As things looked like they were about to turn for the worse, suddenly the phone rang, grabbing my mother's attention.

While she went to answer the phone, from the inside of my pocket, I nervously thumbed Marisol a text: "Must be on Death row—just had what was tantamount to my last meal."

Marisol responded, "Is it that bad?"

I responded back, "Yeah, that's why I'm making sure that someone knows exactly what happened if shit goes left. Oh, my mom just hung up I gotta go!"

As my mom approached the table, I eased my hand out of my pocket. I could tell by the look on her face that something had been said on the phone that had changed her aggressive demeanor. She was once again a soft-cookie-baking soccer mom, if there even is such a thing.

Resting her hand on my head, she gently said, "Hoodie, I really need you to understand that giving the shooter up is the best thing that you can do for both of us. You wanna live in a bigger place, don't you—in a better neighborhood. You can have a much bigger room to fit all of your toys in, and you can even have a new bike." I had to admit her offer was sounding really tempting. You just couldn't offer a kid a bigger room and a new bike, expecting him, I mean him or her, not to take it or at least be interested. I hated my room. It was the size of a closet. I think it was a closet because one time I was watching this movie, and the White lady walked into a closet that was bigger than our living room. My room was definitely a closet. As a matter of fact, our entire apartment was a closet.

"A new bike," I squeaked out.

"Yes, baby, a brand-new bike," she said, continuing to con me.

"A BMX dirt bike," I inquired.

"Yes, whatever you want," she muttered, sounding like I was wearing her patience out. She continued, "Look, Hoodie, they gave me this credit card and promised to move us into Section A Housing… " Cutting her off, I blurted out, "Witness protection."

"No, just a new place, honey," she smiled. Now she must really think I was stupid or something. I didn't even know how many cop shows I had seen throughout my lifetime, but one thing I was certain of was that whenever the snitch got moved, it was witness protection! And somehow, the bad guys always located that snitch with a little help from the cops, of course. I didn't know if a new bike, not even a BMX, was worth all this trouble-trouble.

"Hoodie," My mother yelled. "Don't you hear me talking to you, boy?" But before I could answer her question, she went on. "Now I done told your ass to listen to me when I'm talking to you. Something is seriously wrong with you. You always in God damn la la land. Your uncle was like that too, and you see where he end up. In the crazy house that's where and that's just where yo ass gonna end up if you keep acting crazy."

Now I thought to myself, *'something is wrong with me? Shoot, she's the one who has different people living inside of her. One minute she's cool and the next minute its World War Three, but I'm crazy.'*

"I heard everything you said, Ma," I spat out in rapid speed, realizing my little trip to la la land would get me in trouble.

"Well, if you hear me then ass better say something. I'm not playing with you, boy. I tried to do it their way, I mean, I tried to do it the nice way. Now you're wearing my patience. You gonna tell those cops what they want to hear or I'm gonna beat the skin off your body. Shit, if you think I'm going to jail because your little black ass wanna protect these mother fucking hoodlums, you outta your got damn mind. I'll beat the shit out of you first!" she finished off. She was now fumbling through a pack of cigarettes until she retrieved one of the cancer sticks from its pack. "Now pass me my got damn lighter," she gestured at the clear pink lighter right across from my plate.

Without hesitation, I grabbed the lighter and handed it to her. Any other time, I might jokingly flic the lighter to light her cigarette just so she could snatch it from me, but I knew that she was not in the mood for games. Besides, I had to figure out a way to convince her that I didn't see shit. All the promises the police were offering were just complicating things. She would never let up, knowing that she had something to gain. If anything, they played right into her hands. She got to do everything foul under the sun just to be rewarded by the man—*ain't that a bitch*, I thought to myself.

"Ma, I don't know what the cops are talking about because I didn't see anything," I said as smoothly as possible.

"You gonna sit here and lie to my mother fucking face," she grunted, squinting her eyes as if she could feel the hate she had for me in that very instant. "Now say it again, you little lying mother fucker, and I'm gonna bust you right upside your big ass head," she warned.

I sat there silent, knowing my next words could be my last. "I don't know why you got tears in your eyes. Your ass should have thought about that before you went outside. Now, I'm not playing with you. You'd better tell the cops what they want to hear. I don't give a damn who you tell them did it. Shit, you can tell them you did it for all I care. But, yo ass gonna tell them somebody did it. Now wipe that stupid look off your face," she threatened with a menacing look covering her face. In between, steam puffed out of her once long cigarette, and she stared at me with a grimacing look, forcing me to look down in shame.

"I ain't got all day. What are you gonna tell the cops when you speak to them?" she demanded.

"I'm, I'm," I tried to get the words out before being interrupted.

"I don't know what the fuck you're stuttering for. Now spit it out before I beat yo mother fucking ass," she yelled and then smacked me clean in the back of my head, forcing my face down into the place. Her voice rose to the point that the neighbors could clearly hear her. I wished they could hear her threatening me. In fact, I knew they could hear her, just as I'd heard the neighbors upstairs and across the hall physically and verbally abusing their kids. I'd grown accustomed to the high-pitched screams of kids as young as five years old and the overpowering voices of mainly mothers and a few fathers who relentlessly whooped their children like they were chattel slaves. Each beating ended with the threat of being beaten longer if the child didn't stop crying. Abusers often said stuff like: *"Stop crying like somebody is killing you."* Or, *"If you don't quit crying, I'm a really give your ass something to cry about."*

Sniffling, stuttering, and trying to hold back my tears, I finally muttered, "I'm, I'm, gona, gonna tell them what you said."

"What the hell you mean you gona, gonna tell them what I said?" she mocked me, then continued. "Yo ass gone-gonna tell them who did it, and I don't care if you make the shit up. Yo ass better tell them something because I'll be damned if they gonna keep harassing me! Yo ass will be dead first, shit!" she yelled, dropping the butt of her cigarette to the floor. She'd steamed well past Fort Greene and deep into Brownsville as the heat from the cigarette's fiery tip burned her lip and charred the midsection of her fingers.

Just in case you were wondering, Fort Greene symbolized the green line that circled a Newport cigarette's base, just before the brown-wrapped filter began. You guessed it! Brownsville symbolized the filter portion. So when someone said a smoker is past Fort Greene, it was a slight on that person's fiend habits, and if you smoked to Brownsville, that's cause for burst-out-laughing ridicule. Now back to the regularly scheduled cycle of generational violence, hurricane Katrina-ing every third-world ghetto across this great nation.

"Now take your ass to your room and don't come out until I tell you to come out," she ordered, pointing in the direction of my room. I didn't like the feeling of the first slap to the back of my head, so I made sure to exit stage left immediately. My mother was good at following up with another blow if I moved too slowly or eyeballed her. When I got up, the only thing that my watery eyes made contact with was the floor. In all actuality, I was thinking how lucky I was to escape with just an ear-ringing slap. I had come to realize that the only reason I was still breathing was because of the person on the other end of the phone. I don't care if she never told me to come out of my room because I don't want to be around her anyway.

"I-I don't-don't care if she is-is is my mother. God didn't make me to be her punching bag. She's evil. I hate her!" Stuttering, I mumbled to myself as I figuratively stomped to my room.

Rude Awakenings

"Hey, beat Officer Day, how's it going?" asked homicide detective Lynch. Lynch had been on the force for decades. His father, grandfather, and his grandfather's father were all former cops. He was just following the family tradition, and the carte blanche treatment of the White men of Irish descent had come to be expected. While both men stood at the same height, anyone could clearly see that age had taken a toll on Lynch as his back hunched over his thin frame, robbing him of at least an inch of height. His hair was a silver grey and no longer matched his red-freckled face.

He stood there holding a fresh cup of hot coffee, awaiting Day's reply.

"Everything is going rather swell," Day replied with a hint of sarcasm in his voice.

"Listen, Day, don't give me that bullshit! Now you begged me to give you some time to work the kid, but as far as I'm concerned, you're not holding up your end of the bargain," wagging his finger, he chided him.

"Maybe if you just let me do things my way instead of intervening, I would be a lot further along than I am now," he fired back.

"What, are you still whining about that call I made to his mother? Well, somebody had to do something. Maybe you need to grow a pair," he barked as he walked off down the hall to the homicide detective squad room. Day just stood there, not knowing if to respond or if to take it on the chin. He took it on the chin. Shaking his head in disbelief and laughing it off, he walked in the opposite direction.

The homicide squad room was a small office with desks piled on top of one another. In pairs of twos, fourteen desks were squeezed into a small area with each desk facing the one next to it. Each detective sat directly across from his or her partner. The reality was that White men dominated the squad, and there was only one female detective and a lone Black male detective.

"Hey, Lynch, how's it going?" the two-hundred-pounds-overweight detective asks, swiveling around in a chair that suddenly disappears behind him. If it weren't for the visible wheels at the chair's base, anyone would think he was suspended in the air.

"Nothing much, except I just got through chewing Day – a new asshole," he said with a sly look on his face.

"I was wondering when you were going to put him in his place. That guy has a lot of nerve, thinking he can tell any of us how to do our jobs. If it weren't for affirmative action, he wouldn't even have a job. If it were up to me, no Blacks would be on the force," he rambled before being silenced by another detective.

"Yeah, that's exactly why you're not in charge, because we wouldn't have any women or anything that doesn't look white on the force. You're stuck in the dark ages. It's time you wake up and smell the coffee because we all know you can smell the donuts," Detective Tori said, followed by a chorus of laughter.

"If it were up to me, you certainly wouldn't be on the force because you're still a momma's boy. You're just mad because your mammy doesn't include donuts in your lunch bag. You hear this fifty-year-old virgin," Detective Maloney says, twirling back around in his chair to face the other eight detectives in the room, as another burst of laughter erupted. Directly across from his desk hung a target-practice poster with the capital letters B. L. M. emblazoned across the top.

"Yeah, whatever," Tori said, then got up to exit the room, with a coffee and a donut in hand.

"Goodness gracious, I thought he would never leave. Alright, this is what we're going to do about this kid. His mother already assured me that he would give the shooter up or someone who fits the description of the shooter. Either way, somebody will be going to jail," Lynch said, then takes a sip of his coffee.

"But don't you think we should just arrest the mother to let the fucking kid know we're not playing games. We should just go down to Brown Housing and bust some balls," Maloney insisted.

"In due time, but for now, let's just work the angle we've got. These Black kids that come from single homes in the projects are terrified of their mothers. They beat the shit out of these kids. I remember about thirty years back, when a Black mother arrived on the scene just as we'd apprehended her son for stealing some candy. She commenced beating the handcuffed kid with her purse, her fist, and she even tried to grab my knight stick to hit him with that too. I decided to let the kid go because I knew that she would eventually kill him or we'd eventually kill him one day anyway," Lynch reminisced.

"And I thought I was cold," Maloney said, and all the other detectives started laughing.

"That's because you haven't met my great-grandfather, Paddy Irish. Now, he was cold. They didn't even bring nigg, I mean Blacks, to the precinct back then. They'd billy club 'em out on the street, leave 'em there to bleed out, and take the stolen goods. That's cold!" Lynch professed.

"I guess you're right. I only get to waste precious lead on their asses," Maloney replied. "Okay, is anyone going to say something about your fellow officers breaking every ethical code known to man?" said a detective sitting way off to the end of the room.

"No," a chorus of officers chimed in, as another burst of gut-wrenching laughter filled the room.

"Hey, Maloney, scoot over here," Lynch requested as he took a seat at his desk. His desk sat at the opposite far end of the room, next to a single row of dusty windows. Maloney looked like a professional, effortlessly making the wheeled chair slide across the room, spinning, and coming to a halt right in front of Lynch's desk. The two men sat in the corner and started to whisper, mapping out their plan to ensure that Hoodie talked.

"I have a CI who confirmed to me that Little D, also known as Derrick Martin, is our guy. He is the shooter. But we need to get the kid to say he's our guy, so my CI can be the witness number two. The D.A. refuses to give us the go-ahead without the kid's or some other eyewitness's statement. They need someone who was actually on the scene as a safety measure," Lynch informed Maloney while hunched over. Their faces were less than a foot apart.

"What is the D.A. worried about, some evidence suddenly popping up that proves your CI wasn't at the scene?" he asked with a hint of sarcasm in his tone.

"I guess you must have forgotten about the Rashad Bell case or the Anthony Gurley case, and let's not forget about the Jessica Rhymes case. As I remember it, you screwed that one up pretty bad. I'm surprised that conviction is still standing to this day," he pointed out with his voice rising an octave.

"Well, Lady Justice is blind for a reason, just not the reason these fucking niggers think," he whispered, followed by a chuckle.

"Listen to me, you idiot. I'm not about to lose my pension after all these years. Practically every detective in this squadron has skeletons in his or her closet," he said, placing emphasis on the word 'her.' Continuing, he explained, "In this climate of the Black Lives Matter bullshit on the evening News every single night, we have to be careful about our approaches to closing cases. We got a rise in body cameras, dash cameras, street cameras, you name it. There's footage everywhere we turn. We can't keep using the 'he tripped' line or the 'I thought he had a gun' line, and I'm even tired of hearing the 'I feared for my life' line." Lynch had a concerned look on his face as he spoke, and Maloney could sense his fears.

The men had come to know each other well, as they had worked together for decades. They both understood that when one bad apple staff member was telling another bad apple that they needed to rethink their approach to being bad apples, it was a cause for concern. It was only a matter of time before people realized that not only was the whole tree bad, but that the tree also grew on a plateau.

There was no hill for bad apples to roll down into good apples.

Straightening up, Maloney agreed, "I guess you're right. There is no doubt in my mind that Detective Tori would turn on us in a heartbeat. He sure likes all the colors in the rainbow. Shit, I think the Black Klan's men will stuff his mouth with blue mortar before Tori would, and it's only a matter of time before that Me Too Movement severely damages you know whose brain."

"So, we're on the same page. We nail the kid down first, and then we can pull the rest of our witnesses out of a hat for all I care," Lynch suggested with a malicious grin on his face.

"I still think we should lock the mother up, plant a crack pipe on her, and charge her with child abuse," Maloney insisted.

"Have you been listening to anything I just fucking said? Plant a crack pipe? We're not locking the mother up! At least not for now! She's on our side," he yelled. He was clearly aggravated by Maloney's doggedness to muddy the waters. Lynch was the senior officer in the squad, and he had a lot of pull with the higher-ups. He'd been getting pressured to add some more minorities to the squad and was repeatedly reminded that Day was a prime candidate. However, the last thing he wanted on the squad was another Black. He'd take a Puerto Rican first or a Spanish Mama, he'd often joked about.

Lynch knew that the more minorities they included on the force, the greater the likelihood that IA would be breathing down their necks and people would go to jail, just not the usual suspects. He was a realist. He had long realized that they over-policed minority neighborhoods and would only show up in affluent neighborhoods when somebody fired a gun. They didn't make drug arrests in White neighborhoods, and they certainly didn't practice stop-and-frisk. This was the only way he and many of the other men and women on the force knew how to police. There were no paradigms for policing Whites, so White neighborhoods largely went unmolested.

Lynch, in fact, knew the history of his ancestors and how they had come to dominate inner-city police departments. He could remember when he was a wee lad and his grandfather Paddy told him how Irish men would get drunk in pubs, cause disturbances, fight, and end up in the back of police wagons so often that they eventually started calling police wagons Paddy wagons. It was a play on Paddy the Irishman. The family secret his grandfather told him to protect at all costs was how Paddy went from being handcuffed in the back of the Paddy wagon to becoming its driver. His grandfather feared the day Blacks figured that out because they would no longer be easy prey, instantly endangering the lives of all the other ethnic groups that remained at the bottom of the social hierarchy, and that included White ethnic groups.

On other occasions, Paddy reminded Lynch of the days when other White men called them smoked Irish, associating them with Negroes. His grandfather even showed him an old news pamphlet from the dawn of the twentieth century, depicting a caricature of hairy Irishmen drawn in the likeness of monkeys. He could still hear his grandfather's heavy Irish voice as he warned him, "If we don't accept the crumbs, then the niggers will get full off them. I'd rather eat scraps than shit any day. You listen to me and you listen to me, good lad!" Lynch lamented the memory of his grandfather slapping him straight to the ground after he suggested that Irishmen should join Negroes and fight against their oppressors instead of taking their crumbs. He even remembered the salty taste of the cherry-red blood that filled his mouth right before he spat a tooth out in a splatter of blood, gluing his painted tooth to the kitchen floor. Paddy stood over him, dug in his pocket, pulled a dollar bill out, and flung it down to the floor next to the bloodied tooth, and told him that the Tooth Fairy didn't exist, and he'd better get up right that minute or he'd knock him down again.

Lynch remembered the teachable moments during his childhood when either his father or grandfather reinforced their ideas to him. Whenever they introduced him to White cops belonging to other ethnic groups, they made sure to give him the history of Irishmen battling with Polish men, Italian men, and other White men for scarce resources. He told him that eventually they were all considered White, and even that didn't guarantee upward mobility. The social hierarchy was set, but at least it separated them from the Blacks, Latinos, and Asians.

They accepted their role as a buffer between White elites and non-Whites.

However, Lynch's grandfather was no dummy. He made clear to Lynch that each time one out of a million lower-class Whites moved up the ladder, it kept the lie alive. The American dream was possible for anyone, except that it wasn't possible for everyone. Even he couldn't understand why Whites didn't mind seeing other Whites taking the Lion's share of resources, but the same Whites would be up in arms whenever Blacks and other minorities simply asked for equality. Contradicting his own practices, he'd lamented, *"Why I tell yah, we just can't get enough of the taste of them bloody crumbs, not even for our own good."* It was in those moments of learning that Lynch struggled to find his own identity, corrupting him, and in some respects, making him unprincipled.

Lynch gathered his thoughts and said, "Maloney, we have to watch our steps a lot more. We're in the endgame now. Now, gear up, we're going on a crusade in the hood." He stood to his feet, slammed the empty coffee mug down on the desk, and adjusted his belt around his waistline.

"See now that's the Lynch I know. Should I bring my brass knuckles?" he joked with a wide grin on his face. Lynch looked at him and shook his head, displaying a grin of his own.

Maloney knew that it never was about what Lynch said. It was always about what he did. Besides, since the addition of minorities, neither of them felt comfortable talking in the squad room. Taking their cues from number forty-five, they often contradicted themselves as a safety mechanism. In that way, they could always point to the times when they were politically correct and downplay the times they weren't. As the two men proceeded to leave the squad room, Detective Jackson flew to his feet and followed them out into the hall.

"Hey, guys, do you mind if I tag along?" Jackson asked, causing both men to turn around at the sound of his voice. They looked at each other for a brief second and then back at Jackson. Jackson stood there awaiting an answer for what seemed like an eternity, but in all actuality was only a few seconds.

"Uh, yeah, why not? Maybe you can help us with the natives, I mean locals," Lynch derided him.

"Yeah, it's probably a good idea to go and grab your dashiki, so that we can look like the brothers," Maloney piggybacked off Lynch, bringing a sly smile to Jackson's face.

"As a matter of fact, I'll bring my spear too, just in case we run into a wild boar," Jackson fired back, raising both of their eyebrows.

"Yeah, you do that, and while you're grabbing the dashiki and the spear, can you grab my radio off the left corner of my desk?" Lynch said while shifting his jacket forward. Jackson was no fool. He noticed the move.

Pointing to the bulge under Lynch's jacket, he said, "I think your radio is on your waist."

"Oh! What do you know? It sure is right here on my waist. But about that ride-along, it's not going to happen. I have some things I need to talk with my partner about. Besides, if we apprehend a suspect in our case, then we won't have the room to put the perp in the back. We'd have to call for a squad car and all that extra stuff, you know," Lynch explained.

"Yeah, we may joke about you looking like the perps, but it would be inconsiderate of us to sit you back there like one," Maloney added, revealing another grin,

"Okay. Maybe next time," Jackson responded.

"Yeah, maybe next time," Lynch said and spun towards the other direction with Maloney in lock step. Neither man looked back as they exited the precinct. Once they were in the confines of their Crown Victoria, they burst into laughter. Maloney put the car in drive and exited the parking lot. Lynch eased back in his seat and then hit the window button, lowering the passenger window. He rested his elbow out the window, watching the sun go down and the pedestrians as they passed them block after block. All of the pedestrians' faces were either black or brown. Some women walked with their children, and others pushed their kids in strollers. Lynch noticed that there weren't many men on the streets for a Saturday. There were plenty of young boys, but even older teenage boys were scarce.

Maloney brought the car to a stop at the red light, and right before their eyes, Little Dee proceeded to cross the street. He raised his head just enough to expose his eyes from the cover the brim of his hat provided. As he and Lynch made eye contact, Little Dee flashed a smile and picked up his pace. Lynch reached his hand out and hit the siren button, making a single "whoop" sound. He nudged Maloney in his hip and pointed in Dee's direction, who suddenly decided to take off running down the block. Maloney simultaneously slammed his foot down on the gas pedal and hit the sirens on full blast. The car's tires screeched as it swerved into motion on the takeoff, propelling the vehicle forward to a speed of sixty in four seconds.

Little Dee bolted left down the next block. The Crown Victoria bent the corner in less than a second after him, fishtailing as Maloney manhandled the steering wheel.

Realizing that the car was right behind him, Little Dee violently stopped on his heels and ran back down the block he had just run up. *URRRR,* the tires screeched, brought the car to a complete stop, and sent both detectives' bodies towards the dashboard. Almost instantly, Maloney slammed the car in reverse, reaching his arm behind Lynch's headrest and contorting his body to face the backseat window. The vehicle catapulted backwards, careening down the street at breakneck speed. Bystanders nearly caught whiplash trying to take in the events that were occurring before their eyes. Some people just moved along, minding their own business as if it were the order of the day.

"I'm calling it in because ain't no way my old limbs are getting into a foot chase with Kuntaur Kente."

Grabbing the radio and raising it to his face, he continued, "In pursuit of one murder suspect, Derrick Martin. Suspect is considered to be armed and dangerous. I repeat, suspect is considered to be armed and dangerous."

The dispatcher said, "Copy that!"

"Copy, dispatch, we're in pursuit on Malcolm X Boulevard. Suspect is wearing all black with a black baseball cap," Lynch screams into the radio. "Don't lose him! He's turning again. He's trying to make a run for the project buildings. Are there any beat officers patrolling in Brown Housing near the Malcolm X entrance?" He screamed into the radio, awaiting a response.

Maloney rammed into the curbside, pulling the car onto the sidewalk directly behind Little Dee. Pedestrians were screaming, darting left, right, or in any direction that got them out of the vehicle's path. The sound of sirens started erupting into the atmosphere as more police vehicles descended on the housing projects. "Run his Black ass over!" Lynch shouted. As Maloney pressed his foot down on the gas; the car's engine rumbled in response. It roared so loud that Little Dee could feel the vibration shake the pavement under his Air Force Ones. Without hesitation, he immediately jumped sideways over the four-foot fence to his left. He barely cleared it as the Crown Vic's bumper scraped the black gates, denting the chrome fender on impact.

"This is Officer Day in foot pursuit of a male wearing all black, heading towards 457 Malcolm X," he dispatched over the handheld radio. They could hear his heavy breathing, the jiggling sound of his keys, and the rustling of the uniform over the radio. He could see the unmarked car up ahead, barreling across the sidewalk recklessly, nearly hitting pedestrians.

"In pursuit of male wearing black," Lynch mocked him. Continuing, he yelled into the radio,

"Black male wearing black and he's armed and dangerous!"

As Little Dee was approaching the building's entrance, Day was closing the distance. He was now within twenty feet of him, and he couldn't see a weapon. He got a good look at both of his hands.

"Dispatch, suspect is in clear view, and he does not appear to have a weapon. I repeat, the suspect is not displaying a weapon," Day informed dispatch. Little Dee just made it up the steps before being tackled by Day, breaking the key off in the door to the lobby. The weight of the two men forced the door open as their bodies crashed to the lobby's floor with Day on top. "Don't move! It's the police! Stop resisting!" he shouted as the men briefly scuffle on the floor.

Little Dee heard the blaring sirens, the screeching of cars, and the slamming of doors, followed by footsteps. He instantly gave up the fight, allowing Officer Day to handcuff him face flat on the ground.

"I have the suspect. I'm in the lobby of 457 Malcolm X," he dispatched over the radio just before Lynch, Maloney, and about ten other first responders entered the lobby one by one with their guns drawn.

"Good work," a uniformed Sgt. said to Day, tapping him on his shoulder as he was kneeling down on the side of Little Dee, holding on to the cuffs behind Little Dee's back. Happy to see backup arrive, Day looked up with confidence.

"I'm glad you guys are here. He tried to give me a little resistance until he heard the sirens. Help me get him to his feet and against the wall. I haven't searched him yet." The Sgt. motioned for two uniformed officers to assist him.

"Nah, we got this," Lynch said, waving the beat cops off. The Sgt. followed suit and waved the officers off. As soon as Maloney and Day pulled Little Dee to his feet, Maloney slammed his hand into Little Dee's back, pressing him up against the wall, instantly knocking his breath clean out of his lungs. Everything went black, and his limp body collapsed to the floor as Maloney pulled his hand back. The force of his body falling to the floor yanked the handcuff chain, jamming Days' fingers.

"Shit!" he yelped, pulling his hand back. He released the cuff's chain, which caused Little Dee's arms to bend upwards, sending his head forward, bouncing off the wall, then crashing to the floor face-first. The eerie sound of his skull cracking echoed through the small lobby. The Sgt. and a number of the other officers winced and turned their heads at the sight of the deadly blow. A pool of blood formed around Little Dee's head with his face planted in the sanguine liquid.

Everyone just stood there in shock.

The sight of a red air bubble popping near Little Dee's nose snapped Day out of his trance, and he yelled, "Hurry up, turn him over on his side, so he doesn't drown in his own blood."

Maloney backed up and played the role of an onlooker as Day struggled to flip Little Dee's limp body over. He was unconscious, but he was alive. "Call a medic!" he yelled in a strained voice. Once he had Little Dee on his side, he checked his pulse to make sure he was still alive. "Sir, can you hear me? Can you hear me? Blink your eye if you can hear my voice," he instructed him. After about a second of no response, he said, "He's not responding. How are we looking on that medic?"

"The ambulance is en route, about two minutes away," the Sgt. responded.

"Hey, pat frisk him, Maloney," Lynch ordered.

"No! You've done enough!" Day said with a hint of excitement in his voice. Continuing, he said, "I'll do it." Day patted him down from top to bottom, emptying his pockets, lifting his sleeves, pants legs, and jacket. "He's clean," he said and stood to his feet. He could see that Little Dee was still breathing on his own. He was just unconscious. He backed up to give him some more air.

Lynch pulled Day to the side to talk to him. "Listen, you did a good job, you got our guy, He's a murderer. You have no reason to feel sorry for him. So, he bumped his head by accident.

No foul, no harm. You hear me?" he demanded, shaking Day's shoulder, causing him to look up. Right when he was about to answer, he noticed Maloney bend down over Little Dee. In the next instance, he reached down to his right ankle, pulling out what appeared to be a twenty-two snub-nosed revolver, and held it up in the air for all to see.

"I've got a gun!" he shouted. Struggling to bring his three hundred pounds to his feet, he finally stood erect, turned towards Day, and waved the small weapon, saying, "You missed this." Day practically shoved Lynch out of the way, trying to get to Maloney.

The Sgt. and two other uniformed officers jumped in between them.

"You fucking liar. I saw you pull that gun out of your ankle. Come on, guys, I searched him twice. Everyone saw me search him thoroughly from top to bottom. Sgt., are you gonna back me up here?" Day pleaded. The Sgt. simply looked at Lynch as if to say It's your call.

"Listen, Day, it's understandable with all the excitement, it's easy to miss something. These thugs are very subtle. Now, you're not suggesting that detective Maloney would plant a gun on an innocent person," Lynch said, emphasizing the word innocent.

"No, I'm not suggesting it. I'm saying that's exactly what he did. Come on, man, all of you guys, seen it," he insisted. Looking from the Sgt. to the other uniformed officers, Day looked for someone to back him up. Each man just stood there and shook their heads as if to say, 'you're on your own.'

"Hey, I think it's normal to see a little blood and get all confused. Blood is a scary sight, especially when it gets on your hands," Maloney said. Day looked at his hands to check for blood. His hands were clear of blood. He immediately understood that Maloney had just insinuated that things could easily be made to appear as if Day had caused the injury.

"You fat fucker! You're not putting this on me in any way," he yelled, trying to break free of the other officers. The loud commotion was followed by the sound of door chains being unfastened, doors unlocked, door knobs turned, and the apartment doors opened.

"Hey, close that fucking door!" Lynch shouted at a concerned female resident. Another resident opened her door to be yelled at as well. Lynch gestured towards the other uniformed officers, ordering them to force people to close their doors. As they walked towards the residents, another door opened, and Chemistry stepped out.

"We live here. We have a right to see what's taking place in our building," he countered.

"That's right," the other residents chimed in.

"I don't have time for this shit," Lynch said, unholstering his gun and pointing it at the residents. Continuing, he demanded, "Take your Black asses back inside before I shoot you in the face. And I'm starting with you with the big mouth," he aimed the gun directly at Chemistry.

Not taking his eyes off of Lynch, Chemistry calmly says, "Mrs. Davis, Mrs. Shirley, go on in and lock your doors."

"Serge! Lynch put the damn gun down. He's an unarmed man," Day pleaded.

"Not from where I'm standing, he has an unidentified object in his right hand," he responded.

"It's my phone," Chemistry said.

"What, you recording me? Toss the object on the ground," Lynch ordered as his hands started to shake a bit. It wasn't because he was nervous. He was actually cool as a fan and wouldn't think twice about taking Chemistry's life. He had bad nerves from all the coffee he drank.

"I'm not throwing my phone on the ground," Chemistry refused.

"I'm ordering you to drop the weapon now!" Lynch screamed.

"Serge, it's not a weapon. It's a phone," Day insisted, still trying to break free from the other officers. Just as the Sgt. appeared to speak up, the EMT unit arrived on the scene, entering the lobby. They immediately rushed to Little Dee's lifeless body.

"He's not breathing!" one of the emergency responders yelled as she squatted by his side. For whatever reason, that made Lynch reverse the course he was taking, and he lowered his weapon.

"Sir, I'm going to ask you one more time to go back into your apartment and shut the door. At the moment, you are obstructing justice," Lynch said while holstering his weapon.

Chemistry shook his head and stepped back inside his apartment, locking the door.

"Hey, give me that phone!" Maloney yelled as he went for the door, but the Sgt. intervened by placing his hand on Maloney's chest. The Sgt. shook his head and then looked back to the EMTs. Maloney got the picture.

"I need someone to take these cuffs off, so I can perform CPR," the EMT frantically shouted.

"Let me go, man," Day said to the uniformed officers who had him in their grips. They looked at the Sgt., and he gave them the okay to let him go. He immediately reached for his keys, diving to the ground to un-cuff Little Dee. He left one wrist cuffed. The paramedic rolled Little Dee over and started performing CPR.

"One, two, three," she counted as she pressed down on his chest, then placed an oxygen pump over his mouth, squeezing the device. She repeated the cycle three times before Little Dee gasped for air, coming back to life with his eyes wide open. He was finally conscious. The sound of peephole covers could be heard moving in the background. You could even hear a muffled 'thank God' come from behind one of the closed doors.

At the sight of Little Dee coming to, Maloney waved the throw-down piece at him and said, "You're going to jail for attempted murder of a police officer."

For a brief second, Little Dee had a confused look on his face, but then his facial expression turned to anger at the sight of his blood. "What? Attempted murder! That ain't my gun. You planted that shit on me," he shouted back, struggling to rise up. With the assistance of Day, both EMTs held him down.

As the female paramedic breathed softly over him, she said, "Calm down, sir. What's your name?" Next, they rolled him onto the gurney, and Day clamped the open cuff around the gurney's metal bars.

Pressure

I looked in the living room mirror, approved my outfit, and smiled as I proceeded to leave the apartment. Before I got a chance to open the apartment door, I could hear my mother getting out of her bed. I sped up and exited the apartment. I was so determined to avoid my mother that I didn't even lock the door. At top speed, I flew down the stairs, leaping whole sections of the staircase to get away. I was moving so fast that I barely noticed what appeared to be a cherry red Cool-Aid stain in the lobby. When I exited the building, I jumped the gated-grassed area right below the building's windows. In this way, my mother wouldn't be able to look out the window, see me, and call me back. I ran through the grass until I reached the edge of the building, jumped back over the gate, and turned the corner out of sight. My heart almost fell into my stomach at the sound of my cellphone ringing. I looked at the screen, noticing it was Marisol's number I let out a sigh of relief. I answered the call.

Full of excitement and without even saying hello, Marisol screamed into the phone, "Did you see the News this morning?"

"Hello to you, too, Marisol. No, I haven't seen the News," I responded.

"Are you still in the house?" she asked me.

"No. I left before my mom woke up," I informed her.

"Oh. I'm on my way out of my building right now. I'll meet you at the corner in about three minutes," she said and canceled the call. I knew she was up to something because the only time she turned a five-minute distance into two minutes was when she had some juicy gossip. I started to wonder if it had something to do with Ms. Mitcheck, as I ran into the corner store to get some candy. I had a long day ahead, and some candy would definitely help the day go smoothly.

"Good morning," I greeted the older Latin-X man named Hoolio, standing behind the counter.

"Buenos dias, Hoodie. Let me guess, you need your grape and apple Now-and-Laters to start the day off right," he said with confidence that I would answer in the affirmative. Sure enough, I nodded my head.

"You know that's right, let me have two of each," I say, and place a dollar bill on the counter. Hoolio placed the four packs of candy on the counter. To no avail, he always tried to convince me to buy an orange or an apple. He even tried to convince me that I was not getting my money's worth because twenty years ago, I would have gotten ten packs of the same candy for a dollar. I would always fire back that, twenty years ago, parents probably only gave their kids a quarter, so that I would have had less candy. Hoolio had to admit I had a point. He would always toss me an apple for free.

"Later, kid, don't forget your apple," Hoolio said.

"Oh, thanks, Hoolio," I responded and grabbed the shiniest red apple I could find before exiting. I looked up to see Marisol staring in my face. With the apple in one palm and the candy in the other, I held my hands out, gesturing for her to make a choice. I knew that she would take the apple as always. Sure enough, she grabbed the apple and sank her teeth into the fruit, creating a loud crunching sound.

As we began our trek to school, I said, "Damn, you must be hungrier than a runaway slave," causing her to blush from ear to ear.

"You know I love apples, idiot," she responded with a mouth full of apple bits.

"Ruhh, Ruhh, Ruhh, is what you sound like. Didn't anyone ever tell you not to talk with food in your mouth?" I asked, being sarcastic. Marisol took a second to dust off the rest of her apple, throwing its core by the wayside.

"Yeah, whatever you say, pal. Anyway, on the News today, the reporter said that Little Dee is in a coma and being charged with attempted murder on police. But Black Lives Matter protesters are questioning the accounts of the police because, although they claimed he had a gun, no shots were fired. To top all that off, none of the officers on the scene had on body cameras," she said in one breath.

With a stunned look on my face, I blurted out, "Huh, this is amazing! Now I don't have to worry about Little Dee no more."

Right on cue, Marisol went into investigator mode, "What reason do you have to worry about Little Dee? I mean, the cops may have put this guy in a coma, and the first thing you say is you don't have to worry about him no more. What are you talking about?" she drilled me.

"Um, IDK, he uh… he was bothering me. Yeah, that's it. He was bothering me about some nonsense, nothing major. He probably won't even remember what it was about when he wakes up. Shoot, I don't even remember what it's about," I lied.

"I must look like I'm stupid to you and have no plans of going to law school one day. Maybe you think I was born last night," Marisol insulted.

"Maybe not last night, but you may have been born the night before last," I said and started laughing. Continuing, I bragged, "Boy, I should be a stand-up comic the way I crack me up."

"Ha ha, making those corny jokes on stage, the only thing you're going to get is some rotten tomatoes to the face." As if having an epiphany, her face lit up all of a sudden. "Does it have to do with that shooting the other night? The reporter said that he was wanted for a murder that took place in Brown Housing. That's right. Hold up! That blood on your sneaker didn't come from—oh my god!" she exclaimed.

"No, no, no, you got it all wrong. Our dispute had nothing to do with any shooting. No guns, no blood, no sneakers," I tried to convince her.

"I'm not buying it. If I found out, then how long do you think it will take the cops to find out?" As the words left her mouth, I could tell that her brain was working again. After a moment's pause, she voiced, "Oh, the cops already know. That's what all the visits to school have been about and your mom acting crazy about." I had to admit the girl was good. Even I hadn't completely tied my mother to the cops yet, but Marisol knew that she knew that she knew that was the case.

"Wow! You really are crazy. You obviously don't know what you're talking about, and that's my cue. I have to go," I pointed out, responding to the school bell. Not giving her a chance to respond, I darted up the school steps and disappeared into the crowd. Marisol stood there with her 'he escaped again' look on her face.

At the sight of Ms. Mitcheck, I stopped dead in my tracks, making an about-face down the hall. I ran into Billy, who was on his way to class. Billy took one look back at me and acted like he didn't see me. I realized that he was trying to reach the classroom before I caught up to him. In that way, Billy could enforce his no talking in class rule on me. I sped up to beat him to the punch.

"Hey, Billy, what's up?" I inquired, tapping him on the shoulder. Billy turned around, amazed at how fast I made up the distance between us.

"What's up?" he answered flatly.

"Did you happen to catch the News this morning about Little Dee?" I asked. I was trying to make small talk, but I also knew that Billy likely remembered every detail about the report.

Happy to engage me on a relevant topic, he smiled and revealed, "I watch the News every morning, and once I heard about our neighborhood, I paid close attention. The reporter said that due to the swelling in Little Dee's brain, he was placed in a medically induced coma. Later reports claimed that the first detective arriving to the scene had to wrestle a gun away from him, as he tried to fire the weapon. During the struggle, they claim that his head accidentally slammed into the floor as they fell to the ground. The mayor is calling the detective a hero and considering giving him the keys to the city. The president of the PBA claimed that the detective is a decorated officer from the good old days of law enforcement, arguing that Little Dee's record attests to a broken system. He argued that criminals like Little Dee should not be allowed back on our streets because they are vicious animals."

I thought he would never stop talking. It was bad enough that I had to hear Marisol all day. I refused to allow Billy to talk my head off as well. I knew if I let him, given the right subject, Billy would talk all day long without sharing the microphone. Being that he already revealed some nuances that Marisol failed to point out, I was happy with what I learned. Little Dee would be awakened once the swelling in his brain went down. Besides, I dodged Ms. Mitcheck, and that was my main objective. Now I need to find out why she's back, and more importantly, what that means for my safety. I heard she once sat on a kid until he couldn't breathe, and she didn't even go to jail for it. They claimed that the kid had ADHD, and he was strung out on the drug Ritalin. I don't think that's a good enough reason for someone to lose their life. He was only a kid, but even the educational system treated him like a vicious animal. *'Great equalizer, my ass! Only in America,'* I thought to myself as I shook my head.

"Hey, Hoodie, snap out of it," Marisol said, waving her hand across my eyesight.

"Yeah, what the hell was that man?" Billy questioned.

Landing back on earth, I say, "Oh, I was just thinking about what you said about the News report. The stuff that Marisol," I place emphasis on her name, then finish, "didn't tell me."

"What are you trying to call me incompetent?" she demanded.

Instigating, Billy chimed in, "I think that's exactly what he just called you."

"What, no. I was just pointing out the fact that you must have been listening to fake news because you missed a whole lot of important details," I patronized her. Before Marisol could fire off, our first-period teacher popped her head out of the classroom door, looking for stragglers. She gave us one look, causing us to B-line for class. We didn't want that drama. No sooner than I took my seat, I heard my name blaring over the intercom to report to the principal's office.

"Let's see who's incompetent now," Marisol shouted from across the crowded room with a smirk on her face. *'Boy, she has some nerve. This is serious business. There are times to play and times to be serious,'* I thought to myself. I completely ignored her as I grabbed my book bag and nearly tripped over four different students' backpacks before exiting the classroom with all eyes on me once again. Out of frustration, I field goal kicked the last backpack, sending it flying over the teacher's head, crashing into the chalkboard, and causing a cloud of dust to cover her glasses. Before she could realize what had just transpired, I dipped out of the room while she dusted her lens off. I could hear the classroom erupt in laughter.

In many ways, I was happy to leave that stuffy room. We were packed in like a can of smelly sardines. All forty of us! A bull pin in Central Booking had more room than our classroom, and Billy's brother Chemistry told me that detainees either clutter the benches, stand shoulder to shoulder, sprawl out on dirty floors, foot to behind, foot to face, and even butt to face. He said just imagine ten or twenty people playing the popular game Twister with everyone on deck, yikes! I remembered imagining five filthy panhandlers, at least two wayward teens, a fat, drunk guy, and two mental health patients all locked inside of a cage, tangling, and twisting over a twister board. The images of worn, piss-stained clothing, soiled, funky socks, and dirty, holey sneakers have contributed to my nightmares. I was traumatized and ever since then, I haven't been able to shake the thought that our overcrowded classroom is preparing us for Central Booking twister. I couldn't hear shit in the classroom. I could not even hear myself think in the classroom. What were we doing in the classroom? I lamented as I reached the principal's office.

The principal's twenty-four-year-old secretary filled the office with the smell of expensive perfume. She reminded me of a Victoria's Secret model ripping the runway, as she sashayed her way over to meet at the entrance.

"Mr. Hoodie, the principal will be with you in a minute. Have a seat over there," she said as she pointed towards the plush burgundy leather love seat with two room-friendly palm trees sitting at each end. The plant's leaves hung over head, giving a paradise effect. I was in paradise. The room was cooled by central air, and I could kick my feet out. There was only foot space under your individual desk in the classroom. I was cramped up in the classroom. Only I was able to hear myself thinking, 'what we doing in the classroom?' No sooner had I sat down and felt my behind absorbed into the cushiony sofa, than I couldn't help but blurt out, "How this was what I needed after an ass whooping."

"What did you say?" she asked.

"Oh, it's nothing. I was just thinking out loud," I lied. She sped on her red-bottom heels, and the sound of her heels click-clacking was violently interrupted by a sudden rumbling vibration under my feet. The leaves of the trees started shaking, the water in the water cooler started shifting from side to side, and I was becoming seasick. The next thing I knew, the office door opened and Ms. Mitcheck's size fourteen shoes pounded the office floor as she stepped into the room, bringing everyone to full attention. Just as she looked in my direction, I couldn't be happier to see the principal magically appear from his office. Instantly, she softened the menacing look she gave me. It was as if she picked up the principal's scent. I swear I saw her nostrils widen, sniffing the air.

"Great! Good morning, I'm glad you both are here," said the principal

In unison, Ms. Mitcheck and I said, "Good morning."

"Follow me into my office," Principal Joe said.

I slowly got up out of my seat to make sure that Ms. Mitcheck went ahead of me. There was no way I would give her my back. She might sucker punch me in the back of my head, and I'd probably deserve it, but that was neither here nor there. She could sense my hesitancy to go ahead of her, so I stalled moving forward, and she stalled too. We were in a Texas stand off until, thinking quickly on my feet, I politely gestured with my hand for her to go first. She remained reluctant to move and one-up me.

"After you, Mr. Hoodie," she gently said, returning her on gesture and more importantly gaining the principal's attention. He turned around to find me at a standstill.

"Come on, Mr. Hoodie. We're not going to the electric chair or the guillotine. Isn't that right, Ms. Mitcheck?" he asked.

"No," she said loudly and then whispered to me, "That would be too nice for a little liar." Looking at the principal becoming impatient, I thought it best to move along. Not taking my eye off of her for one second, I nervously squeezed passed her down the narrow hall. I actually sped up as I passed her, but it felt like she pressed her weight down, shifting the floor, and suddenly I was in an uphill battle. I put on my Barney Rubble feet and steamrolled ahead. By the time I reached the principal, who was no more than five feet away, my brow filled with nervous sweat. My heart was pounding so hard that I could hear it beating, and I was willing to bet they could hear it too.

"Mr. Hoodie, are you okay?" the principal asked.

"I'm fine. I just have claustrophobia," I said, causing the principal to blush.

"Claustrophobia, this kid is funny. Isn't he funny, Ms. Mitcheck?" he asked rhetorically.

He was trying to clean up his inability to refrain from laughing at what was clearly a shot at Ms. Mitcheck. *'Shoot,'* I thought to myself, *'people body-shamed me all the time. Like Billy's brother, Chemistry would say: all is fair in love and war. And, this was war!'* I knew Ms. Mitcheck wouldn't let this down. She would make sure to try and get her revenge, but I was determined to deny her revenge against me. She left me no choice but to launch preeminent strike number two.

I just needed time to figure out what that would look like.

"He should be a comedian," she answered as we entered the office.

"Everyone, please have a seat. I'm sure you both have an idea of why we're here, and full disclosure, more so you than Mr. Hoodie," he said, causing my spider senses to fly up and get me thinking, what the hell does that mean? He continued, "Your mom and the detectives cleared everything up for us, and we know that you said, or rather implied, some things about Ms. Mitcheck that weren't true. Unfortunately, Ms. Mitcheck was arrested, but her record has been cleared. Thankfully, her reputation has been restored for the most part. At this point, no one is in trouble, and we understand that you previously had a traumatizing experience that we've been advised not to talk about. So, at this point, we believe it is best to let bygones be bygones. Ms. Mitcheck has agreed that she harbors no ill feelings toward you for your part in this very inconvenient situation. Isn't that correct, Ms. Mitcheck?" She nodded her head in the affirmative.

Continuing, he asked, "Mitcheck, is there anything that you would like to say to Mr. Hoodie?"

"I think you pretty much covered everything. I just would add that I have always viewed Mr. Hoodie as one of East Side's brighter students," she said, turning towards me. She continued, "Although this has been an experience I regret, I can see us moving forward in a positive direction. I still believe that you are a bright young man, and I completely forgive you."

"Mr. Hoodie, is there anything that you would like to say to Ms. Mitcheck or me?" he asked me.

"I think you covered everything, pretty much. I'd only add that I was strongly advised not to speak about this unfortunate situation. I was assured that it was in all of our best interests to refrain from any mention of it," I lied with a straight face.

"Oh! Well then, that settles it," Principal Joe said.

"I guess so," Ms. Mitcheck responded.

"Will that be all?" I asked. I was dying to burst out in laughter, but I held it in. Ms. Mitcheck looked at me like she wanted to strangle me.

"Uh, I guess that's about it. Ms. Mitcheck, thank you for your time, and that will be all. I need to speak with Mr. Hoodie for a moment," he informed her. She stood to her feet, and it felt like the whole room raised about two inches, causing my stomach to turn. I was happy to see her exit. I just had to avoid her now, for the rest of the day. I found myself wondering what did the principal wanted to talk to me about. Before I could assume too much about it, he started to fill me in, "Mr. Hoodie, have you ever thought about joining the debate team? We have a pretty good team, and I think you have a public speaking ability that fits the debate club."

'I have to admit that he caught me off guard with that one. I had no idea he was going there. Debate who? Who does he think I am, Barack Obama? The only thing I'm debating is sports, music, or sneakers. He must have been watching too much Kid President or something. He must be on that deuce. Whatever it is, I don't care. He won't have me on stage looking like an idiot. What do I know anyway?' I thought to myself while sitting there.

"Well, are you going to say something, a yes, no, or you'll consider it?" he insisted.

"I'll consider it," I said before realizing what I even said. Boy, I wished to take those words back. I should have said no to put an end to any thoughts of me saying yes. For a second, I thought about telling him, on second thought, that was a no. It was quite lucky for him; I hate to look confused or unsure of myself. My motto was never let anyone see you sweat. Of course, that was minus a deranged mother wielding an extension cord. I think a grown me would confess to crimes they didn't do after being threatened with an extension cord. And if it was wet, that was a cause for blood, sweat, and tears. Yikes! Just the thought of it stung.

"Mr. Hoodie, are you okay?" he asked, realizing that I was off in never-never land.

"I was just having a moment. Are we done here?" I asked. My patience was wearing thin, and at this point, I was tired of playing Mr. Nice Guy. Being nice didn't get me anywhere but into another situation that I didn't want to be in. *'Boy, what a tangled web we weave,'* I thought to myself.

"Yes, Mr. Hoodie, we're done here. Please give it some thought. You really would be a great addition to the team," he said, standing to his feet and gesturing for a handshake. We shook hands, and I laid my extra-firm Hulk Smash grip on his fingers. His eyes widened with surprise as I clamped down hard, smashing his fingers together. His college ring only made matters worse.

He nearly pulled my shoulder out of place, yanking his hand out of my grip.

"Shoot, maybe I should sign you up for the wrestling team. What do you have some gorilla glue in that palm? That's one hell of a grip. I think you'd give Ms. Mitcheck a run for her money," he finished with a wide grin. I couldn't help it. I had to laugh at that one. Ms. Mitcheck would make a real gorilla snatch its hand back. I left the office thinking that Principal Joe wasn't that bad. Even he knew Ms. Mitcheck could be a tenor. Don't get it twisted, I'm not letting my guard down. Doctor's candy never fooled me. Principal Joe wanted something, and whenever someone with sense wanted anything, they used honey to get it. You know the saying about attracting more bees with honey.

Anyhow, I had a reason to feel good about myself. I applied Chemistry's hand gripping technique, and it worked on a grown ass man! You see, the trick is to grip the fingers rather than the palm. Now I was not the only one who knew what it felt like to have the squeeze put on them. I was tired of being pushed around. It was time for me to rise like a phoenix from my own ashes. And I knew just what I needed to do to start my new life as a gangster.

"I'm on top of the world. On top of the world, I tell ya," I voiced aloud down the empty hall. Just as the words left my lips, I felt the ground rumbling and a shadow bending the corner up ahead.

Hey, I knew everything I just said, but it was time to put shit in reverse, put my Barney Rubble feet on, and live to fight another day. By the time Ms. Mitcheck bent the corner, I was around the other corner, exiting the school building, intentionally setting off the fire alarm on my way out. There was a method to my madness. I could always claim that I left school with everyone else in response to the fire alarm.

Stand 4 Something

"Yesterday, in Brooklyn at the Brown Housing Projects, detectives from the precinct were met with attempted gunfire from a wanted murder suspect. The quick thinking of decorated detective Maloney saved the lives of several officers and residents of this crime-ridden neighborhood. Witnesses claim that the detective sprang into action. Relying on his training, he avoided the gunman's line of fire. According to the Police Chief, before the suspect had a chance, Detective Maloney was on him, wrestling him to the ground, disarming the suspect. Other witnesses claim that as other officers arrived on the scene, the suspect, Derrick Martin, became belligerent, forcing a uniformed officer to wrestle him to the ground once again. In the midst of all of that, somehow the suspect hit his head on the ground, knocking him unconscious. At some point, he stopped breathing, and detectives Maloney and Lynch performed CPR until the paramedics arrived on the scene and applied a defibrillator to restore the suspect's heartbeat and breathing. The Police Chief said that Derrick Martin is a known violent criminal with a long rap sheet. He went on to say that the suspect should never have been on our streets. The suspect is now fighting for his life in a medically induced coma. Walter Crosby, reporting for Channel Six Evening News," the news reporter disclosed.

I sat in my room thinking, "attempted gunfire." What did that even mean? I didn't even think Walter Crosby knew what that meant. "That's bull sugar!" I vented aloud. My mother could hear through walls, see out the back of her head, and read minds. I knew better than to cuss in the house because she heard everything. She heard when I didn't flush the toilet, didn't wash my hands, or didn't brush my teeth. One time, when I was about seven, she even heard when I forgot to wipe my behind. I never forgot to wipe my ass again. "Oops!" Covering my mouth, I sat there thinking, I hope she didn't hear that thought. After about a second, I was convinced she didn't hear my thoughts. My room door remained shut, and I didn't see any movement under the door. I learned that trick from the movie Child's Play. I remembered Chucky scaring the poop out of me when he looked at the shadow under the door and tricked Andy's mom, giving her his my buddy voice as opposed to his Charles Lee Ray voice. I didn't want any parts of Chucky, and I damn sure didn't want a My Buddy doll either. It reminded me of Chucky too much. But at the end of the day, it was my time to be tough like Andy was in the end.

One thing I was certain of was that the story being reported on the News was very different from what the streets were saying. I heard that it was a Black officer that apprehended Little Dee, and it wasn't much of a struggle. The melee occurred when all of the White officers arrived on the scene. And word on the street was it was ten on one, and it looked like Rodney King part two, more than anything else. On top of all that, Little Dee didn't even have a gun. One of the White cops planted it on him, is what I heard. Chemistry always said, "Where there's smoke, there's fire." I sat there playing the scenario out over and over in my head, and I realized that the cops made it seem like everything took place outside the building. But it actually took place in the building lobby. Everyone knows that the lobby cameras don't work, so that couldn't be the reason for the cover-up. I was confused, wondering where I would fit in with all of the recent events. I meant, *'would this get me off the hook and prevent the cops from forcing me to say what they wanted me to say?'* I laid back and dozed off into a deep sleep.

*****

Day looked dumb founded after hearing the News report. He flopped back in the black leather love seat, looking depressed. He couldn't believe that they were trying to put everything on him. At that point, they were saying it was an accident. However, he knew that could change in an instant, and once he played ball, he'd lose any leverage that he held. He understood that going along with their lie now would make it harder to get the truth out later. He was confused because it was his word against possibly nine other officers' words. Obviously, the Sgt. agreed to go along with their version of the events, making Maloney look like some kind of hero. Day rehashed the events that led to the young man ending up in a coma. On top of everything, Maloney planted a gun on him! This was all wrong. The kid hadn't even identified Little Dee as the shooter. The detectives claimed that they had a reliable informant other than an actual witness who insists Little Dee was the shooter. He couldn't help but sense that something was horribly wrong. Things weren't adding up. It was time for him to start investigating on his own. For all he knew, they would have him demoted to desk duty any day now.

In that very moment, he decided to march down to the precinct and set things right. If he was going to go down, then he would go down fighting. He'd heard too many stories of Black officers being thrown under the bus for trying to fight the system. However, he'd heard about the ones that tried to play ball and ended up in worse positions than the fighters. The top brass were predominantly White men, and that was the way it had always been. Day knew that the White men at the bottom provided a level of protection for those at the top so that the top would protect the bottom to an extent. The reality was that even White officers, at the bottom of the totem pole, were expendable.

But for some reason, White officers at the bottom didn't mind being used, and that could be said about many Whites across America. He didn't even want to think about the few minorities who made it into positions of power only to become pawns in a racist structure. He thought, *"Sure, they'll make a few of us chief of police, but we'd never dominate the ranks along with control of leadership."* Day was sick of News reporters using Baltimore to undermine efforts to create more Police Departments that actually looked like the neighborhoods they served. Critics argued that the Baltimore PD was predominantly minority, but that didn't stop Freddie Gray from being killed or countless other men, women, and children of color from being brutalized by law enforcement. Sometimes, he wondered why he had even become a cop in the first place. It was bad enough that he had to deal with the disdain he felt at work, but he received harsh looks from Black people and other minorities. They claimed he was a sellout, calling him Uncle Tom and all sorts of house niggers, big-headed house nigga, dark-as-night house nigger, yes-uh-boss-ass house nigger. *You name it.* The derogatory renditions of house nigger were endless. Nevertheless, what kept him going were the many others who thanked him for trying to make a difference. His very last thought filled him with the energy he needed to confront Lynch and Maloney.

Day arrived at the precinct, storming up the steps to enter the lobby. He disregarded the night Sargent's greetings and headed straight to the homicide squadron. He knew that Lynch and Maloney were nocturnal creatures. They were actually more like vampires. Blood suckers who used the cover of night to help conceal their corrupt actions. The night provided cover for their drunken stupors, drunk driving, and random assaults on citizens. NYPD had a reputation for enabling what they conveniently called a few bad apples. Shoot, corporate leaders claimed individuals like Bernie Madoff and companies like Enron represented a few bad apples. The housing bubble and stock market crash in 2007 were the result of a few bad apples. When the Good Old Boys committed crimes, the controlling narrative always scapegoated a few bad apples. Day decided that it was time to upend the status quo. Maloney and Lynch were at the top of his hit list. They would pay for underestimating him. '*Shit, they don't know, I move like a Black Klan's man,*' he thought to himself as he furiously shoved the door open. The door smacked against the doorknob bumper attached to the wall, shattering the glass and creating a loud thud that vibrated through the tiny office. The commotion startled everyone in the room, causing several detectives to reach for their weapons, and some even went as far as unholstering their weapons.

"Shit! What the hell is wrong with you, Day?" Maloney shouted, then holstered his chrome forty-four magnum.

"Yeah, man, you scared the shit out of me," Detective Tori said and holstered his weapon.

"I told you he's a freaking lunatic and some people in brass have the nerve to tell me to consider him for this squad," Lynch said, then took another sip of his cowboy-boot-black coffee before standing to his feet. Continuing, he said, "With Antifa, anarchists, looters, and Black Lives Matter extremists out there threatening to defund the police, burning down precincts, and attacking our officers, you want to try and get a rise out of people. What are you testing our reactions? I even heard that some of your people on this force have been out there protesting, taking knees and shit," he taunted, exciting laughter in the room.

"Yeah, he thinks he's Kap-Uh-nigger. Get it? Cap a nigger. I'm sorry, I mean Kapernick," Maloney said, causing another round of laughter. He even caught Detective Tori off guard with that one, causing him to exit the room in an attempt to hide his laughter. The look on Day's face was priceless. He looked like someone had just smashed his face with a pie. He stood there for a moment, looking dumbfounded.

"Well, you burst in here like an idiot. What's on your mind?" Lynch asked confidently, knowing that the five men left in the squadron were all handpicked by him. Even if they didn't wear their feelings about Blacks and other minorities on their sleeves like him, they sure as hell thought like him. At all costs, they would side with him. Day didn't have a single ally in the room. He might as well have been in a room full of Klan's men outfitted in white sheets and coned hoodies.

Clearing his throat and taking in the six sets of gawking eyes, he started off slowly, choosing his words wisely, "Now I've been on this force for fifteen years. I haven't made a beef with any man in this room who hadn't beefed with me. Every day, I put on my badge and uniform faithfully. I wear them with pride. I put my life on the line for my fellow officers. Shit, I put my life on the line for fellow soldiers in Afghanistan, Iraq, Libya, and Somalia. I proudly served and continue to serve my country. I face the disdain from my own people and from White people who don't respect a Black man in uniform. Through it all, I have never crossed any officer, and I've even adhered to the Blue Wall of Silence, many times against my own people. But this shit you're trying to put on me, I don't deserve this shit. Lynch, you and Maloney are wrong for this, and any of the rest of you who condone the denigration of a fellow officer. Own your shit, man. I'm not going to let you turn me into a fall guy." After his last words, he stood there wagging his finger at them.

"Somebody please give this guy an Oscar," Maloney said, clapping his heavy hands together. Now standing to his feet, in a threatening tone, he continued, "This ain't Training Day and you damn sure ain't Denzel Washington. I tell you what, though, you sure are looking to have an epic ending like him. Now get the fuck out of here before I toss your Black ass out."

"Yeah, if I were you, I'd get to stepping," said a steroid-diesel detective sitting at the set of desks directly to Day's right. As the words left his lips, muscles and veins bulged out of his neck, matching the bass in his deep-threatening voice, evoking Batman's cadence. When the door slammed open, it shook the family pictures on his desk, knocking one of them to the floor. He wasn't the least bit pleased with that. But his interjection was all about preventing Lynch from saying anything that might come back to haunt him. Maloney and all the other detectives in the room would shield Lynch because they knew if he went down, they were all toast.

"You heard him. Now I suggest you leave before things get really bad for you," Lynch warned, placing his hand next to his weapon.

"It's like that, huh," Day responded.

"Just like that," Maloney said, following suit and placing his hand next to his weapon. Realizing he was outnumbered and outgunned, Day took two firm steps backwards until he felt his heel hit the base of the door. Reaching his left hand back, he found the door knob, twisted it, opened the door, and exited without taking his eyes off them. As he gingerly walked back down the hall he'd stormed up just a few minutes ago, he immediately started to regret his actions. He allowed his emotions to control his thoughts. He failed to strategize, and he knew that it would cost him. But what he wasn't sure of was just how much it would cost him.

"Hey, Day, is everything all right?" the night Sargent yells at his back, as he exits the precinct. Day bounced down the steps one foot at a time until he hit the pavement. The ground felt like it absorbed all the pressure he was feeling, filling him with a temporary feeling of relief. He let out a sigh and took a deep breath of the fresh night air. It was slightly cool outside, and the night sky was starlit and clear. By the time he reached the end of the block, his ginger pace turned into a brisk pace. For some reason, he regretted not driving his car. He had to be about five blocks away from the precinct when he realized a dark car was tailing him.

"He's right there! Pull right up on his side!" The front-seat passenger of the dark colored vehicle said while twisting a silencer around the nose of a pistol. Simultaneously, the back-seat passenger concentrated on twisting a silencer on the muzzle of an AP-5 machine gun, peering in the direction of Day. Day noticed the sedan slowing down, and he could see the occupants inside focusing on him. His mind started to race, thinking Lynch wouldn't send a hit squad after him. Would they? He pondered. The thought gave him chills, as goose bumps covered his entire body.

"We're about to reach the end of the block. I'll just swing the car right in front of him at the corner," the driver said.

"No. Why don't you just speed up now and make the turn as if we're moving along, and then back up, and we'll have a clear shot at him," the backseat passenger said.

"I like that idea, except when you turn the corner, pull out of his sight, and let me get out in case he tries to flee. I can track him down on foot," the front seat passenger said in his baritone voice. The driver pressed down on the gas pedal, pulling the sedan forward at a normal speed. Day tried to get a better look inside the vehicle, and he thought the passenger in the backseat had a mask on. He slowed up his pace, noticing the right taillight signaling a turn up ahead. He was relieved to see the car continue to drive on. But suddenly, he felt uneasy at the sight of the brake lights reflecting off the corner street pole. Stopping dead in his tracks, he unsnapped the button that kept his weapon in its holster. The brake light disappeared from the light pole, and just as expected, the vehicle backed up into his line of view. He was prepared for the car's appearance, but he didn't prepare for the shooter who popped out of what seemed like nowhere, firing a weapon at him.

"Theu-theu-theu," the silencer sounds off. Two bullets smacked Day clean in the chest, knocking him back, causing the third bullet to skip across his scalp. Day's body crashed to the ground, and he gasped to retrieve the air that the bullets had just knocked clean out of him. His eyes nearly popped out of their sockets, snapping him back to reality. Lying on his side, he could see a tall, shadowy figure approaching fast to finish the job. He rolled over to his back, yanked his weapon out and unleashed a salvo of bullets.

"Pop-pop-pop-pop-pop," sounded the department-issued Glock 9 mm. "Tinktink," sounded the bullets that hit the sedan as the fleeing shooter jumped in the front passenger seat. I know that frame! *'That was the big lurch from the office,'* Day thought to himself. But before he could waste any more time thinking, the back window slid down, and the muzzle of a machine gun was now hanging out the window. He scrambled to his feet as the deluge of bullets tore from the weapon. He could hear bullets crashing into the pavement and the row of cars he split through to get away. Tires screeched behind him, letting him know that they meant business. They wanted him dead tonight. Day's heart pounded in his chest as he ran for his life down the block. The car's engine revved as it jutted forward in pursuit. As Day hit the corner, the sedan fishtailed out, bending the corner right behind him. He could still hear bullets ricocheting off the pavement, hitting the garbage bags that were left out on the streets, and the black gates aligning the buildings. All of those missed shots fueled his efforts to get away because he knew that any one of them could easily end his life.

As the engine roared behind him, he dug his feet even deeper into the pavement. He thought he had a chance if he made it to the next corner. He figured the vehicle had picked up too much speed and wouldn't be able to make the turn ahead. Day edged around the corner, feeling a bullet tear through his army jacket's collar. Just as he figured, the sound of tires screeching and dented metal filled the air as the sedan slammed into the parked cars on the corner.

He knew that slowed them down, but he was getting tired. He could already hear the engine revving, followed by screeching tires. Looking up ahead, he could see a band of protesters marching horizontally across the street up ahead. He never thought he'd see the day that he would be happy to see a swarm of Black Lives Matter protesters in the middle of the night.

"Black Lives Matter-Black Lives Matter-Black Lives Matter," he could hear them chanting. He also realized that there was a sharp decline in the vehicle's roaring engine. He looked back to find the vehicle at a complete stop. He made it to the crowd and blended right into the immediate sea of Black and Brown faces. As the protesters shuffled him along in what seemed like a bed of salmon swimming against the current, he felt his shoulders bumping into protesters as they moved along at a determined pace. The more he looked around, the more he realized the many different shades of pigment in the crowd. There were a lot of young Whites, some Asians, and even Indians embedded in the crowd. In fact, he noticed there were a lot of Whites. His head started to turn from side to side, taking in the faces that passed him. Suddenly, he no longer felt safe. His assailants could easily get up on him and shoot him with their silencers and move right along with the crowd. No one would hear a thing. He thought to himself.

In his peripheral vision, he could swear down that he saw that tall dark figure.

"He's right up ahead of me," the front-seat passenger whispered into a headset as he brushed through the crowd.

"I think he made you," said the back-seat passenger, as she brushed by protesters just a few feet away from Day. "Just distract him. He doesn't see me. I can get him," she said, closing the gap. Day looked nervously to his right, noticing the figure again.

"No justice. No peace. No racist police!" the protesters chanted, bellowing at a loud pitch. The back-seat passenger was directly on Day's other side, slowly raising the weapon against his back, when a protester brushed past her to get to Day.

"Hey, Day, what's going on?" an old buddy asks, but before Day could respond, he continued, "Hey guys, we got an 89er with us. It's my squad buddy Day from the academy," the Black gentleman said to the immediate group of what appeared to be Black and Brown off duty officers. A bald male, standing at about six feet five inches tall, turned towards Day and flashed the beaded metallic chain that hung around his neck, linking his badge. A few other officers made the same gesture. Day realized that this group represented One Hundred Black Officers in Law Enforcement. Day's assailant recognized the move as well, and the banners that read Black Officers in Support of Black Lives. She immediately waved off the other assailant, and as if they were never there, they both faded away into the sea of protesters. They would have to get him another time, but now was definitely not the time, unless they wanted to end up in Guantanamo Bay.

Day was really beside himself now. Not only did a group of protesters save his life, but a group of Black police officers also protested police brutality. It was incredible. Never in a million years could he have imagined this display of unity within the Black ranks of the department and the community. Although he had to admit that times were changing because in response to the killing of another unarmed civilian, a police chief recently took a Kaepernick-style knee in solidarity with protesters, a White police chief at that! He sighed in relief as his old academy squad captain patted him on the shoulder, gathering his attention.

"Hey, man, is everything okay? You seem a bit disturbed," Kurt, the man they called Cap, inquired as they moved up the block.

"Yeah, Cap, I'm fine. I'm just a little taken aback by the way times have really changed. I mean Black officers marching for justice. I don't know if that's a good thing or if it means that things are getting worse," Day resentfully said, hating the fact that he remained confused.

"Man, we've always been marching in one way or another. Once I took the oath to serve and protect, I knew I had added to the cause of marching. Now some Black folks claim that marching don't do no good. I beg to differ. Marching brings awareness to social issues that go unnoticed on a day-to-day basis. Today, we have the most diverse crowds of protesters in the history of this great nation. More people are willing to get out and protest against injustices that have gone on for far too long in America," Cap ranted.

"I get what you're saying and all, but the Civil Rights Movement had a diverse crowd of protesters. Pull up any film and you will see that it's not just Black people marching. Man, even the Freedom Rides, Sit-ins, you name it, they all had some White, Brown, and other folks involved. My point is, what makes this time any different?" Day demanded.

"To be honest with you, I think that everything in life takes just the right amount of time to produce fruit. In other words, Grandma's corn bread tastes so good because she knows just when to turn the oven up, just when to bring the temperature down, and just when that golden brown crisp signals that the cornbread is ready, not a minute too soon or a minute too late, as my Ga-Ga would say," Cap replied.

"Your grandmother, huh, she sounds sagacious. So I guess what you're saying is the right amount of ingredients must be added to the corn bread as well. To put it another way, the Civil Rights Movement had some older people of various backgrounds and some younger people. Today we are witnessing loads of young and older people from various backgrounds, equaling the right brew of ingredients," Day added, seeming to get Cap's point.

"Exactly, there you go! Now, are you going to tell me what's going on or do I have to pry it out of you?" he probed.

"Cap, I think I got myself into some deep intra-departmental trouble with homicide. I may have rocked the boat a bit too much, sending these piranhas into a feeding frenzy," he responded.

Nodding his head, Cap said, "I recognized your name on the News the other day with regard to the incident in Brown Housing. I was hoping that it wasn't anything that went sour. Something just didn't seem right about it. I mean, different reports between the Police Chief and the so-called witnesses. Do you feel like going into details?" He finished with a question, but before Day could answer, the crowd burst into even louder chants.

"No justice, no peace, no racist police!" they loudly shouted in response to the police roadblock up ahead. Their movement was effectively being stopped.

"Ah man, I hope things don't go left," Cap said, realizing that police in riot gear were deployed to the peaceful protest.

"This is a peaceful protest. We are asserting our right to protest the injustices against Black and Brown people in this country. We are tax-paying citizens. We are Americans, and we demand justice for the killings of unarmed Americans. An injustice to one is an injustice to all!" the six-foot-five bald male shouts over a bullhorn.

"Injustice to one is injustice to all!" The crowd repeated, directing the slogan at the blue wall of silent officers in riot gear that formed in front of the protesters.

"Cap, I think this is my cue to get out of here. I've got too much going on right now to have to explain this to top brass," Day informed him before parting ways.

"Alright, Day, remember you have a lot of friends from the academy. We're brothers. Don't you forget that either. If you need me for anything, I'm not hard to find. Come down to the six-nine and ask for Cap. You hear me. All you got to do is ask for Cap," he shouted out to Day as he faded away deep into the crowd.

Day proceeded with confidence once he was certain that he had lost his trail, or rather, the trail retreated once they got wind of the other officers surrounding him. He saw the tall, shadowy figure vanish into the crowd. That's what gave him away to Cap. It was obvious that Cap noticed his eyes scanning the crowd. He couldn't hide that, nor did he try to hide it. In the line of duty, you didn't gamble with your own life. The academy tacitly taught them to value their lives over the civilians they were supposed to serve and protect. Their mottos promoted the idea that no matter what happened on the job, you made sure you got home to your family. In a very real sense, Day knew that meant the lives of the people in the communities they served were counted as less than an officer's life. He remained perplexed because the people of these communities all looked like him. They were Black and Brown bodies: the undeserving poor.

Zero to a Hundred

I sprang to my feet, stood erect on my tiptoes, stretched my arms to the sky, and let out a lion's yawn. My eyes zoomed in on the black television screen. Finally, putting my feet flat on the ground, I walked over and turned on what Chemistry referred to as *the tell lie vision*. Immediately, I noticed that the News topic concerned me. So, I turned up the volume and plopped back down at the foot of my bed.

"There have been some startling revelations that have recently come to light about the apprehension of Derrick Martin, an alleged murder suspect. New reports have been surfacing about one of the arresting officers. According to credible sources, Officer Day struggles with Post Traumatic Stress Disorder. He served numerous tours in Afghanistan, Iraq, and possibly a tour or two in Kuwait. As we know, Don, there is a great possibility that many soldiers who served in Kuwait were exposed to mustard gas, among other biological grade weapons. No one truly knows the long-term effects of exposure to any of those chemicals, but that's another story, Don. It appears in this case, preliminary reports suggested that the injury to Derrick Martin was an accident. However, we are now learning that several witnesses and possibly some officers are now claiming that Officer Day's conduct was intentional. If any listeners are just tuning in, then you heard me correctly. Reports now claim that Officer Day intentionally used excessive force, harming the alleged murder suspect, leaving him in a coma."

He paused to take a breath and then continued: *"Reports are coming out that Officer Day even used a derogatory term towards the suspect, repeatedly calling him the N-word. The Police Chief said that they are hopeful that the camera footage can be recovered from the camera facing the building's entrance. The Police Chief went on to say that the department is launching a full investigation into the matter and cautions the public not to rush to judgment. Don, with all of the protests against police brutality going on, this appears to be another case where excessive force reared its ugly head. However, I would caution folks out there that the one thing that's different about this case is that the suspect was wanted for killing another Black man. According to police reports, he allegedly had a gun on him and even tried to fire at unsuspecting officers. I think people are smart enough to know the difference in this situation. Well, that will do it; this is Walter Crosby reporting for Channel Six News. Back to you, Don."*

I sat there stunned, thinking to myself that there must be some kind of mistake. Officer Day was one of the nicest cops I had ever met. He was the embodiment of the neighborhood caricature known as Officer Friendly. When I thought of him, I thought of McGruff the crime-stopping dog, who encouraged us to take a bite out of crime. Why would Day call another nigger, a nigger? This didn't make any sense. Black people call each other niggers all the time. There's nothing duh – rog – derogatory, yeah, that word, about that either. In fact, we actually say nigga with "a" at the end, not "e" "r" at the end. White people pronounced the "e" "r" and that's where all the problems started. That was why they couldn't use the N-word because they couldn't pronounce it correctly. I didn't think that the N-word existed during the time of slavery. That was a long-long time ago, like dinosaur long ago. We didn't even talk about slavery in the classroom because the books about slavery were obviously way too old for the classroom, and so the conservative White teachers kicked those books out, and yelled "kick them out the classroom—," "What they doing in the classroom?" Shoot, I'd have to go to an antique shop to find a book about slavery now. I would have never been a slave. I didn't care what Chemistry said. My name wasn't Kunta Kente. I had never been to Africa and didn't plan on going either. In Africa, Africans didn't wear J's. They dressed like the Flintstones. They would have to shackle me and put me on a slave ship to take me back to Africa, and then, I'd still jump off the boat and would definitely have outswam the sharks. 'I ain't no African booty scratcher,' I whispered to myself.

Just then, "Bang, bang, bang," the loud thuds pounded on our apartment door, immediately followed by a voice demanding, "It's the police! Open the door!" The alarming noise snapped me out of my daze, and I knew it had woken up my mom, too. I heard her bed creak to the weight of her springing up like a dead person in a casket. It was her ritual because every time my mother woke up, she always sat straight up in the bed like Count Dracula. Normally, she'd have cussed at the top of her lungs at whoever was banging on our door. But I guessed that the word police must have made her think twice. I wondered what the cops were even doing here. It wasn't even seven o'clock yet. It was barely fifteen minutes past six a.m. This couldn't be good, but at least they knocked. They usually just kick the door in without even saying, '*It's the police!*' After hearing my mother's slippers shuffling across the living room floor, I nervously sat in the bed awaiting the response. I heard her unlatch the chain and unlock the door. I could hear the door violently slam open, and a brief scuffle ensued.

"Get on the ground and put your hands behind your back! Stop resisting!" were the last words I heard before hearing the sound of troops marching to my room door. I wanted to dive under the covers, under the bed, or under anything that would shield me from the occupying army that lay siege to our apartment. My body wouldn't move. I was like a deer caught in the headlights. My heart pounded, trying to break free from my chest, as my breathing took on a sudden struggle for air. The force of a storm trooper's foot flung my room door open, with such force that it was off its hinges. I couldn't hear anything but my mother screaming after a bright flash followed by a bang. My ears were ringing, I could barely see, and I swore it felt like someone just inserted me into PlayStation's Call of Duty game.

'*Oh boy, Jumanji is real!*' I thought to myself, staring down the barrels of three AR-15s. One soldier squatted down at the doorway's entrance with the butt of his weapon pressed against his shoulder, another soldier wrapped his assault rifle around the door's left frame, and the third soldier swiftly moved into the room, pointing his rifle at my head. For a moment, I thought he was the character Cyclops from the X-Men until I noticed three separate red beams bouncing across my frail body.

"Get on the ground," the soldier shouted. But before I could even think to move, he snatched me up from my bed like a rag doll, tossing me to the ground. His knee pressed into my back, knocking the air clean out of my hysterical lungs. Next, my arms were yanked back so hard that I thought they were about to pop out of their sockets. He zip-tied my wrist, and I had to hear about four different voices, throughout the apartment, yelling "clear" one after another. My mother and I were chained by the four six-foot centurions and were ushered out of our apartment and down six flights of steps. We reached the bottom in record time. Neither my mother's nor my feet ever touched a step. They literally dragged us through the air. However, once we reached the lobby, the troops were abruptly stopped by their commander.

"What the hell is this? You can't take this kid out of here hog-tied like that. There's a crowd of angry tenants outside. Take those zip ties off the kid now! Jesus Christ, he's only a fucking kid," The Sargent of the ATF squad shouts. The gentleman to his right, whose tag read captain, just shook his head.

"Excuse me, sir, why am I being arrested?" My mother pleaded with the man in charge.

"You'll find out once you get to the precinct," is all the Sargent said.

"Why are you taking my son? His grandparents live right there in apartment IA," She screamed, calling attention to the neighbors. The men in charge were obviously affected by her screams as the look of embarrassment spread across their countenances. The door to Billy's apartment opened, and his grandfather nervously showed himself.

"Please leave the boy with me, sir. He's my grandchild. The precinct ain't no place for a child," He pleaded in an unsteady voice. The two men in charge looked at each other and simultaneously shrugged their shoulders. '*It was clear that they didn't want any more bad publicity. After all, our building made the News early this morning, and the News people may even be outside,*' I thought to myself.

Before I knew it, I heard myself blurting out a lie, "The Channel Six News crew is outside. Is that Walter Crosby?" The looks on each of their faces were priceless, looking like kids with their hands caught in the cookie jar.

The Captain didn't even waste another second to confirm my sighting before demanding that the centurion free me. He ordered the men to proceed with my mother out of the building through the growing crowd of stakeholders, shoving her into the paddy wagon. Billy's grandfather unsuspectingly caught me after the oversized men had recklessly shoved me into his arms. Neither man cared if he caught me or not. Clearly, they didn't believe in catch and release. They probably bit the heads off undersized fish before throwing them back into the water as bait.

Mr. Dave rushed me into the apartment before the officers had a chance to change their minds. Like clockwork, Mr. Dave locked each of the three locks on the door, slammed the door bolt into the floor, and latched the chain. His eye was glued to the peephole with his face awkwardly adjusted to press his ear as close to the door as possible. I followed suit and attempted to squeeze my itching ear through the door's crack.

I clearly heard another man enter the lobby, asking where the kid was. He certainly was referring to me. By the sound of it, he wanted me badly. If I had to guess, then I would say he wanted me more than he wanted my mother. When the Captain pulled rank on him, I realized that he was a detective. The Captain ordered him to get his you-know-what in the car. He complained about the presence of the agitated residents, and Channel Six News actually being outside. He yelled, "We don't have a warrant for the kid. All we have is for his mother, Lynch." He revealed his name, and it scared the crap out of me. I imagined he must be known for lynching people. Actually, where I was from, if your name was Murder, Killer, or even Diesel, you had to live up to that name. People certainly would test you to see if you were who you said you were. Just anybody couldn't go around claiming the name Debo. With a name like Debo, everyone expected you to be the neighborhood bully. Did the movie Friday ring a bell? I had to stay alert. There was a detective named Lynch who had it out for me, and I wasn't taking any chances.

I raced to the window to witness the men exiting the building one after another. I spotted the man who had to be Lynch, being the only one that I didn't recognize from the lobby. He was a tall, White man with silver-gray hair, an unusually long nose, and freckles that littered his wrinkled face. The fleet of police vehicles mobilized in unison, evacuating the premises. I could see my mother's watery eyes beaming out of the back window of the middle paddy wagon. She looked defenseless and, above all, terrified. My heart sank, watching them take her away. I couldn't stop the tears that magically appeared, rolling down my cheeks. The angry crowd trailed the envoy, chanting, "Take back our streets!" It became obvious that they were trying to retrieve the agency and dignity that had been momentarily stripped from all of us. I could see the look of relief on some of their faces as they returned to their individual corners. Some remained in small groups to voice their frustrations, but the unity vanished with the conquerors.

"Hoodie, you get from that window and go on in the room with Billy. I'm going to make some calls to check on your mom. She will be fine. The police officers know that a lot of people witnessed them take her. I doubt very strongly that they would do anything to harm her. You hear me?" He asked, trying to convince me that it was okay to go on and worry about the kid stuff. Easier said than done, as if I didn't just experience my mother being abducted by a clan of White men.

I was horrified at the thought of what they might do to my mom. I couldn't help but recall the stories Chemistry had told me about slave masters. About how they stripped slave children away from their hysterical enslaved mothers, and went on to sell the kids down the river to other slavers. He even told me about slavers who were so cruel that they ignored the wailing of their own young children, who were horrified at the violent destruction of friendships. Sometimes, slavers not only tore slave mothers away from their own children, but they also tore them away from the slave master's children. Chemistry would boast that they traumatized those White kids so bad that they wouldn't dream of making friends with any other Black slave children. *'Now, that's some post-traumatic slave syndrome for your ass,'* he'd end with. I guess he was trying to say that was the reason that most White people don't have Black friends today.

I went to Billy's room door and tried to push it open, only to be met with the resistance of his body. He had his ear glued to the door on the other side. I gave an extra hard push that flung the door open and knocked him to the floor. He sprang back to his feet like he wanted some smoke, but realizing that it was me, he immediately relaxed his stance. "Hey Hoodie, what's up? What's going on?" Billy asked. He was probing for answers about the way things unfolded this morning.

"What's going on?" I repeated in a kind of agitation at his feigning ignorance. But before he could say a word, I unleashed on him. "What's going on is G.I. Joe just went rogue in my humble abode, and they were more akin to Cobra and the forces of Dark Vader. They stormed in, thrashing the place, treating my mom and me like illegal aliens. I thought they were ICE agents, looking for birth certificates and green cards. You never know. If number forty-five can claim that number forty-four doesn't have a birth certificate, then you know they can say my mom and I were illegally smuggled into the country. Now, I'm a refugee. That's what's going on!"

"Hoodie, you're not a refugee," Billy said, sighing loudly.

"Yes, I am. I don't have food or shelter. Your grandfather took me in. I fit the classical definition of a refugee, someone seeking refuge," I responded with loads of spit foaming in my dry mouth. My breathing remained erratic, and I could feel the pace of my heart speeding up as each syllable left my lips. The next thing I knew, I was having a panic attack. I couldn't breathe, causing me to scream, "I can't breathe." Immediately, I was terrified and filled with emotions about all the Black men, women, and children whose encounters with police ended in cries that fell on deaf ears. That same cry: I can't breathe, and now I was the one pleading that I just couldn't breathe. Just before everything went black, I remember Billy sprang to action and called for his grandfather.

When I came round, I saw Chemistry. He was hovering over me as I lay in Billy's bed. Chemistry had just been released from the lockup. Apparently, he was arrested at a peaceful protest the night before. I think what awoke me was the pungent odor fuming off his filthy body. He looked like he had been rolling around in the junkyard. He was beyond musty. I could smell the stench of at least five filthy panhandlers, at least two wayward teens, a fat, drunk guy, and two mental health patients. All of those funky orders mingled with his odor to make one powerful formation of a musky cloud that hovered around his body. I thought I even saw a fly or two, buzzing around his matted-nappy afro. 'Yep,' I thought as one just zipped and then landed on top of the black power fist, crowning his pick. 'Now that's what you call a rude awakening!' was all I could think to myself.

"You stink. Ooh, you stink!" I muttered before rolling over and retreating under the pillow. I could hear his muffled laughter as I pressed the pillow against my ears, smothering my face into the mattress. I imagined a dark cloud swarming with flies, parting his mouth as he laughed. By the smell of his body, his breath had to be kicking like a newborn crack baby that didn't want any milk, not even from a sober breast. I could even hear Chris Rock's voice shout: "Somebody get that baby a crack pipe," followed by the roaring laughter of an audience. Chemistry snatched the pillow out of my clutch, yanking my head up, but it snapped back down from the force of a lost battle of tug-a-war. I reburied my face in the mattress.

"Come on now, get up. I have a sandwich for you. Are you hungry?" he asked. I turned over at the mention of food. I would brave his horrid smell for that moment only. He extended his arm to hand me the sandwich that was wrapped in sandwich paper. My hunger must have clouded my judgment because without thinking, I snatched the sandwich out of his hand, tearing the wrapping open, and sank my teeth into the almost dry-stale bread. By the time my teeth reached the rubbery baloney meat and hardened cheese, I knew I'd been cast for the Ridiculousness TV show. My face turned to disgust as I slowly released my teeth from the grips of the soggy bullpen sandwich.

I just had my first taste of a cop-out sandwich.

"Yuck! What the hell is wrong with you, giving me that garbage? I'd take a murder burger and suicide fries over that any day. Yikes! That was disgusting. Where did you get that from the cemetery? I could have choked to death,"

I raved. He just stood there laughing, clutching his gut. He obviously found his transgression humorous, and I was the butt of his joke. "Hey, man, you brought that one on yourself. What did you think I wrapped that sandwich for you all nice and pretty in the kitchen?" he mused.

"You must mean nice and shitty. Did you just pull that out of your ass?" I shoot back.

"I just got out of lockup, and you just took a full bite of the bullpen special," he informed me.

"What? So, you really did have that sandwich in your butt cheeks," I said before taking another look at the sandwich, then launching it at his head. He tried to duck, but the baloney separated from that bread, slapping him right in his forehead.

"Bull's-eye!" I shouted.

"You little," was all I heard before he jumped all over me. I thought I was in a fight with a blanket of funk. Rather than being snuffed out by the powerful odor, I tried to hold my breath.

"Hey, what's going on in there?" Mr. Dave yelled out.

"Nothing," Chemistry shouted.

And right on cue, I began to yell out, "Mr. Dave, he's trying to kill me with his stink jailhouse odors. Get off of me!" Billy stormed into the room and leaped on Chemistry's back. Right when I thought I had some help, Billy sprang right off him and flew in the opposite direction, brushing by Mr. Dave, who started to enter the room, stopping dead in his tracks and making an immediate about-face.

"What the hell!" Mr. Dave shouts. Continuing, he demands, "You need to take your butt in the shower." Chemistry laughed loudly and heartily. "Man, it ain't funny. You're on your own, kid," Mr. Dave said and headed back down the hall. Billy was nowhere to be found, so much for boys having each other's backs. Just when I thought all hope was lost, Billy showed up with a bucket of ice-cold water.

"If I were you, I'd look behind me," I warned Chemistry. Just as I had hoped he'd do, he turned around and immediately let me go and started towards Billy. He gave us just enough separation when Billy extinguished him with the bucket of water. I rolled over completely off the bed to escape the splashing water. The next thing I heard was the bucket fall, followed by Billy's footsteps tearing in the other direction. Chemistry knew that it made no sense to chase after him, especially hearing the apartment door slam. He turned on me with vengeance in his eyes.

"Hey, I tried to warn you," I pleaded. He took one look at me and then stormed off to the bathroom, where he belonged. Billy came back when the coast was clear. We cleaned up the water and the soggy sandwich off the floor. Ironically, I found myself thinking how the sandwich looked more edible after soaking in water. I figured if I ever found myself in lockup, I'd wet the sandwich to make it edible. It was one more piece of information that I added to my tool belt.

Since a young age, I had to deal with the reality that one out of three Black men is destined to end up in prison, like Don King would say, "only in America."

I stood there thinking, especially in my case, Black juveniles were six times more likely to be sent to a detention center than their White counterparts were for the same criminal charges. I was conscious of living in a country that incarcerated more youth than any other country around the globe. I wondered how that can be when many other countries have child soldiers like the character Baby Gangsta in the movie Blood Diamonds. Although America made up much less than ten percent of the world's population, America imprisoned a quarter of the world's prisoners. Chemistry told me that it had something to do with the New Jim Crow, and then he said I should read more. I told him we didn't even talk about the Old Jim Crow in the classroom, so how was I supposed to know about the New Jim Crow? He countered that true leaders learn outside of the classroom and that classroom learning is designed for followers. Once he started talking about indoctrination, workers and people who take orders, Rockefeller, and the Persian school system, he had really lost me on that. I wondered what the hell fast food or restaurant workers had to do with anything. Speaking, or rather thinking of the devil, Chemistry entered the room more like his usual self. I turned around only to realize that Billy darted under the bed.

"Billy, you can come out from under the bed. He has us surrounded," I said, giving up Billy's location on purpose. I was being facetious. I always found the joke extremely funny about how the two criminals who tried to escape from the cops, and one of whom hid under a car. The cops arrived and nabbed the one who failed to get under the car. Before the cops even got a chance to look under the car, the criminal who got nabbed shouted, "Hey Jim, they got us. You can come out from under the car." I couldn't control myself and burst into laughter. Even Chemistry found it funny. We could even hear Billy's muffled laughter coming from underneath the bed. *'Nothing like some good old laughter to lighten the mood,'* I thought to myself. Chemistry forgot all about beating the brakes off us and instead, he wanted to talk to me about some serious stuff.

I was not mentally prepared for what he was about to tell me. I wish I'd taken a seat because I started to feel queasy as he revealed the details. Chemistry insisted that he and I had a bone to pick with the same people. I stood there thinking that I didn't have a bone to pick with anyone, especially not the cops. After the way that SWAT Team stormed our apartment, after the way they ragdoll dragged me and my momma down six flights of steps, after seeing Mr. Dave visibly shaken, after seeing all of our residents scramble like roaches at their presence, and nobody attempting to help my momma, I flat out told Chemistry that he must be crazy if he thought I was enlisting in his Black power movement. I tried to convince him that the Blue Power Movement was real. My mother got an instant black and blue eye to prove it.

How I didn't get choked, but I still couldn't breathe when Sargent Slaughter plunged his adult knee into my infant back, cracking my spine in fifty different places. I saw stars and stripes. I told him that although I believe in King's, Malcolm's, and even Hampton's words, the Ku Klux Klan puts its hands on niggers. How even he said that they ain't wearing white sheets no more because, according to a twenty-first century FBI report, the KKK and other White extremist groups traded their sheets in for Blue uniforms. Your exact words were that they infiltrated law enforcement. "I'd be listening when you're telling me stuff," I threw back in his face.

Furthermore, I said that they don't care about anything, and never about what you got on videotape. I asked him, "How many unarmed innocent Black and Brown people had he witnessed die on camera at the hands of police, and not one officer be tried and convicted of murder? All the top brass was going to do with your video is tell people not to rush to judgment and how the video doesn't show moments before or after whatever the fudge they want to make up! And you don't even have the video in your possession anymore." I was literally screaming in the end. By the look on his face, I could tell that he not only heard me loud and clearly, but he also got my point. Even Billy was stunned at the amount of information that I had lodged in my mental arsenal. For a second, I was even impressed, thinking maybe Principal Joe is right about me being a perfect fit for the debate club. 'Nah,' I shook my head and quickly erased that thought.

"You finished?" Chemistry asked and paused a second before adding, "Listen, little nigga, we're gonna go in there and smoke all those fools. Them niggas shot yo cousin and you ain't gonna do shit," He mimicked the character O-Dog from the movie, Menace to Society.

"Both of ya'll niggas sounding like," Billy got out before Chemistry gave him one of those looks that said he'd better not even think about finishing MC Eights' line from the script that ends in. Deep in my heart, I knew that Chemistry was right. Those cops nearly scared the poop out of me. I literally had to hold my grippers. They got a lot closer than my mom ever did.

Besides, I was not even a teen, and something told me that Lynch would make sure that I didn't see my thirteenth birthday. He'd probably do me like some people claimed they did, Little Dee. The only difference would be with me; he'd probably just have to plant a toy cap gun on me. I imagined him even getting away with claiming that I fired it, and him mistaking it for actual gunfire, how the headlines would read. He feared for his life, making mines not matter. If I had anything to do with it, Lynch wouldn't get to be rewarded with a two-week paid vacation for killing me. 'Not this Black kid,' I told myself. 'I wouldn't allow Lynch or anyone else to make me a statistic.'

Chemistry was searching my eyes, observing my body language, and he must have been reading my mind too. He went into a long spiel about how he understood that I was afraid and how I needed to be brave. I wanted to tell him, like my mother would say, that the only thing I needed to do was eat, sleep, and shit. But he went on and on about the people in the Black Lives Matter movement risking their lives for me. How Dr. Martin Luther King Jr. walked so I could fly. I wanted to yell out, "Nigga, I never even been on a plane." What the hell was he talking about? I don't know Rosa Parks. The only thing I know about her was that she didn't like the rap group Outkast's song lyrics that say "everybody get to the back of the bus," If it hadn't been for their song, I still wouldn't know who she was, never mind the pregnant girl Claudette Cloven who didn't relinquish her seat to a fat White man either. Well, it was the South, so in my mind, it must have been a fat White guy. Who else would want to take a pregnant woman's seat, but someone else who looked like they themselves were nine months? Shoot, he probably was happy about the boycott, more food for him. Boy, I cracked me up was my last thought before Chemistry snapped me back to reality. Only this time, I was all ears.

The Sun Don*t Shine Forever

"Now, I'm going to say this one time only, so you'd better listen to me real good. If you have any plans to see your child again, then you're going to do exactly as I tell you," Lynch said as he stood over a seated Ms. Hoodie. She was handcuffed to a metal ring that was attached to the cold steel table that was bolted to the ground. The small room was grey and gloomy. A two-way mirror adorned the wall to her right. The walls were cold blocks of cement splattered with gray paint. Only one door allowed access to the room, and she sat on the opposite side of the desk, pressed against a corner. It did not allow passersby to get a good look at the room, and it looked as if she weren't even there. Normally, Lynch would feel like he had his perpetrator right where he wanted them, but there was something different in her eyes. He quite couldn't place what it was.

"Are you finished? Let me tell you something. You can keep that little bastard for all I care. His little ass is the reason I'm in this mess in the first place. You'd better hope I don't see him again because I'm gonna beat him to death when I do see him, and there goes your witness. Shit! Got me locked the fuck up!" She vented and punctuated her statement by crossing her arms over her breast. Her hair was disheveled. They didn't even give her a chance to get dressed. She still had a nightgown on and a pair of flip-flop slippers that barely covered her feet. Her calloused heels hung off the backs of the slippers, brushing the ground. She looked the part of a deranged woman. Lynch hadn't expected such a response from her, but he'd been doing his job long enough to avoid raising an eyebrow. He knew that most people could be easily broken. He just had to find out what her weakness was, and it wasn't really that hard. Most perpetrators revealed their deepest fears in their own words. They talked too much and always unconsciously gave up information. She did the same thing, and now he would use the information she revealed against her.

"How about we start over," Lynch said, reaching inside his blazer and pulling out a pack of New Port cigarettes. He opened the box and continued, "Do you smoke?" he asked, pulling the butt of a cigarette up just enough for her to grab with her fingertips. Without waiting for her response, he extended the box of cigarettes out for her to take one. With her free arm, she raised her shaky fingers and pulled the cigarette out of the pack, placing it between her dry lips.

"You got a light?" she demanded with the cigarette dangling from the corner of her mouth like a cowgirl in an old western movie. Without saying a word, Lynch dug in his pocket, pulled out his lighter, and lit the cigarette. He walked to the other side of the table, pulled the other chair out, and sat down directly across from her.

"I think I'll have one on me too," he pulled another cigarette loose and lit it. They sat across from each other in silence. She didn't take her eyes off him. She steam-pulled on the cigarette, causing her cheeks to sink in after every inhale. She tilted her head up slightly and exhaled, releasing a purple cloud of smoke towards the ceiling. All the while, she kept an eye on him through the corner of her eye. He pulled on his cigarette, analyzing her body language. It didn't take long for her to finish her cigarette, but Lynch was only halfway through his. Seeing there was no ashtray anywhere in sight, she didn't even bother to ask for one. She just dropped the cigarette to the ground in a pile of ashes and ground it into the floor under her slipper. For a brief second, he wondered if the fire tip would burn through the worn slipper. He sat there with a smirk on his face.

He leaned forward and asked, "Would you like a cup of coffee? Let me guess, no sugar, no creamer, steaming black, right?" he said, emphasizing the word black indirectly referring to her ethnicity. He revealed a twinkle in his eye at the snide remark. Hoodie's mom wasn't stupid. She recognized the slight comment, but a hot cup of coffee this early in the morning sounded like a good idea after a smoke. Besides, she didn't know how long they planned on keeping her in the precinct or when she'd be able to get her own cigarettes and coffee. Not to mention, she had no idea where Lynch was going with all this. She hadn't committed any crime. She held up her end of the bargain and forced Hoodie to agree that he would tell the cops what they wanted to hear. For the life of her, she didn't understand why they were harassing her or why they stormed her apartment and treated her like a common criminal. None of this was right. *You damn Skippy, she would have her some coffee, with warm milk too,* she thought to herself.

"Yeah, a cup of coffee sounds good. It's the least you could do after snatching me out of my bed and violating my civil rights. I do know I have rights that you never read to me," she said, doing quite a good job at hiding her fears.

"Well, I guess that will be your word against my word, and you know how he said she said goes," he chided. Shrugging his shoulders, he continued, "I guess I was right about the steaming black, steaming- southern-cotton picking black."

As he finished, he smiled.

"No, actually, I'll have some freshly squeezed seventeenth-century smoked-Irish milk with it. Straight from the field alongside the cotton pickers. I don't really care for late-nineteenth-century monkey-Irish milk. The taste just doesn't have the same integrity," she said, revealing her own smile.

Although he forced a cunning smile, his face was beet-red, effortlessly blending his freckles in with his skin.

"Oh, so you're ugly and funny. We'll see who gets the last laugh. One steaming black cup of Joe with smoked Irish milk coming up," he said, and exited the room.

Ms. Hoodie sat there having second thoughts about drinking any coffee from him. If she hadn't known any better, she would have thought that Hoodie had tried to poison her coffee. The thought had certainly crossed her mind more than once. She damn sure wouldn't trust a cracker. She sat there thinking to herself. *'But what if they tried to trump some charges up on her? It wasn't like things like that didn't happen all the time. What makes her different?'* She pondered. It felt like an eternity as she sat there in dead silence. She felt like the walls were closing in on her, making the closet-sized room even smaller, nearly suffocating her lungs. There were no windows, finally causing a sense of capture to sink in. She felt trapped and started to panic. Her chest moved up and down as her breathing sped up out of her control. Now hyperventilating, she struggled for air. Not knowing what to do as her eyes widened, she felt as if her life was slipping away. She clutched her chest, realizing she was tumbling into cardiac arrest. A thunderous shock cracked through her chest, sending a violent tremor through her heart. Instantly, her body fell off the chair, crashing to the ground. Her lifeless arm hung from the top of the table, still chained to the cold ring.

Lynch entered the room with the coffee in his hand and stood there for a second, taking in the sight before him. He didn't think that she was the type to faint or act a fool. But he figured to himself that he must have been wrong. He'd seen one too many perpetrators, fake seizures, heart attacks, and even one perpetrator who acted like he had a sudden case of amnesia. He stood there for another second until he noticed her fingers had turned a dark greyish purple, indicating that the handcuff was cutting off the blood and oxygen circulation to her fingers. Within the next second, he placed the coffee cups on the table and sprang into action.

"Ms. Hoodie, can you hear me?" he asked nervously, fumbling in his pocket for the handcuff key. He retrieved it and freed her hand from the cuff. Flipping her body over, he could see that she'd been foaming at the mouth. He checked her pulse and was relieved to feel a faint sign of life. "I need a medic in here. I need a medic!" he shouted at the top of his lungs.

The first one through the door was Maloney. "What the hell!" he said, surprised to see Ms. Hoodie down and out for the count.

"You're not a damn medic. Get me a medic. Get me a defibrillator. Do something," Lynch shouted. Maloney ran back out of the room, and within a second, he was back with an oxygen pump. He handed it to Lynch, and he immediately placed the device over her mouth and pumped air. Next, he pushed down on her chest three times, followed by a squeezing of the oxygen pump. He went through the process at least three times before Ms. Hoodie started showing signs of taking deeper breaths of air. Right on time, a female medic entered the room, rushing to aid Lynch.

"How long has she been like this?" she asked.

"It couldn't have been more than five minutes," he responded. Maloney just stood back as an onlooker. Other medics entered the room with a gurney. They all worked together, swiftly moving Ms. Hoodie from the floor and onto the gurney. Maloney made sure to clamp the handcuff down around the gurney's metal rails. He then instructed a uniformed officer to escort them to the hospital and remain with the prisoner. The medics wheeled her out of there and off to the hospital.

Maloney plopped his behind on the table's surface and asked, "What the hell happened?"

"I went to get coffee, and when I came back, she was unresponsive. I thought she was messing around until I noticed that her hand was practically grey. I know the media is going to have a field day with this nonsense," he said, scratching his head.

"You could have at least let me play bad cop before you knocked the cunt out," Maloney joked.

"What the hell is wrong with you? You can't see that this isn't the time for jokes and laughter. I have to explain this shit to the Captain. He's already complaining about the Chief of Police breathing down his neck about this case because the Mayor's breathing down the Chief's neck about a record number of complaints. I'll tell you what it is. It's Black Lives Matter and all this protesting bullshit! So, we cracked a couple of heads. How else are we supposed to do our jobs? That's what the Chief needs to tell the Mayor. That cock sucking Mayor wants us to tell these criminals to be careful that they don't hit their heads when we put them in the back of the wagon. Over my dead body, I'm with the President on that one. I'll bang every last one of the scumbag's heads into the hood of the car that I lock up," Lynch vented.

"That's the price of doing business. Crime doesn't pay. Hey, Skipper, don't worry about it. The cunt probably overdosed on crack. I think this is her crack pipe right here," he said, holding up a crystal-clear three-inch glass cylinder in his hand.

"Yeah, and when did she get a chance to smoke crack? That damn pipe you have is brand new. It doesn't even have any smoke residue in it, you idiot. What the hell is with you with this crack pipe shit? Don't tell me you're fucking smoking crack," he lambasted.

"What me no, I wouldn't dream of it. I like being fat," he joked.

"Do you take anything serious?" Lynch asks.

"Not any of this shit because at the end of the day, America is pro police. I can do no wrong. I am the judge, jury, and executioner. Here's my license to kill right here," Maloney bragged, patting the forty-four caliber weapon on his hip.

"You'd better be glad that no one important gets to hear half of the things that come out of your mouth, because you'd be out of a job. You'd probably get me fired as well," Lynch said, shaking his head. Before Maloney could respond, the door opened to an angry Captain staring at them with his arms crossed over his chest. Maloney stood to his feet, and Lynch just stood there awaiting the onslaught of grievances that were sure to be hurled at him.

"Hey, Cap," Maloney squeaked out.

"Don't you 'hey Cap' me. What the hell is wrong with you two? Does everything you touch suddenly turn to shit? I asked you to keep things quiet, but you couldn't do that one simple thing. I'm letting you both know that I'm washing my hands with your shit. You're on your own from here on out. If I were you, I would think really hard about how you're going to explain this shit to top brass," he barked and slammed the door before either man had a chance to respond.

"One minute we have the whole precinct dispatched on our behalf and then the next thing you know we're up shit's creek," Lynch lamented.

"Hey, Skip, why don't we go to the hospital and see if our girl is doing better? It may not be as bad as you think," he offered.

"That may be the smartest thing you've said all day. Jesus Mary let this woman be okay," Lynch said, looking to the ceiling as if he were praying. Then he drew the symbol of a cross over his head and torso. Maloney repeated the motion, drawing an imaginary cross over his wide body. All eyes were on them as they exited the interrogation room. An officer or two even had the nerve to shake their heads in disapproval. Bad apples spoiled a bunch; at least that's what minority communities believed. Who would know better than them? Police saturated Black and Brown communities, not White communities, exponentially increasing their encounters, interactions, and relationships with the police, whether good or bad. Unfortunately, most of the time, Black and Brown contact with the police was a 'European-Indigenous-encounter', bad.

Deep down inside, Lynch felt uncomfortable in a place that he'd always taken ownership of at all costs. It seemed as if things were rapidly slipping out of his control. The python stranglehold his people enjoyed over the city during the Tammany Hall days was all but gone. Men like George Washington Plunkitt believed in what he called the spoils system, affording all Irishmen first dibs on the best city jobs. Now they had to share the spoils with Blacks, Asians, and Latinos. In fact, the Italians didn't even have numbers back then, as his grandfather remembered it. The Irish ruled the town, and his grandpa boasted about it. From ward bosses to the city council members and mayors: could you believe that he'd ask, not expecting an answer. Lynch was indoctrinated into being nostalgic about a time he only experienced through the stories of his grandfather.

"Hey, Skipper, you okay?" Maloney asked just as they were about to enter the unmarked vehicle.

"Yeah, I was just taking a trip down memory lane, remembering who owns this town. It ain't the damn protestors and so-called activists, I can tell you that!" He said with excitement building in his tone. He had that pissed look in his eyes that was borderline reckless. That was what Maloney had become accustomed to. That's the Lynch he appreciated the most. The Lynch that took the Lion's share and didn't give two shits what anybody thought about it either. Maloney knew there was always plenty of meat left on the bones to fill his stomach after a slaughter.

However, Lynch had them on a diet, and Maloney was becoming hungrier by the day. They hadn't taken from the scum of the earth in months. He didn't want to believe that Lynch was going soft on him. Little Dee's slip-up gave them the leverage that they craved over the hustlers operating out of Brown Housing Projects. The complex was massive. It bolstered over a hundred buildings and was surrounded by townhouses, stretching into an affluent neighborhood.

Brown Houses were rumored to gross over a million dollars a week in drug money, and it was all run by one crew. Little Dee would have to pay up to make the murder go away. Maloney wasn't ready to let that up when they finally had the crew by the balls. The way he saw it was that he and Lynch were good at making criminals cough up stashes to get away with murder. They'd just put the murder on some other Black or Brown sucker. As long as one was off the street, they didn't care. And they even relished the thought that the scumbag they left on the street would continue to participate in a slow genocide. Then, the process would start all over again.

As they drove to the hospital, Maloney couldn't help but wonder what Lynch was so worried about. They had a safe backup plan for any of the hustlers who failed to play ball. He could just envision the morning News headline reading: "Dangerous suspect wanted for murder shot by decorated officer who feared for his life." It hadn't failed them yet. Besides, they only cleaned house when it was absolutely necessary. It had been a while since they sent some drug dealer to meet his or her maker. Nearly everyone in their squadron had at least one killing of the sort. And nearly no one in their squadron had a mortgage to pay either.

While other officers struggled to pay off their mortgages and even took out second mortgages on their homes, many of them had already paid off a second mortgage on an additional home or were halfway through paying off for an even bigger home. Quiet as kept, Lynch even owned a home in the Hamptons. Homicide detectives in their squad didn't lease or finance cars. They paid in full in cash. They paid off their kids' college tuitions and sponsored little leagues in their communities. With the money they extorted from scumbags, they did a lot of good for their families. At least, that's the way they saw it.

Well, maybe Lynch did have a lot to lose, Maloney pondered for a brief second. But then he thought they also had a lot to gain. This was the one that Lynch always spoke about. Little Dee was the big catch. If they did things just right, they could keep their hooks in him until they retired comfortably. They could convince the District Attorney to string out the murder charge on whatever poor sucker took the fall. It was never their intention to send Little Dee to prison. His arrest was necessary to let him know they meant business. All their chips were in place, but Maloney had no idea that Day was the real reason Lynch remained sleepless at night.

"Hey, look at that, we're here already," Maloney said, noticing that they were approaching the hospital parking lot.

"Now let's just hope our girl is okay," Lynch responded.

"What the hell, that's a News van right there," Maloney complained and then frowned.

"Well, the coast looks clear right now. Let's just hope that none of those leftwing-Black Lives Matter-loving reporters are upstairs," Lynch grumbled as he parked the vehicle. As soon as the two men exited the vehicle, they were swarmed by a reporter and camera crew. Wasting no time, the female reporter threw her body in front of Lynch's path.

"Detective Lynch, is it true that you have numerous excessive force complaints against you?" But before he could respond, she continued, "Rumor has it that you and other officers from your precinct beat up the female suspect who was apprehended earlier today, and she is now hospitalized." Removing the handheld microphone from her face, she pointed it directly towards Lynch's face, awaiting his response.

Lynch stopped dead in his tracks, looking directly into the camera, he said, "Next time, get your facts straight before spewing the lies of Black Lives Matter looters and rioters. Thanks to reporters like you and your fake news, the safest big city in America is becoming lawless. I'm not going to let that happen. This city was built on law and order, not Black Lives Matter, not defunding the police, and certainly not this crap about police reform."

Before she could react to any of that, he brushed right by her and the cameraman, with Maloney following up the rear. Relentlessly, the female reporter sped around and gave him a little chase, pestering him with questions, "You didn't answer my question. Was the woman hospitalized as a result of police brutality?"

"You had better get that camera out of my face," Lynch warned. Right on cue, Maloney shoved the camera lens back into the cameraman's face.

"Hey, you can't do that!" the female reporter shouted.

"I'd like to see you try and stop me," Maloney cautioned. The two men entered the elevator, and Maloney blocked the entrance and said, "This elevator is full. Please watch the closing doors."

He ended with a smile.

The female reporter thought it would be unwise to try to push her way past the over-three-hundred-pound bear-sized human.

"Well, there you have it, folks. There are no Officer Friendlies here," she emphasized, letting them know she got the last word. She even flashed a conniving smile once the camera was off her. Maloney responded with a hateful look, evoking the old cliché if looks could kill, you'd be dead.

"It works every time," the cameraman said, aiming the camera directly at Maloney to capture a potential front-page shot of an overly aggressive cop. Right on cue, the female reporter turned on her heels, giving them her back as the elevator's door closed. Maloney settled on pounding the elevator door with his clenched fist, sending a thudding noise through to the other side. The reporter and the cameraman both jumped at the sudden banging sound.

"Somebody needs to call the fire department because the elevator obviously exceeded its weight capacity," she shouted at the top of her lungs, hoping they could hear her.

Then the two of them burst into laughter before climbing into the back of the News van and surprising some other unsuspecting candidates for their news story.

Lynch and Maloney exited the elevator and headed directly to room seventeen-B. Each man exchanged a simple nod as they walked past the uniformed officer standing outside the room. To their amazement and delight, Ms. Hoodie was wide-eyed and clearly responsive.

Full Court Press

I had a lot on my mind since Chemistry informed me that he had managed to video the events that took place with Little Dee. 'He had the whole thing on video!' My mind was jumping inside with the news. He had even picked up audio, so heads were sure to roll once the video got out. If he hadn't gotten his property back from the precinct, I didn't believe I would even be entertaining his plan. Although I felt his plan was well thought out, it had quite a few holes. For one, Chemistry couldn't account for the people he entrusted the video to, that it would go into the hands of the right people. I might not have known much, but I had heard enough about the Blue Wall of Silence. I distinctly remembered about ten officers contradicting what everyone else clearly saw on video, concerning a police involved shooting in Chicago. The teen was clearly walking away when he was shot multiple times, but the Blue Wall of Silence dictated what each officer claimed had taken place.

I couldn't help but think about how all those officers didn't care that the teen was dead. The only thing they cared about was their Blue Wall of Silence, which seems a lot like the infamous Code of Silence that the Italian Mafia touts. *'You know, as in The Godfather I, II, and III, Omertä with the Sicilians, never sing like a canary to authorities under any circumstance, and not to forget Cosa Nostra with the twenty-plus organized crime families of the United States whose motto is Our Affair.'* My mind was working hard. *'I always wondered why White crimes are called white collar crimes or organized crime.'* I thought it was done to make it sound more sophisticated than regular old street crime. Instead of calling Mafia figures common criminals, people in society tend to call Mafia figures mobsters or gangsters. But the average corner boy was called a thug or a lowlife. 'And why is it that mobsters do crimes until they're seventy, old, and gray and then retire in a gangster's retirement home in the Federal penitentiary,' I said in a whisper to myself.

However, the street criminal or thug had less than a five-year run. They were almost always convicted in their teens or early twenties, and were hit with football numbers for sentences that keep them imprisoned until they're sixty or seventy. It was the exact opposite! Chemistry expected me to dismiss all of these observations and ignore the fact that these cops won't think twice about ending our lives. I knew I was rambling on and on in my brain, but when did it become my responsibility to upend the status quo?

My brain was on fire. It was ranting, *'I mean, seriously, all this stuff about youth finding an identity and wanting to make an impact on the world is overrated.'* Besides, I was thinking to myself, *'I am way ahead of schedule. Certain things shouldn't be expected of me at least until I reach my teens, and I've even heard an expert or two speak out against the high expectations that society places on teens. Technically, I'm not even a preteen. I was convinced that my time should be spent thinking about G.I. Joe, Transformers, or scuffing my knee on a sidewalk, not about murder suspects and killer cops. I haven't even begun thinking about the opposite sex—you know, girls and how they pee differently. Well, I thought about it a little bit, but I still don't understand why God made it so girls have to sit down and pee. One girl I know peed standing up because she said she didn't think it was fair that only boys got to pee standing up. I told her, 'me too: let's start a movement! You go, girl!' But then she peed down her leg, and it got all on her underwear and socks, giving me an instant change of heart. All I could think after that was how lucky she was that it wasn't poop.'*

That ended all thoughts I had about the possibilities of pooping standing up, ewe. All I knew at that point was that I didn't want to take my last poop shaking and end my life curled up like a baby. Something changed in me. I started to come to grips with the reality that my favorite artist could very well be outlining my infant corpse with orange chalk. I found myself wondering, *would yellow ribbons flap in the wind at my expense?* A loud voice was screaming in my head: *What the hell was Chemistry thinking about! Black Lives Matter is a slogan used as a talking point for politicians on both the right and left sides of the aisle.*

What happened to me and my mom was a prime example of how powerless we still were. I couldn't forget how the invading army hauled my mother away. I could still hear helicopter propellers in my head, saw red beams in my vision, and felt the phantom plastic restrictors around my nude wrist. It became clear to me, as Chemistry would say, *Black people didn't have any rights that Whites needed to respect. Plessey v. Ferguson,* I recalled him always ending with. Why would they respect my mother's rights? She was a single mom who didn't work, and we were on welfare for crying out loud. Chemistry always told me that I had it good with my fancy food card because, in his day, he was sent to the store with rainbow colored food stamps. He said that kids would actually cry about being sent to the store with food stamps, fearing that they would be targeted by other poor kids who would make fun of their poverty.

However, Chemistry explained to me that once the Chinese restaurants started accepting food stamps, those same hecklers ordered four chicken wings and French fries, demanded extra duck sauce, and proudly paid with colorful money. He said he always found it funny how it was shameful to purchase groceries with food stamps, but it was okay to buy Chinese food with them. He joked about the government limiting poor people from purchasing Chinese fast food with food stamps because it helped control the city's stray cat population. He'd say, "There ain't no cat in a chicken Mc nugget so that you won't be getting any Mickey Dees with food stamps." *Boy, I sure wish they'd let us bail my mother out of jail with our food card.* I thought to myself as I sat at the edge of Billy's bed.

"Hoodie, you have a phone call," Billy shouted from the kitchen. As usual, he was in there, hovering over the food that his grandmother was preparing for dinner. I was surprised that he wasn't fat because he never missed a meal. He'd eat his food, my food, and anybody else's food that took their eyes off him. They should have named him Mikey because he'll eat anything. As I stood to my feet, I wondered who could be calling me. Detective Lynch was the first person who came to mind. His cronies must have told him where I was, and it wasn't hard for him to track me down. *What if they stormed the apartment*, I thought to myself. A dizzying feeling suddenly came over me, and I lost my appetite. I wanted to vomit. Each step I took felt like I was moving in slow motion. Anxiety hijacked all of my reason, and I dreaded finding out what awaited me on the other end of the line.

"If you walked any slower, a turtle could beat you in a foot race. Don't you want to talk to your mom?" Mr. Dave asked as he reclined in the plush burgundy leather living room sofa that made a U-shape.

"Oh, my mom is on the phone! Why didn't Billy say so in the first place? Shoot, he had me thinking it was a bill collector. He got me all nervous and sick. I said sick." I pointed out jokingly, as he shifted in his seat, clearly wondering if he heard me correctly.

"I thought I heard you say shit. Don't play with me, boy. I know how that saying goes, and it doesn't end with sick either. You thought it was a bill collector. Boy, what could you ever know about bills?" He asked, not expecting me to answer.

"I know my credit score is a seven," I boasted.

"You know your credit score is a seven, shit. Then lend me some money. Boy, you're a trip. You'd better take your seven-score-crediting-having behind to that phone before your momma whips your butt through the phone line. Like T&T, reach out and touch yo butt," he finished, bursting into an obnoxious laugh. I thought to myself, *this old fool must find something funny about me getting my butt whipped as if my mother were auditioning for a slave-master role. That's why his old ass smells like Bengay mixed with Geratol and underarm odor. I bet he got grapes hanging out of his behind. That's why he's sitting on his hip. He just reminded me why I hated my mom. Why should I care what happened to her? He's right. If she could, she probably would beat me on the phone. It's not like she never whipped me with a telephone cord.* All of my anxieties were replaced with the raw emotions of hate and love. I was ambivalent about speaking to my torturer. It didn't make sense; it was like willingly waltzing to the guillotine and greeting my executioner.

Snapping myself out of the thought, I turned to Mr. Dave and asked, "Are your hemorrhoids okay? It looks like they're really troubling you." Although I wanted to flip him the finger, I settled for a smirk and turned towards the kitchen.

"Hey Hoodie," he called out. I turned around to find him clenching his fist, then doing an uppercut motion until he slapped the open palm of his other hand down on his bicep, completing an Italian-style Up Yours. Making sure I got the message, he doubled down. Then he finished with a smirk of his own. The only thing I could do, at that point, was laugh. I had to admit that the old man cheered me up, lightening the mood for my unexpected phone call. As I slowly approached the kitchen, Billy's grandmother stood there with a wide grin on her face, extending the phone out for me to take it. Grabbing the phone, I told her 'Thank you.'

I put the receiver to my ear and said in a timid voice, "Hello, ma."

"Hoodie, how are you doing? Are they treating you okay?" she asked me. I was wondering the same thing. I was thinking to myself, was this some sort of role reversal because I should be asking her those questions? After all, she was captured. She was the only detainee in this situation. I couldn't help but conjure up James Cagney's famous line: "You'll never take me alive, coppers." I guessed number forty-five had a point about not liking his heroes captured because once they were strung on a meat hook, they would tell you whatever you wanted to know. After watching the remake of the movie Carlito's Way, I even knew that. Naturally, I worried that someone was listening in on the call. Doubt overwhelmed my senses, leaving me speechless. Was my mom trying to set me up?

"Hoodie, Hoodie, Hoodie, are you there?" she repeated.

"Uh, um present," was all I could come up with, as if she were a teacher taking attendance in class rather than my mom. I was confused. No one could blame me for taking precautions.

Besides, for much less on several occasions, my mom made an effort to beat me half to death. There was absolutely no reason for me to believe that she wouldn't prefer me in a cell and her lying back in bed, smoking a cigarette, and watching one of her shows on television. She killed me, too. Always talking 'bout not interrupting her while she was watching her show as if they made the show especially for her. I was sure of one thing: that I wasn't trading places with her, not after all the hell she had put me through. *'Let's see how tough she is when Big Shirley comes for her cornbread,'* I made a snide remark.

"Hoodie," she called out my name again, snapping me out of my thoughts.

"Yes, Mom. Are you okay? How are they treating you?" I threw back at her.

"I'm fine baby," she said. The word baby echoed in my head. *Baby*, who was she fooling?

Now I knew something was up because my mom hadn't referred to me as *baby* since I was dropping gems in Luv's diapers. Deep down inside, I was screaming, "Spit it out, woman." However, even with her in restraints, I wasn't dumb enough to get beside myself. I could see her now, breaking the restraints and leaping over a thirty-foot wall just so she could hunt me down and whoop my ass one last time.

"That's good, ma," I responded, making small talk. But before she could say anything else, I asked, "Ma, is there something that you need to tell me?"

"Don't worry about anything, baby. You don't have to tell anybody anything," as the last words left her lips, Det. Lynch snatched the telephone. I could hear him complaining in the background, asking her what the hell she thought she was doing to his case. At the sound of his voice, I nearly dropped the phone.

"You listen to me, you little," Lynch paused for a second. He must have realized that he was not on a secure line. He took a deep breath and said, "Don't let your mother get you in more trouble than you're already in at the moment. Do you understand Hoodie?"

"Don't say anything to him, Hoodie!" I heard my mother yell out in the background, and then her voice sounded muffled like someone had covered her mouth with their bare hand. From somewhere, I mustered up the courage to say, "I heard you loud and clear. Now, how 'bout you speak to my man Tone?"

"Tone, Tone who?" Lynch asked.

"Dial tone, mother sucker," I said and slammed the phone down on the receiver. I could imagine the look on his beet-red face. His platinum white hair probably stood straight up on his head. I didn't care if I made matters worse. It felt good to stick it to the Man. Unfortunately, Billy's grandmother didn't realize that I was talking to the Man. She looked at me like I lost my damn mind. She didn't have to utter a word because the look on her face said it all.

"If I didn't know any better, I would think you were talking to your mother like that. That wasn't your mom, was it?" she asked to confirm her intuition.

"No ma'am. That was the 'opps," I politely said.

"Who?" she asked with a confused look on her face.

"The cops," butting in, Billy answered with a proud look on his greasy mug. Apparently, Fatboy stuffed himself eating before anyone else. I stood there shaking my head. He should know better than to start eating before a guest has a chance to eat. His grandmother noticed the astonished look on my face and straightaway admonished him for his lack of Northern hospitality.

Breaking the momentary silence, Mrs. Pearl acknowledged, "Oh, the cops. Well, they say you learn something new every day. I bet it will only be a matter of time before they add that word to the dictionary. These days, it's like they add a new word to the dictionary every single day. It doesn't make any sense. Ya'll kids make up your own words for words that already exist.

"Then the homojis, that's a, how ya'll say it, a whole 'nother language – a whole this, a whole that. It's a whole lot of nothing, " she finished. It only took her a second to realize that me and Billy were laughing, die-hard, clutching our stomachs.

"What are you two laughing at?" she asked suspiciously. She'd seen our laughing response many times before. She knew she had said something wrong and wanted us to correct her.

"Homoji, grandma? You said homoji. It's an emoji," Billy explained to her.

"Ya'll know what I meant. It ain't my fault. Ya'll keep coming up with all these different words and expect somebody to remember them all. Dinner's ready!" she yelled out. She turned and went about her business, letting us know she was done with the Ebonics lesson for the day. Mrs. Pearl had snow-white hair that clung to her shoulders. She was a dark-skinned woman with green eyes, something you didn't see too often. Although she was an older woman, she was in good health. Unlike Mr. Dave, she sat on her hip as a matter of preference. The two complemented each other, making a nice elderly couple. There weren't too many elderly couples in my neighborhood.

In the hood, you'd have a better chance at seeing Bigfoot than seeing more than one elderly couple in a ten-block radius. So much for Black love, I guess. It wasn't that Black folk didn't love each other and wanted to grow old together. Chemistry always said that the life expectancy of a Black man may as well be counted in dog years. We went to meet our maker way too early, he lamented: If it wasn't the streets that killed us, it was the cops, and if it wasn't the cops, it was heart disease, lung disease, high blood pressure, too much salt, or too much fried chicken, hence cholesterol. A Black man almost never lived a long, prosperous life and died in his sleep from natural causes. For the life of me, I still couldn't understand what was so natural about dying in your sleep.

While a part of me wanted to live forever, another part of me hated the misery that came with living in this world. I understood that Black people unnecessarily had it way too rough. However, I knew as well that there were poor, sick, and what they called undeserving White people. Like any other ethnic group, there were Latinos and Asians who wouldn't survive a bout of cancer. Chemistry said that all Americans were obese, and thanks to the fast food, tobacco, and gun industries, our life expectancies were shorter than the life expectancies of people living in other industrialized nations. He made mention of a book called Lethal but Legal by a German author, I thought, whose last name begins with an F. I was not even going to fool myself and try to sound it out either. Besides, once you got the title of anything published, it was not too hard to find out the writer's name. One thing I knew for sure was that I was not giving my happy meals up for anybody. Shoot, they would cost less than five dollars, and you got a free toy. You couldn't beat that! So what if it might have been made in China out of some toxic product? I had no plans to eat the toy.

At that moment, what I planned to do was devour this scrumptious food Mrs. Pearl prepared. I haven't had any good-tasting home-cooked food in months. My mother's favorite seasoning was a dash of hunger, and you'd think she really could throw down when she threw a pinch of starvation in the pot. One time, my stomach cramps were so bad, I ate a stale piece of toast with butter and swore down it tasted just like basket bread from the Olive Garden. Other times, I went to sleep clutching my air belly and, like the rapper Beanie Siegel would say, those were the times I ate sleep for dinner. Though breakfast was better, at least I had baking soda and plenty of sink water to quench my thirst. I recall my stomach being so empty one morning that I could hear the water splashing up against my intestinal walls.

At school, later that morning, I was embarrassed. I could swear down that everyone else heard the splashing water too. I stood still as a tree, and just when I thought it was safe, my stomach made a horrible grumbling sound. Oh, you should have seen the look on my face when the prettiest girl in my fourth-grade class excitedly raised her hand and asked our science teacher, "Could people fart with their stomachs?" When the teacher said, "No, that was just ridiculous," she responded, "Nuh-un, I just heard Hoodie's stomach farting, and it was loud too." I sat there and tried to shake my head only to find my stomach rumbling like I was a belly dancer, followed by an extremely loud farting sound, sending everyone, including the teacher, into an unforgettable fit of laughter that sparked back up every time my stomach rumbled. At the sight of my stomach bubbling, one kid yelled out, "Hoodie's having contractions." Another kid chimed in and said, "Hoodie's gonna have a doo-doo baby." I hauled ass out of the classroom, hearing the chorus "doo-doo baby" trailing behind me.

"Earth to Hoodie, Earth to Hoodie," Mrs. Pearl repeated, pulling me out of my trance. She continued, "Is the food okay? Are you at all hungry?"

"The food is fine, Mrs. Pearl, and I am hungry. I'm like a wine connoisseur, but I specialize in food tasting, that's it. I like to smell the aroma of the food before I eat. Sometimes really good food hypnotizes me and I become spellbound," I responded.

"A food connoisseur," Mr. Dave repeated and let out a chuckle, signaling that he didn't take me seriously. You had to see it. He was at the table, sitting on his hip, and he had the nerve to take me for a joke. "This kid is a riot. You should be a stand-up comedian because it damn sure ain't any money in food tasting, not for Black people," he finished.

"Dave, we're at the table," Mrs. Pearl cautioned.

"My bad, excuse my language, but it's the truth. There ain't no money in food tasting. It's a lot of free loading in it. That's what's in it. Shoot, I wish I would pay somebody to eat for free," Mr. Dave vented.

"I wanna be a food connoisseur," Billy said, sounding muffled with a mouth full of food.

"I bet you would, honey," I heard Mrs. Pearl muffle under her breath. I let out a small chuckle, noticing that Billy tried to act like he didn't hear her. Then she said, "Now that Chemistry has finally arrived, we can pray and then eat," she finished and looked down at Billy, who stopped chewing mid-sentence, obviously knowing that her comment was directed at him.

Taking one huge gulp, Billy cleared his throat just enough to say, "Well, since Hoodie is our guest, he should say grace over the food." He looked at me and grinned from ear to ear. What he didn't know was that I was extremely thankful to be eating some good food. I didn't have a problem with letting the world know how thankful I was for Mrs. Pearl's cooking. I smiled right back at him before commencing a seven-minute-long grace. Apparently, he didn't know who he was jiving with. By the time I finished saying grace, Billy was done eating all of his food. He put an exclamation point on it, letting out a loud belch.

Unbeknownst to me, their family had agreed to a sixty-second rule. The only exceptions were made for Thanksgiving. Any other time, you either finished saying grace or got the picture when you heard forks and spoons scraping against their plates. They even had measures for people who went way overboard, too. They would just start talking while the person continued to put on a show, which was what they called it. In their minds, it was the false preacher who was out of line, not them. Mrs. Pearl said, "God's speech wasn't even that long when he kicked Adam and Eve out of the Garden. The serpent didn't even take that long to convince them to eat the forbidden fruit. In fact, they ain't say no grace." She had me cracking up. Everything was going smoothly right up until Chemistry told me that we needed to talk after dinner. I was hoping he'd forgotten about his ill-advised scheme. This was real life. *My life, this ain't a movie, dog!* I was screaming inside.

All of a sudden, I felt like I was on death row, and the food was so good because I was eating my last meal. Chemistry and his bone-headed plan were ushering us to the electric chair. I wasn't about to let that happen. It was time that I started thinking for myself. I had to come up with my own plan just in case things went left. I knew just who I had to get in touch with if we were going to come out of this unscathed at best or alive at worst. I needed someone who thought like a cop. There was only one person who would know what the opps' next moves were, and that person was a district attorney in the making named Marisol. After my talk with Chemistry, I gave her a ring to set up a meeting with her in a public place. I picked a place where the cops wouldn't try anything, so we agreed to meet at the downtown mall's McDonald's.

Point of No Return

The next morning, I told myself to get up before everyone else, so that I could duck Chemistry for at least another day. Besides, it was Saturday, and I had my own plans. I didn't want to risk Mr. Dave telling me that it was too dangerous to go out, so I snuck out. Not making a sound, I eased out the front door. I made my way through the lobby and opened the building's door to find Chemistry standing there as if he were waiting for me. Even though I knew I was caught red-handed, I tried to play it cool.

"Hey, what's up, Chemistry? Nice morning, isn't it?" I said, making small talk.

"You weren't trying to sneak out on me, were you?" he asked, getting straight to the point. It was now or never. I had to voice my concerns and try to change his mind. His plan wouldn't work. It would get us into a lot of trouble. Things were bad, but they weren't bad enough for us to do something so dramatic. Think about it, we were alive. We were still breathing, and we just had a wonderful meal last night. Why mess things up? Why risk being captured like my mom? The cops weren't bothering us. It was just as likely that eventually they would forget about us. I wanted to draw an analogy between the Fugitive Slave Laws and the position that we would be in once all the cops in the city wanted us dead or alive. It wouldn't be long before they issued a nationwide man-slash-child hunt for our immediate capture. I could vividly imagine the hound dogs hot on our trails, and my imaginary hound dogs looked more like overgrown, vicious pit bulls. Chemistry was crazy. I had to put an end to this now!

I started off stuttering and mumbling to get my words out, "I… I… I was going, I was just going for a walk. Why would I be trying to duck you, man? I… I wouldn't do that. I'm all in. I'll be back in a flash." I said and tried to walk off. Chemistry was right behind me. I could see his enormous shadow engulf mine across the pavement.

"A walk sounds like a really good idea," he said, confirming my suspicions that he wasn't going to let me out of his sight.

This could only mean one thing. It was going down today, and I wouldn't get a chance to meet Marisol before he willingly led us to the firing squad. What an idiot I was this morning, believing that I was ahead of the game. I should have looked through the glass on the building's door before I exited so recklessly. I'm lucky it wasn't Detective Lynch, or I'd really be screwed. Well, none of that mattered now because Chemistry would lead us right to Lynch anyway. I scolded myself.

Right as we were about to cross the street, I felt Chemistry's big grizzly hand wrap around my hand. With all of my might, I yanked my hand free and said, "Excuse me. I've been crossing the street on my own since I was five years old. Thanks, but no thanks. Now, I'm going to go along with this charade, but there ain't no way I'll be caught dead with a grown ass man holding my hand while I cross the street. Do you know out in these streets that will certainly make you look like a pedophile?. And even worse, it will make me look like a sucker for strangers' lollipops."

He just looked at me and burst into a fit of laughter. "Lil man, you crazy. Ain't no fool out on these streets, in their right mind, gonna confuse me with no pedophile. But I have to admit, I kind of like your way of thinking. You're pretty shrewd, Hoodie. However, you were trying to slip out on me, and for that reason, I will be holding your hand until we reach our destination."

Before I had a chance to do anything, he clamped down on my wrist, and there was no way I would pull free this time. Thank goodness it was early in the morning, so there weren't too many people outside. Man, he dragged me like a ragdoll to a place I least expected the most. This fool brought me to the precinct. My last-ditch effort to pry myself free was useless against his grown-man strength. All I could think was, damn, the boy ate his Wheaties. I was exhausted, and he didn't even break a sweat. And I thought Ms. Mitcheck was strong. I had to rethink my strategy. I couldn't overpower him, so I had to outsmart him. I had to convince him that I wouldn't run. I stopped trying to break free.

"Now listen, Hoodie, I need you to be cool, man. It's not what you think. We're going to meet with some good cops, Black cops. They're on our side," he said in an attempt to convince me. On the outside, I gave him a fake smile, but on the inside, I was screaming, "This nigga." That's right, I said it. *This nigga done completely lost his damn mind. They 'on' our side, he said. What the hell was this fool smoking because I ain't want none of that shit. What? He never heard KRS One's song Black Cop. His lyrics clearly say, "White police trained Black cops to stand on the corner and take buck shots," and everyone knows who they aim those buck shots at. It damn sure ain't at White men, their women, or their children. Obviously, Chemistry had a death wish, and he was dragging me to hell with him.* I was screaming in my mind, kind of hoping that chemistry would hear it.

I didn't want to make a scene, so I unwillingly allowed him to lead me to the slaughterhouse. One thing I was certain about, I would escape the first chance I got. For now, I had to play it cool. I don't know if I was dreaming or what, but as we entered the precinct, it looked like Chocolate City. We were in Harlem and Spanish Harlem all at once. It must have been the end of roll call because it seemed like all of the officers were exiting the building. As we passed each group of officers, they greeted us with a good morning, a how you doin', a what up tho, and even a que pasa. Before I even realized it, I was telling myself, "Officer Friendly did exist." That was short-lived because I immediately heard my interlocutor singing the rapper Phresher's song, "Woe Woe Wait a minute, Hold up, wait a minute." I think I caught a contact from that bull shit Chemistry was puffing on. I clearly remembered him telling me that a wise man once said, 'Power Corrupts.' And even in the small number of instances where power wasn't the problem, most minority cops fell in line because the top brass was predominantly White. To make matters worse, the union hierarchy that protected rotten apples was snow white. In the end, too many minority cops were unwilling to risk their livelihoods for a teenager reaching into a hoodie pocket for Skittles. *IDK, I guess the cops figure that teenagers are no longer babies, so it takes high-grain bullets to take their candy.* I whispered to myself.

Before I knew it, we were at the reception desk, and the desk sergeant was drop-dead gorgeous. She wore her hair in two sandy-brown afro puffs with a sharp part down the center of her scalp, evenly separating each puff. Either my eyes were deceiving me, or she had sparkles gleaming off her curly hair. She smiled, revealing her pearly white teeth that shone like an actress's in a toothpaste commercial. Her white shirt was neatly pressed, tailor-fitted to her upper body, and the black tie that hung down the center of her perfect breast was fixed in place by a gold clip, which read H.W.I.C. I was immediately embarrassed when she caught me gazing in the direction of her breast. The only thing that eased the tension in her face was her reading my lips, as I repeated the letters on the golden clip. The most beautiful smile returned to her smooth, caramel-complexioned face. It was then that she reminded me of someone I hadn't seen in years, my mother.

Just seven years back, my mother had to be one of the prettiest women in the city. At the time, she was optimistic about doing what needed to be done to give us a better life. She believed all of the fables she'd heard about the opportunities that existed in a Metropolis. After about three years, struggling to find work that paid enough money to cover bills barely, she realized that the opportunities she'd heard about were not for everyone. The rent and just enough food to last the month swallowed up practically every single penny she earned. I mean, she really earned that money, slaving like a dog in someone's restaurant, kitchen, or home. Sometimes she crashed dead on the couch after long work shifts that lasted over a month straight, trying to pay back rent, keep a roof over our head, keep food in our bellies, and keep us from starving to death. Not long before, my mother developed a pack-a-day cigarette habit to cope with the constant threat of being evicted. Some nights, I heard her crying until the sun came up just to drag her sleepless, thin frame to punch a clock. Reflecting back on that time, I wish I could punch every clock that stole my mother's time for little to no money at all. What sense did it make to work all day and all night to not even make enough for rent and still have to beg neighbors for butter, sugar, milk, or an egg? For the very first time, I realized how much hell my mother had been through to keep me alive. At just twenty-two years old, everyone told her to abort me, especially since my twenty-one-year-old father was killed in a police-involved shooting. To this day, I don't know why it wasn't simply called murder.

According to everyone who knew my father, he didn't have a weapon or a violent bone in his body. The police claimed that his blue Chevy Impala matched a red Chevy Impala reported in a robbery. After following the command over the bullhorn to shut the engine off and slowly exit the vehicle, eyewitnesses said he never had a chance. The local paper's headline read: "Cops open fire on newlywed Black male with prayer hands raised to the Most High." My mother was devastated. Although my father was a good young man, one of our best, the old folks would say no one encouraged seeing him live on through me.

My mother was the only person who thought he deserved a legacy. Her family turned on her in a heartbeat. She was bound for Spellman, Howard, or some other HBCU. At least until my father impregnated her young womb. My grandparents were staunch Christians that worried more about what other people thought than they did about their own daughter. The fact that my parents eloped only made matters worse. My mother couldn't take the ostracism anymore, so one day she picked up and headed north, leaving the South in her second trimester. Eventually, I was born premature.

My mother always said that I knew so much because I had a head start in the world. Chemistry would always say that I would need it because Black men entered the foot-race-of-life with their shoes on the wrong foot tied together. And to make matters worse, he said, "Our White counterparts brought their electric bikes to a foot race."

I surely felt like my shoes were tied together as we stood in a police station, an institution that sifted my father's life like wheat. I began to panic, wondering if I would ever see my mother again. I hated the thought that the last memory I had of seeing my mom was with her manacled and hogtied like an animal, kicking and screaming as her slavers took her away. Her last syllables were muffled, strained, and gagged as she seized the time to warn me. I couldn't trust the same people who were trying to wipe out my father's bloodline. Where were these so-called good Black cops when they killed my father? Where were they when they stormed our home, beat Rodney King, or disgraced Abner Louima?

"Hoodie, are you alright?" Chemistry asked, shaking me by the shoulder and pulling me out of my daze.

"What's up, lil-man? You were gone for a minute," he told me.

"I'm fine," I said, a bit annoyed at how he put me on the spot in front of the lovely woman.

The woman on the desk cleared her throat loudly and asked, "Well, how can I help you all?" She was mostly addressing Chemistry rather than both of us. "Yes, I have an appointment with Cap. Can you tell him that Chemistry is here to see him?" he said.

"Chemistry," she inquired to make sure she heard him correctly.

"Yes, Chemistry," he said flatly. It was obvious that she wanted him to give her his birth name, but she placed the call anyway. She nodded her head to whatever the person on the other end was telling her. After hanging up the phone, she instructed us to have a seat, gesturing to the row of seats to our right.

Sargent H.W.I.C. also told us that Cap would be with us in a minute. For some reason, the woman put me at ease. Hearing her voice calmed my nerves. She was Officer Friendly! My false sense of peace lasted about two seconds before I spotted, of all people, Officer Day. I hunched down in my seat, hoping that he wouldn't notice me. I couldn't help but think that Chemistry was trying to set me up.

My mind started speed racing for answers to the swarm of questions, flooding my mind like a bison stampede. What was Day doing here? How long had he and Chemistry been planning this sting operation? Was my mother somehow involved? No, she couldn't be because she was on the hook like me. Maybe she struck a deal. Did she strike a deal? Would my mother really turn in her only child to save her own ass? Considering the fact that she tried to beat me to death on countless occasions as much as I wanted to, I couldn't put it past her. It wasn't beneath her. I remember one time she beat me to sleep because I threw an ashtray full of cigarette butts out. How was I supposed to know that she ran out of cigarettes and was saving the butts for a rainy day? I didn't know who to trust. I buried my head in my lap to conceal my face. The funny thing is, Officer Day wasn't paying me any attention. I peeked up to find him conversing with the desk sergeant, who appeared to be blushing. A rush of jealousy came over me, acting as if I ever had a chance with such a grown-beautiful woman. Who was I kidding? It had only been a year since I quit super soaking the cradle.

I don't know if I was happier to see Day leaving the desk without noticing me or if I was happier to see him leaving empty-handed. Shoot, I thought to myself, if I can't have her, he can't either. I believed in Even Stevens and applauded the like-minded who believed that two wrongs don't make a right, but it damn sure makes it even. Day was harassing me. He was on my back, and I didn't owe him a damn thing. *Talking about it, I remind him of his younger self. That's only because I saw his mind standing to the right of him, so he was obviously out of it!* I chuckled.

"Hoodie, Hoodie, Hoodie," Chemistry called me for the third time, shaking my shoulder to get my attention. "Listen, man, you have to pull it together. We're about to go in here and talk to these people about some serious stuff. You can't be acting like you're still wearing diapers," he finished, disrespecting me. He had my full attention now. *Me still wearing diapers, and he was the grown ass man still living with his grandparents.* I meant he had a momma and a daddy, what was his excuse for not making something of himself? Sure, he knew some things, but where did it get him besides sharing a room with his younger brother? He had a lot of nerve, shaving all his facial hair to appear younger. In his thirties, yelling for his grandmother to let him in the building, how uncool is that! "Hoodie, it would be nice if you would say something," he snapped.

"You're the one acting like a baby. This is your plan, not mine. Since when did it become okay to work with 'them' people? They're killing us out on these streets every day, all across the country. And you want to make a deal with them. Do you really think they're going to help us over their cronies? You taught me that the Blue Wall of Silence is thicker than blood and cuz put together. Cosa Nostra ain't got shit on the Boys in Blue. It all balls down to the Blue line and not even a Black cop is going to cross it for me and certainly not for you," I went all in on him. He just sat there stunned as if Hello Kitty were keeping him speechless. '*Who's the baby now,*' I thought to myself.

"Are you done? I just want to know, are you done?" he rhetorically asked. Smiling, he sat all the way back in his chair, sizing me up. "Hoodie, I got to give it to you. You are a very smart young man, and you're very good at regurgitating information. But what you fail to realize is that life is not as cut and dry as you make it out to be for your comfort. You see, you're at the stage where you're just happy for an answer. You're only brushing the surface with your view of the world, and especially with complex topics like policing Black neighborhoods. I'm sure your mother gave you The Talk a long time ago, way before you were ready to receive it. As a result, you think you know about the Black man's struggle in White America. Since you know everything, tell me why you think it's okay for Little Dee to take another Black man's life? I'm waiting. I don't hear you," he patronized me.

'I don't know who Chemistry thought he was messing with, but he had the right one,' I thought to myself before answering him. "Oh, that's easy. I don't think it's okay for another Black man to take another Black man's life. But we're talking about apples and oranges if you're going to compare drug-dealing Little Dee to an Officer of the Law," I said, placing emphasis on the words Officer of the Law. Before he could respond, I continued, "Little Dee ain't ever sworn an oath to serve and protect Black or White America. Shit, he prays to a bandana. Little Dee makes his money from selling illegal drugs, not from collecting taxpayer dollars transformed into a paycheck. Wasn't it you who said, or rather regurgitated the quip: 'No taxation without representation,'" I remonstrated with him.

Chemistry started clapping his hands, smiling from ear to ear. He knew I was telling the truth. The only thing he could do was give me my props. Just when I was about to take my victory lap, I heard him clear his throat like an orator about to give a long-winded speech. All I could think to myself was, he's about to go Barack Hussein Obama on me. I should have never started an intellectual tango with the man who practically taught me everything I know. He really took his time explaining to me about how the world worked. In my foolishness, I overstepped my boundaries, so I prepared to be put in my place, or better yet, I prepared to be G-checked.

"That was impressive. You even stuck the tip of your shovel into the ground and dug up a little dirt, too. What you didn't do was provide a solution. It's easy to point out the things that are wrong. Now, highlighting solutions is where the real hard work begins. Since you want to paint all cops with the broad stroke of a paintbrush, what do you suggest Black people do about policing their own neighborhoods, because by the looks of things, policing is necessary?" he asked, waiting for my answer. I knew what he was up to. He was taking me to task. We've been down this road a time or two. I took my time to make sure I didn't sound like a fool. This time, I would make certain to dig six feet deep, end of discussion. I stalled just enough to hear the voice of an angel. It wasn't the eleventh round, and I was saved by the bell, for now.

"You two can take it to the back. Cap will see you now," she told us, showing off her pearly whites once again. Simultaneously, we got up and nodded in her direction. She simply smiled and turned her attention to the papers littering the counter. The next thing I know, I start voicing aloud the letters H.W.I.C., once again revealing my thoughts.

"Head Woman In Charge," Chemistry said, breaking my concentration.

"Huh," I responded halfheartedly.

"H.W.I.C., Head Woman In Charge. It's a play on the more popular H.N.I.C.," he informed me.

"Huh," I was even more confused because I had no idea what he was talking about. When he tried to brush me off with a never mind, I became suspicious. It was clear to me that H.N.I.C., meant something provocative. Lucky for me, he already revealed what three of the letters stood for. Naturally, I zoned in on the letter N.

"Head N in charge, head N in charge, head nigga in charge," I blurted out in excitement just as we reached the ajar door to Cap's office. The next thing I heard was a chorus of astonished Hoodies, leaving the lips of everyone present.

"My bad," is all I could come up with, and no one even had a gun in my face. I don't know how the hell the man, who I'm guessing must be Cap, knew my name.

"Excuse me, gentlemen," Chemistry jumped in, busting up the awkward tension that seemed to be building in the room. The man, whom I assume is Cap, stood up from his cushioned brown leather chair behind the cherry wood desk. He greeted Chemistry with a wide smile as he looked down at me as if he was happy to see that Chemistry came bearing gifts. All I could think to myself as he stood there grinning, is that he was in for a rude awakening because I, for one, was not down with the program. Immediately to my right sat Officer Midnight, looking like a dark mist in an army jacket. I have to admit, he was wearing that thing because if my eyes weren't deceiving me, he had some bullet holes going for him. From where I was standing, it looked authentic.

Continuing Chemistry said, "I was just explaining to Hoodie what the acronym H.W.I.C. stands for."

"Oh, I thought lil man was referring to me, "Cap replied jokingly.

"I thought he was talking to me," Day chimed in. Then there was light, I heard my interlocutor saying. I sneakily giggled to myself, or at least, I thought.

"Would you like to share what's so funny with the rest of us?" Cap asked. The cop just came right out of him, always trying to bust somebody. And to think that Chemistry expected me to trust these guys with my life, he must be crazy.

"Well, since you asked. I had no idea officer Midnight, I mean Day, was sitting over there in that dark corner camouflaged, and I don't mean in his fatigue jacket either," I said rather bluntly. The moment the words midnight left my mouth, Cap and Chemistry caved in and burst into laughter.

"Hoodie, have some respect for your elders. I'm sorry, Day," Chemistry managed to squeeze out in between horribly concealed laughter.

"Hey, no need to apologize. I know the kid is quite a character. We had a couple of run-ins already," Day said. *What!* I was screaming in my head. I didn't like the way that sounded one bit. It was like he was implying that we had some kind of relationship. Everyone knows that if you're talking to the cops in my hood, then that means you're a Huggie Bear and I ain't no Huggie Bear. He left me no other option but to defend my impeccable reputation.

"Hold on now. You come in here looking like you're auditioning for Spike Lee's movie Da Five Bloods, talking about we had some run-ins as if they weren't forced. I don't know you, man. Besides, don't you suffer from PTSD because that's what the news said," I poured it on heavy.

"Okay, young man, that's enough. You've made your point. You're nobody's informant. We get you. I really mean that Hoodie. No one is going to put you in any position that makes you uncomfortable. You have my word on that," Cap said, extending his hand to shake on it. I had to admit, the OG was smooth. He was much smoother than Day, and his hands weren't crusty. I shook his hand and thought against the urge of introducing him to my killer grip. The muscles and veins wrapped around his forearm made me think twice. With his left hand, he gestured for us to have a seat in the chairs to his right and to my left. I felt relieved to be sitting down instead of standing on Front Street.

He continued, "My name is Cap, or at least that's what everybody calls me, so you can call me Cap, too. I know you're probably wondering how I know your name and what's all this about."

Before I could say anything, Chemistry barged in, "Cap, hold on for a second before we get into that. I think you owe my lil bro a full introduction, especially since me and him were just having a conversation about Black cops and well, Hoodie seems to think you're not too different from White cops."

"Well, we all do wear the same color uniforms. We all swear the same oath to serve and protect. And I believe we all hope that we make it home to our families at the end of our shifts. Outside of that, many of us like sports, good food, catching a movie every now and then, and just enjoying family and friends. So, I guess in many ways we are the same. Is that what you're talking about Hoodie?" Cap asked with a hint of suspicion in his voice.

"Maybe," I said, then paused as everyone looked at me, beckoning me to continue. "Well, no. Black cops don't care when White cops shoot and kill unarmed Black men, women, or even kids. It has become so bad that ordinary White citizens emulate White cops and kill kids armed with only a pack of Skittles. Then the killer has the nerve to claim a stand-your-ground defense, yet the Black victim does not have a right to stand their ground. To make matters worse, the 911 operator tells the wannabe cop to stop pursuing the kid he presumably wants to kill and indeed ends up killing. Then the killer's White father, who happens to be a judge, interferes with the investigation, giving his killer son carte blanche treatment in the Just-Us-System. Is anyone surprised that an all-White jury acquitted the villain? No, I certainly am not! Next, I have to skip the hundreds and thousands who came after the three little angels bombed to death for praying, or the northern kid who ended up in a casket for not knowing what White-Jim Crow-southern hospitality meant for Black kids that supposedly whistled. A young Black man graduates from high school in America, only to be compared to a charging bear with his claws up in the air. Why, I didn't know that charging bears charge backwards, ending up with bullets in their backs. Oh, I'm not done. White cops can respond to a call reporting someone with a gun and show up at a playground of all places, not to a grocery store, mind you, and ignore a 911 caller's caution that it's probably just some kid with a toy gun. Nope, the cops shot the kid. I still can hear him scream, and not a kid on the playground laughed. Mr. Officer decided to shoot him dead because he might one day turn into a gangster. He's a Black Boy, he can't possibly one day want to be a cop. Maybe he would have grown up and been revered by pre-school kids, but after complying with orders to retrieve his license and registration, White cops gun him down in a car with a Black woman and child. Moreover, the whole world can't get a four-year-old's words: "Mommy, are you okay?" out of their heads. We hadn't even gotten the words "I can't breathe" out of our heads, minds, or souls. We certainly haven't been able to scorch from our memories the sight or the sounds of that same man being placed in an illegal choke hold and choked to death. Only, it wasn't the 1980s. It was the twenty-first century. We weren't Bugging Out. We weren't watching a bad rendition of cops forcing Radio Raheem to fly like Mike and click his heels like Dorothy. No. It was real for all to see that the Black victim unequivocally was placed in an illegal chokehold. And what do White cops say, "Stop Resisting." Mr. Black cop, would you resist if someone choked the life out of you? That's a rhetorical question," I paused when I sensed Cap wanted to respond.

But, as no one said anything, I took a huge breath and continued. I lambasted, "Or when a White cop demands a Black woman to put her cigarette out, she ends up in a cell looking like strange fruit. Even if she was a young girl sleeping on her grandmother's sofa, White cops can serve a no-knock death sentence, set her on fire with a flash bang grenade, and then shoot her to put the fire out this time." By this time, both of my cheeks are glazed and glistening with rage. However, I pressed on, "You would think they have a fetish for the smell of a Black girl's burnt pigtails. No, that can't be the case because that young girl can grow up to be a Black first responder with dreams, and they will still serve a no-knock death sentence. And how many times do we have to hear that it was the wrong apartment or faulty information, to realize that it begins with White cops not caring about the lives of Black citizens in the first place. Don't dare ask me why we shout Black Lives Matter. Would you believe that far too many Whites have the nerve to feign ignorance when a professional sports player takes a knee for justice during the National Anthem? And then turn right around and tell the world not to rush to conclusions, when a White officer mocks the knee for justice as he kneels on a Black man's neck, and we all hear that all too familiar plea, 'I can't breathe,' complemented by death. Please tell me where you see the Black cops standing when peaceful protesters speak out against this slow genocide," I finished, placing emphasis on my last statement.

For a moment, there was silence in the room, and everyone looked at me, as if I were some boy asking them to join the girls' cookie summer team. The Cap then sighed, "Well, I stand with you. At some point every day, I have to take my uniform off. I can never take off my Black skin and wouldn't want to if I could. It hurts me every time I see another Black person gunned down by an officer of the law. It hurts me when we gun each other down as well. However, I know the difference between someone from the criminal element killing citizens and someone who swears to serve and protect killing citizens. When the people who end up dead at the hands of police so often look like me, it definitely strikes a nerve. Many times, I have wondered about wearing the same uniform that symbolizes a constant threat to Black lives. It frustrates me when people dismiss the repeated murders of unarmed Black men as a training issue…" Cutting Cap off, I blurted out, "I be saying the same thing. Oops, my bad," then I let him continue his point, as he raised his eyebrow. I had to let him complete his point, as they had let me.

"We all receive the same training, and I bet you won't find one Black cop that tells you it's a training issue. It's clearly a systemic racism issue. I believe that as long as Blacks continue to stay on the periphery of the system, the racism within the system will continue to affect us. That's why it is my challenge to upend the status quo from within the system," Cap ended with a smile.

"Wow, my friend Marisol says the same exact thing. One day, she's going to be a D.A. and help put a stop to this madness," I said.

"Hoodie, would you believe I ran into a Black Lives Matter rally the other night, and a lot of the protesters were Black, Latino, and Asian police officers. I couldn't believe it myself. I felt like I went to Mecca and discovered White Muslims," Officer Day chimed in.

I just couldn't return the smile just yet. All I could do was listen to what he had to say

"Some of the officers were White, too, as were many of the protestors. We are living in different times, and it's no longer as easy as Black and White. It's the younger generations that have a more inclusive vision of America's future," Cap threw in.

"Unfortunately, the old guard is still in place, and they're trying to maintain the status quo. I think Black people would benefit from learning more about the system and politics in general. I mean, I couldn't believe that a president who hasn't resided since the '80s still has more federally appointed judges than twenty-first-century presidents." Chemistry enlightened us.

"You're talking about Ronald Regan, aren't you?" Day inquired.

"That's right, and that's why I don't believe in ageism, because there are a number of White sitting justices and White politicians who were young men during the Jim Crow era. I always ask myself who they were then and who they are today. Do they have their great-granddaddy's photo album of Black bodies hanging from trees, I question. I mean, seriously, the museum pictures are not the only ones that exist. The lynching of Blacks was like a circus spectacle for many Whites. What happens when Whites raised off those kinds of mentalities become cops, policing predominantly Black neighborhoods?" Chemistry asked. I was sitting there soaking everything up. This conversation was getting extremely rich, and I couldn't stop scratching my ears. Boy, I wish Marisol and Billy were here. I guess they would have no option but to get my version of what was said in this room. I mean, I felt like I was in a room with Malcolm X, Dr. King, and Fred Hammond. Cap was clearly King, Day had the positive skepticism of a Malcolm, leaving Chemistry as Hammond, and I was happy with being a fly on the wall, a buzzing fly.

It really made a difference, for me, to hear Black cops talk about how they felt the same oppressive system and, more importantly, were working to do something about it. These guys were the evidence of everything Marisol was talking about. Chemistry hadn't led us into the lion's den after all. He just got us some desperately needed allies. I figured that once Marisol and I got a chance to put our heads together, there would be no stopping us. It was time for the empire to strike back, and I planned to hit them where it hurts. Now, all I was thinking about was how I could convince them to give me a bulletproof vest. The Black power cum-bi-yah moment was dope: it really was dope, but I didn't lose my common sense. Lynch had a bullet with my name on it, and I didn't plan on taking an early trip to my grave, especially not at the hands of some silver-haired, decrepit gatekeeper with a penchant for destroying Black bodies.

I have to be honest, though. Our conversation was not nearly over with and I had a boatload of questions for the Black men who appeared to have at least some of the answers. I promised myself that I would not only walk away from all of this unscathed, but I would also walk away armed with fire from the gods, and just as Prometheus did, I would give all the knowledge I obtained to the little people of this world. For now, I would just pay close attention to all the nuances in the scheme we were cooking up.

Stick to the Script

"Una dos si esta, I said, uh, east, uh, west. I met my boyfriend at the candy store. He brought me ice cream. He brought me cake. He brought me home with a bellyache. I said Momma, Momma, I feel sick. Call the doctor quick, quick, quick. I said, Doctor Doctor, will I die? He said Close your eyes and count to five. "I said one, two, three, four, five, I'm alive," I could hear Marisol and the group of young girls cheering as they jumped Double Dutch in McDonald's parking lot. Every Saturday, we all hung out at this location. Sometimes we actually had enough money to order a number one or at least a milkshake, and I mean that with the utmost respect. Unbeknownst to many people, it was the milkshake that made McDonald's what it is today: a cheap burger and a shake. I mean, like fifteen cents cheap. I would have been eating burgers every day, three times a day, and I'm sure I would have had plenty of strawberry shakes too.

"Hoodie and Marisol sitting in the tree K-I-S-S-I-N-G, first comes love, then comes marriage, then comes Hoodie with the baby carriage." I finally snapped out of my thoughts as Marisol snuck up on me again. Actually, the change in the cheerleader lyrics grabbed my attention. Whenever Marisol and I got together on Saturdays, all of our friends tried to turn us into a couple. Although we did kiss once, we were playing spin the bottle, and it landed on us. I couldn't back down, or everyone would have labeled me a Sippy-cup, and if you know me, then you know I wasn't having that, so I tried to French kiss her, sending her spitting and running in the other direction at the sliver of my slimy tongue. When I opened my eyes, everyone was pointing and laughing at me, saying, "He slimed me, he slimed me." The crew called me Slimer for months, and as you know, the little ugly green ghost from the movie Ghostbusters. Their taunting finally died down just for Halloween to arrive and start it up all over again.

"Mr., don't you see me standing here?" Marisol said, annoyed.

"Oh, I'm sorry. I didn't even notice," I responded, being funny.

"Anyway, I have some scoop for you. Hot off the Press and it's a game changer too!" she bragged.

"Well, spit it out, woman," I replied. I always wanted to say that.

"Don't play with me, boy. You better watch your tone before you get jacked up," she fired back. I knew she was serious because technically, this was their turf. The girls outnumbered us, and they had more loyalty than we did.

"Oops, my mistake, I was just playing. I don't want no smoke," I copped out.

"That's what I thought," she said, trying to provoke me to engage her in a verbal confrontation, so her girls could come and back her up. I wasn't stupid, so I swallowed my pride.

"Look, Marisol, I need you as an ally right now. I can't afford to be beefing with you, knowing the man is on my neck. We have to stick together, girl," I poured it on, speaking her language.

"Whatever, do you remember Big Shi-shi from the first floor right across from the playground on your block?" she questioned me.

"Yes," I answered, unsure of where she was going with all this.

"Well, my cousin Meeka was talking to Shi-shi the day that the murder took place on your block. The girl was taking a selfie in the window, and guess who's in the picture?" she quizzed.

"Who are you?" I say, confused.

"Not me. You, dummy. You're in the photo and that little girl who always wears the pigtail hairstyle," she revealed, grinning.

"So, what does that mean?" I pressed her.

"That's not all. She captured the shooting in the background of her selfie. When she zoomed in on the picture, she said she noticed your big head, the little girl, Little Dee, the man who got shot, and someone else behind Little Dee," she now smiled from ear to ear.

"What you talking 'bout, Marisol?" I asked, doing my best Arnold impression from Different Strokes.

"You really never saw the shooter, did you?" she investigated.

"I never said I saw the shooter. Nor did I ever tell you I was there either. Maybe it's someone who looks like me," I lied, trying to throw her off course.

"No, it's you, and you forgot that I know all about the blood on your sneakers," she reminded me. Then she continued, "If you want my help, then you're going to have to trust me. No secrets between us, deal," she insisted, extending her hand to shake on it. I shook her hand in agreement, and I didn't even think about trying my death grip on her. I remember the last time I tried that, and that didn't work out too good for me. I ended up on my knees pleading for her to stop crushing my knuckles.

"Okay, from this point on, I will brief you on any new intel that I receive, no need-to-know basis. You are authorized for the highest security clearance level. Yes, that means classified material. I mean the top-secret Pentagon stuff," I said in my most professional tone.

"Boy, please, who are you supposed to be, the Black Doogie Houser or something? Please remember one thing. You're doing yourself a favor by keeping me in the loop. You're not doing me any favors on this one. I'm putting my neck on the line for you, not the other way around. So, get with the program or end up swimming with the fishes. It's your call," she said, crossing her arms over her chest.

I guess she told me because I was speechless. She had a point. The detectives were out to get me, not her. By getting her involved in my mess, I was putting her in danger. Up to that point, everything history had shown me let me know that Black girls were just as vulnerable as Black boys were, and to be honest, they were the ones most likely to end up on a milk carton. Moreover, when I dug deeper, it became apparent to me that many Black girls who went missing never made the cut for the milk carton in the first place. That one in a million gets our attention, even though the media conveniently overlooks the million for freckled-faced Tommy or Becky with the good hair.

"You are one hundred percent correct, this time," I said with emphasis to let her know that I'm seldom wrong.

"This time and every other time," she fired back, not missing a beat. I had nothing. She showed me up again. Boy, I had to get my stuff together. I think all of the drama was hurting my ability to be my best self. Just as I thought of something slick to fire back, I noticed an unmarked vehicle slowly rounding the corner. When it came to a complete halt, I figured that was my cue to leave.

"Uh, Marisol, I'll call you later," I abruptly informed her without taking my eyes off the tented-out Crown Victoria. As I started backpedaling, the vehicle inched forward at a barely noticeable crawl. No one else was seeing all this transpire but me. I turned completely around, and sure enough, out of the corner of my eye, I could see the vehicle moving at a more assertive pace.

"Hoodie, what the hell, we weren't even finished with our conversation," Marisol said, and I could hear her voice closing in as she trailed me.

I took off running and the only thing I could hear were her friends cheering as they clapped their hands and stopped their feet in rhythm, "A, she thinks she bad. B, she a dirty crab. Jump high, touch the sky, break low to let you know that you," were the last words I heard before the sound of screeching tires filled my eardrums, causing my heartbeat to speed to a rapid pace. I never ran so fast in my life. I hit the end of the block within a matter of seconds. I must have been running a three-point-seven-hundred-yard dash up the block. The sound of the Crown Vic slamming on the brakes suddenly exploded into the airwaves. I kept running, but I couldn't help but think that the breaking sound was a bit premature. I ran another five blocks before I was convinced that no one was chasing me any longer. Maybe they were just trying to scare me, I pondered. Something wasn't sitting right with me. I found a stoop hidden in between the alleyway and decided to cop a squat and replay the events over in my head. By the third replay, I could hear the soft pounce of footsteps behind me along with the screeching tires. My eyes widened, and as my mouth dropped, I whispered, "Oh no!"

Instantly, I realized why the driver of the Crown Vic slammed on the brakes so suddenly. They seized Marisol, and it was my fault. If anything happened to her, I wouldn't be able to live with myself. While I was wallowing in self-pity, the homicide detectives were moving right along with their plans. Obviously, they were a step ahead of me, and I had no idea about the chain of events already underway.

"Bang, Bang, Bang, the loud thuds pounded against the apartment door."

"Who is it?" Mrs. Davis asked, a bit annoyed.

"Open up, it's the police," Maloney said.

"The police, no one at this residence called the cops," Mrs. Davis informed him, looking through the peephole without opening the door.

"I'm here on official police business, Ma'am. You can either open the door now, or I'll come back with a warrant and knock the door off its hinges," he said, sounding aggravated. At the sounds of the door being unlocked, he whispers to Lynch, "It works every time." However, the sound of the chain resisting the door opening immediately knocked him off his high horse.

"Grandma, don't open that door," Billy said with a worried tone in his voice.

"Boy, hush up and go wake your grandpa up, so he can know what's going on," she ordered him. Then, turning her attention back to the door, she shows her face through the cracked door. "May I see some Identification?" she demanded in a loud, thunderous voice to wake up the neighbors. Her actions stunned Maloney, catching him off guard. He recognized that she was putting her neighbors on point.

"Here you go, Mam," Maloney said, reluctantly flashing his badge and then immediately handing her his police identification card. He was hoping that she would calm down and open the door. The old woman's bold actions even concerned Lynch. Although he didn't buy the family relation between her and Ms. Hoodie, he had to admit that they both seemed to be cut from a similar cloth. Clearly, Ms. Hoodie refused to play the role of a pushover, and he knew that was rare from many of today's Black women. At least when it came to standing up to White men of authority, too many Black women opted against expressing. The strong, angry Black women that they expressed towards their Black male counterparts. To him, they seemed more inclined to participate in the culture of respectability even in minor confrontations with their White bosses, landlords, and police officers. However, they surely knew how to castigate Black men and often competed against them for pillar of community status. He always found that ironic.

While Coretta and Betty were alive, King and Malcolm were tarnished as something other than the grassroots. He chalked it up as a win-win because divide and conquer ruled the day, just like his Paddy told him it would.

"Well, I see your ID, homicide detective Maloney, but you have to give me a moment before I open this door. In this home, my husband and I make all of our decisions today as we've made them for the past forty years, and that, sir, is side by side. So if you will wait a moment, my husband will be with us shortly," she said, handing him back his ID. Once again, Mrs. Davis stunned Lynch with her response. He thought he was a character in a 1970s film with Black characters that were reminiscent of movies like Super Fly and Foxy Brown. He felt like someone had put him and Maloney in a time capsule. She defied the stereotypical Black woman who lacked respect for her Black man. That depiction didn't exist in this home. In that very instance, he realized that the normal scare tactics wouldn't work.

"All righty then," Maloney replied as he took the ID and then raised his eyebrows, looking back at Lynch. Lynch just shrugged his shoulders. It hadn't even been ten seconds before they heard the sound of the chain unlatching from an open door. Just as Mrs. Davis said, she and Mr. Davis were standing side-by-side to welcome the detectives into their home. Billy was no longer anywhere in sight, even though he wasn't very far. He crouched down in the hall to get an earful of what was going on, and he had his phone on hand, ready to record.

"Good afternoon, detectives. Is there something that we can help you with?" Mr. Davis asked to resume control of the conversation. Then he looked at Lynch with a glint of recognition on his countenance. Lynch acknowledged Mr. Davis's expression that spoke a thousand words, and it was clear that he was signaling that he didn't forget about their last encounter.

Stepping forward, Lynch cleared his throat and proceeded to address why they were there, "Yes, I'm sure that you are aware of, at least some of, the events that took place in and around this building over the past weeks. In fact, just the other day, we turned over the young kid Hoodie to your care. Now I'm not here to harass you or make your life any harder than it already is, but we really need to talk to Hoodie. He may be in a lot of danger because he is an eyewitness to a murder." As soon as the last words left Lynch's lips, his cellphone started to ring. He retrieved it from his jacket pocket and looked down at the incoming caller's number. He looked at Maloney, signaling for him to take over, as he told the Davises, "Excuse me, I have to take this call." He takes a few steps towards the hall where Billy was still eavesdropping. Billy could overhear the conversation that he was having with the person on the other end of the phone.

"What do you mean you nabbed a girl?" Lynch demanded with a hint of aggravation in his voice.

"Listen, just tell us where the kid is and nobody has to suffer the consequences of obstructing a police investigation," Maloney said rather bluntly.

"Are you threatening us?" Mrs. Davis asked in a stern voice.

"Mam, I don't make threats. I'm just stating the facts. This is a homicide investigation, and by not helping us locate an eyewitness whose whereabouts you know, is the equivalent of obstructing justice," he responded.

"Now hold on one minute, we never refused to give you any information about the whereabouts of the child, nor did we give you the slightest reason to believe that we knew of the child's whereabouts. In fact, we haven't seen the child all morning and happen to be looking for him ourselves. Unless you and your partner can help us with that, then I suggest you leave this apartment right this minute," Mr. Davis said with his voice elevating a pitch or two. Lynch could hear their voices rising and abruptly ended his call. Billy stayed in place as he heard the apartment door being unlocked. Chemistry opened the apartment door to find his grandparents being interrogated by Detective Maloney. Before he could say anything, he noticed Lynch tapping Maloney on his shoulder to get his attention.

"Okay, thank you for your time. We were just leaving," he said, urging Maloney to follow suit. The two men walked past Chemistry, who remained standing with the door ajar. He, Lynch, and Maloney had the same look on their faces that tacitly acknowledged their earlier encounter. Tension filled the air between them, as the opportunity for engagement was not only quite apparent but also quite tempting on Chemistry's part. Deep down inside, he knew they weren't there on official police business and that dramatically heightened the level of danger that the detectives put his family in at the moment. Knowing better, he wouldn't do anything to jeopardize their safety, which was the main reason that he remained standing like a doorman. As soon as they cleared him, he stepped in and locked the door.

Chemistry took a few quick glances around the apartment and then emptied into a barrage of questions: "Where's Billy at? Did Hoodie come back? Why did you let them in here without a warrant or anybody knowing what was taking place? Ya'll do know that what ya'll just did was completely dangerous, don't you?" he finally finished.

"Billy is in his room, but we don't know where Hoodie is at the moment. We were hoping that you could fill us in on that one, since the two of you left together. And as far as us letting them in this apartment, we know how to take care of ourselves just fine," Mrs. Davis said, placing her hand on her hip, wishing he would respond in any way but apologetic. Sensing her stance, Chemistry knew better, and he clearly noticed his grandfather's silent nod. It wasn't often that someone or something pissed Mrs. Davis off, but when it did, they all knew that they didn't want any part of her bad side.

"Sorry, Grams, you know I'm just concerned about you all. And today's cops are just different," he pleaded.

"Don't tell me about any cops of today being any different than the cops of my time, as if we're not still here experiencing today's cops. A bad cop is a bad cop, no matter what era they policed in America. If my memory serves me correctly, the police have yet to bomb another black organization the way they did the MOVE headquarters in Philadelphia in the 1970s. So don't you tell me about today's cops," she admonished him, straining her voice, ignoring his apology.

"Grams, you're right, and I should know better than to make that statement as if you haven't taught me better. It won't happen again. I'm still uncomfortable with those detectives being in here on unofficial police business." As soon as the words unofficial left his mouth, both of their eyebrows raised, and Billy, still crouched down in the hall, scratched his ears. Continuing Chemistry decided to bring them completely onboard to avoid anything close to what just transpired ever happening again: "Those detectives were not here on business as usual, and targeting Ms. Hoodie and Hoodie is not a coincidence. Detective William Lynch happens to be a close relative of the cop who killed Hoodie's father." He paused as a chorus of "What's" erupted in the apartment, even giving up Billy's position.

"Get out of here, Billy," Chemistry demanded. Billy rose to his feet slowly, thinking about the many times that Chemistry warned him about eavesdropping on adults. Once Billy entered the section bordering the kitchen and living room. Chemistry resumed the family debriefing and said, "Although Ms. Hoodie fled the South several years ago, leaving the Internal Affairs' investigation cold, these cops have tracked her down. We believe Hoodie's name coming up in the homicide investigation is what triggered it. They know she's the Ms. Hoodie that they were looking for. It seems that the cop in the South is running for sheriff, and he's trying to tie up any loose ends that would prevent him from being elected. Ms. Hoodie happened to be an eyewitness to the murder, and there is dash camera footage of the incident. However, without Ms. Hoodie, it seems that the justice department won't touch the case.

"To make matters worse, the situation with Little Dee is more personal to the New York detectives. It seems that they were on the dealer's payroll in the territories surrounding Brown Houses. They promised those dealers that they would clear up the areas around the projects, forcing all the drug traffic into the projects. The detectives held up their end of the bargain, but a federal investigation took all of their dealer friends down before the detectives met their contacts in the projects. To make a long story short, Little Dee's crew cleaned house, wiping out all the competition, making Little Dee's crew beneficiaries by default. They refused all of Detective Lynch's offers, infuriating him in the process. Unless Little Dee plays ball, he will be a fall guy for a murder that he likely didn't commit. Before you ask, we have accurate inside sources that the detectives least suspect," Chemistry finished. He honestly didn't want to tell them because, under different circumstances, the less they knew, the better for their safety.

In this case, they needed to know exactly what they were dealing with concerning the detectives. Chemistry understood that these accusations were serious, and the evidence leveled against them was the key to putting them away for a long time. Lynch and his crew didn't leave the type of evidence that was written down, copied, or recorded. People were the only ones that could screw up their organization. They knew that they only had to get rid of the people to get away with their crimes. For them, these were poor people that no one cared about, wouldn't miss, and the news reporters would overlook for more sensational stories.

Shifting Gears

Once I saw the Crown Victoria bend the corner, I breathed a sigh of relief. I rose to my feet from the squatted position I was in on the side of my building's stoop. The detectives descended the steps without even noticing my position. I couldn't help but think that it was the perfect opportunity for someone to ambush them like they steadily ambushed us with prayer hands raised, while we were fettered, or when we aggressively ran in the opposite direction. I also couldn't ignore the fact that I took a big risk, placing my life in jeopardy. My intuition told me that I was playing a dangerous game with men who killed people for a living wage. My mind raced as I thought about what if they snatched my body without anyone knowing what happened. I felt lost as I finally reached the apartment door. I knocked on the door once, but before my knuckles could make contact with the door again, it swung open. Chemistry's muscular arms reached out and snatched me like a lion retrieving its cub.

As I entered, everyone's eyes instantly locked on me, as if I had made an announcement or as if I were the king of Madagascar. Yet when I took a closer look at their countenances, their faces clearly didn't look like a celebration was about to occur. Instead, their faces looked like those of concerned family members who ensnared another family member with a crisis intervention. At that very moment, I wanted to run out of that room as fast as I could. Everything that I'd ever heard about interventions was bad. They never worked because the addict usually claimed that the intervention was too much for them to handle and actually triggered an urge to get high. I was certain about one thing, and it was that I wasn't an addict and wouldn't let them or anyone else treat me like one.

"Hoodie, where the hell have you been?" Mr. Davis asked me in a stern voice. Before I could answer, Chemistry explained that we were together for most of the morning and that he gave me permission to go to McDonald's. He then proceeded to rehash the turn of events that landed the detectives at the Davises' doorstep. At this point, everyone realized that shit just got real. I didn't have the luxury to underestimate the detectives because it would be my life that I gambled with, or someone else's life. Instantly, I thought about what transpired with Marisol and decided to bring everyone up to speed on my suspicions.

"Marisol," I unintentionally blurted out. "I think they took Marisol. She was running behind me, and then there was this unmarked vehicle. I took off running and didn't stick around to find out if they were there for me or not. But once I got away, I took a moment to reflect on what had just occurred. First, I recalled the sound of tires screeching as if the driver of the unmarked vehicle slammed on the brakes in the middle of the block. Second, I recalled the sound of footsteps behind me when I took off. I think that was Marisol running behind me. The kidnappers probably thought Marisol was trying to escape capture along with me. They couldn't catch me because I went into sixth gear. They must have grabbed her instead..." I stopped for a moment to see if anyone was grasping what I just said.

"I heard the detective with the silver hair mention something about a girl on the phone. He sounded like he wasn't happy about it," Billy informed us.

"Are you certain that you heard him say something about a girl?" Mrs. Davis asked.

"I am one hundred percent certain," he confirmed, looking directly into Mrs. Davis's eyes.

"That has to be Marisol," I said excitedly, and no sooner than the words left my mouth, my cell phone started ringing. It was as if we were in a movie because everyone's eyes turned towards my phone. Billy and Mr. Davis were shaking their heads in a no gesture, signaling me not to answer the call. My phone had to ring three times with everyone either standing or sitting in silence until Chemistry broke the rank.

"Hoodie, answer the call. It might be about Marisol," he didn't have to tell me twice. I answered the call without hesitation.

"Hello, yes, this is he," I informed the caller on the other end.

"I suggest you turn yourself in before you get your little girlfriend into big trouble," the caller said in a grim voice.

"Marisol doesn't have anything to do with this. Leave her alone," I nervously shouted. My hands were shaking like leaves. The caller sounded like the Terminator, and it was clear that the big trouble he was talking about was termination.

"As long as you do what I say, she'll be fine. However, if you try to involve anyone else or do anything other than what I tell you, let's just say your friend will be the one who suffers the consequences," the caller warned.

"How do I know that she's okay? I want to speak to Marisol," I demanded, trying to buy time to keep him on the line so that the call could be traced back later.

"Here, just tell him that it's you and nothing else," I heard the caller order.

"It's me, Hoodie. I'm on a beach!" I hear Marisol speedily shout out before the phone was snatched from her, and her voice was muffled.

"If anything happens to her," I said, but before I could finish my threat, the caller cut me off midsentence. "If anything happens to her, it will be your entire fault, Hoodie. Now, you remember that, ok? Do you hear me?" he asked me, in a grimacing tone. I was speechless. He scared the poop out of me through the phone. All I could hear in my head was the killer's voice in the movie Scream saying, *"Do you want to die, Sydney?"* This was intense, and I wasn't prepared for what this psycho was offering me.

Noticing that the caller terrified me, Chemistry had had enough and snatched the phone out of my hand. He raised his voice instantly, letting the caller know that he was messing with the wrong one. At least he thought he was about to let the caller know that he was serious. Then he had a dumbfounded look on his face as he mumbled, "He hung up on me. The son of a bitch hung up on me. These people mean serious business. He wasn't even willing to hear me out. Grams, you all have to go to Uncle Phil's house. It's no longer safe for any of us here. We have to go now because if they went to the extreme to snatch a little girl, then it's no telling what they're willing to do. I'm going to make a few calls to let our friends know what's going on, but we have to get out of here. Hurry up and pack some things! We have to go!" Chemistry shouted with fear, filling his voice. He was frightening the hell out of Billy and me. We weren't built for this type of stuff. Clearly, the Davises didn't hear him because they weren't flinching when Billy and I sprang to our feet and headed for the bedroom.

"I'm not going anywhere. Ain't no jive turkey gonna run me out of my home. They'd better at least put some sheets over their heads if they plan on terrifying Mrs. Ruby's son. I never ran, and I never will. Over my dead body I'm leaving this home," Mr. Davis barked with Mrs. Davis, right by his side.

"You damn right, you heard what the man of this house said. They picked the wrong folks to mess with this time. We were here during the riots, and we didn't leave then. There ain't no way in hell that we're gonna leave now," Mrs. Davis agreed.

"And, we damn sure ain't leaving without a fight," Mr. Davis added.

"Look, I don't want to run either, but we have these kids to worry about. From the looks of things, these people don't give two shits about killing a Black Child. Shit, the way they shoot and kill our kids, you would think they put that down on their résumés," Chemistry lamented, trying to make them see logic in his words and plan.

"Listen, son, you do what you have to do and take those babies somewhere safe. There's no need to tell us where you're going, either. We will be right here when you get back, and if you need us, then all you have to do is pick up the phone. I have my daddy's rifle right here, and Mama has her great uncle's rifle. These barrels done stared down dozens of clans men in states north and south of this country. Defending Black Wall Street, they saw action in Tulsa Oklahoma too—right down Greenwood Ave. Blacks weren't the only people that died during those horrific nights. They won't tell you that, but the ammo in this here thirty-thirty will knock a wild boar clean off its feet, pun intended," Mr. Davis said as he pulled the gun metal and mahogany rifle from under the pillow below his lap. All Chemistry could do was smile and admire the old man for the fire that remained breathing within him. Mrs. Davis patted the pillow under her, signaling that they were locked, loaded, and ready to go! Deep down inside, Chemistry knew that they would be all right because they lived for, as the late great Civil Rights Activists, John Lewis, would say, "getting into good trouble."

"Come on, boys, let's go," Chemistry shouted out, and as the words left his lips, I stormed out of the room with Billy on my heels. He didn't have to tell us twice. I looked at Mr. Davis with his cowboy rifle and couldn't help but think that he didn't stand a chance. Our enemies had access to military grade weapons equipped with infrared beams, night vision, bang grenades, and armored trucks! The Davises were like kids in some third-world country, throwing stones at a tank that blasted 125-mm cannon shots at them in response.

'Full disclosure, the gun rights activists killed me with their cause to protect Second Amendment rights. I mean, I'm all for the Second Amendment, as all African Americans should be, but the idea was ludicrous that any backwoods militia in the US was prepared for the devastation that an urban police force would deal to anyone who challenged state violence. Many American urban police forces are heavily armed to the point that they could match the combat units of foreign governments in manpower and machinery. New York State alone has more armed police officers than the average country has military personnel. I'm only eleven, and I know that much. I had to give it to them. They weren't the least bit afraid of the detective's intimidation tactics. Maybe one day I too will be that courageous.' I thought to myself, as I took one last look at them and waved what could be my last goodbye to them.

Neither Chemistry nor Billy even bothered to say goodbye. I thought to myself, *'It was because they were afraid that if they said it, then that might mean goodbye for good. I've always been one to believe that whatever's meant to happen will happen.'* To my surprise, Chemistry ushered us into a tented-out black van with Officer Day and Cap as its occupants. I must admit that I was happy to see that the reinforcements were here. I imagined that we had our own Black Stormtroopers in full camouflage, squatting in the trees and the bushes. This was dope! The van reminded me of the popular eighties TV show, The A-Team, and I was Hannibal.

"I love it when a plan comes together," I muttered aloud, once again revealing my thoughts. Cap just gave me this big-old-bright smile from ear to ear. The van pulled off slowly, and I noticed two more black vehicles filed in line behind us and two more filed in line up ahead. "Yes!" I shouted as I looked to the trees and bushes to confirm my other suspicions. That was a negative.

"How are you guys feeling this fine afternoon?" Cap greeted us, turning around in the passenger seat. Day kept his hands on the steering wheel and his eyes on the road, nodding at us through the rearview mirror.

"Fine," Billy and I said in unison.

"That's good. I didn't think that the folk would be coming along with you guys. They are truly some special people. They helped me out plenty of times throughout the course of my tumultuous life. It's very rare to find members of the party still active and willing to engage in good trouble," Cap said, smiling again.

"Yeah, I tried to talk them into coming along with us, but they weren't having it for one minute. I knew they weren't coming, but I had to at least give it a shot," Chemistry complained.

"What happened, Pops gave you his – my – daddy's rifle routine?" Cap asked, and both men burst out laughing without saying another word. It became obvious to me that this wasn't their first rodeo. I was in the midst of a twenty-first-century underground railroad, and I ain't even know it. Billy just sat there, silent as well, sucking it all up, or rather taking notes, literally. This little bleep is an apprentice, I found my interlocutor pointing out. I was officially a member of what Chemistry often refers to as the vanguard. Never in my wildest imagination did I ever think that I would be a part of something so big and transformative. We were fighting back, and no one was being apologetic about demanding equal justice under the law.

    I sat there thinking about BLM activists like the outspoken Tamika, who compelled me to be optimistic about Black civic engagement. Our ancestors slaved, marched, boycotted, suffered K-9 bites, did degrading sit-ins that spawned a culture of prank shows like the Ridiculousness, took rides for freedom, and we're still rioting the rioters and looting the looters, so we can matter, so Marisol and my mom can matter. I fought back the tears that were welling up in my eyelids. There was no way that I would let a single drop slide down my cheeks. Self-consciously, I knew that Billy wouldn't let me live down crying like a baby or a big old scaredy cat. I didn't know where we were headed at the moment, but I trusted that we were going somewhere safe, like Chemistry mentioned. One thing I was now extremely confident about was the fact that Chemistry wouldn't lead Billy and me astray. He was vested in our futures and our success as young Black men, navigating our way through adolescence in a bad city.

RIDEALONG

As our convoy cruised along the city blocks, I couldn't help but feel like a character straight outta one of the Transformer installments. I felt invincible behind the Texas-oil-black-tented windows. I looked up at the rearview mirror to find Cap smiling at me. Out of common courtesy, I faked a smile in return. As soon as I turned my head to look back out the window, I saw the most beautiful woman that I've ever seen, brandishing colorful butterfly tattoos that ran the length of her long, Nestlé's Crunch-toned legs. The butterflies appeared caged behind the hot pink-wide fishnet stockings she wore, matching what clearly looked like a bikini to me. I guess the top-hatted man in the purple and gold Cadillac, reminiscent of one you would see on the TV show Pimp My Ride, planned to take her to the beach. I found that kind of odd because it surely wasn't beach weather.

Although I focused my attention out the window, my antennas remained alert, picking up the chatter in the vehicle. I overheard Cap stating, "That's the oldest profession in the world," as he nodded his head toward the beautiful woman leaning on the Caddy. Then I noticed how Officer Day shook his head in disapproval. For the strangest of reasons, the rapper Kendrick Lamar came to my mind. In particular, the title of his top-selling album, "To Pimp a Butterfly," added meaning to my nymph brain.

"Ohhh," I blurted out, revealing my epiphany. Cap and Day nearly broke their necks to make eye contact with me. Obviously, both men were on point, realizing that I studied them. "Hey, lil-man, what you say?" Cap saluted me with his caught-in-the-cookie jar smile that hung like a hammock from ear to ear.

"Come on now, Cap, I'm not that slow. You'd better ask Chemistry about me," I said conceitedly.

"Oh, I'd better ask Chemistry, huh, I'll pass. I'd rather ask you about Hoodie. Why go to the second hand, when I have you right here?" he suggested.

"Huh," I muttered at his statement. He completely lost me. I sat there, dumbfounded.

Then Billy, who was obviously eavesdropping, blurts out, "A firsthand account, only you can provide a firsthand account about who you are. A third-party account is hearsay, speculation, or opinion other than yours," he boasted. Now you know I'm thinking like the late great DMX barked, "Here we go again!" Does this motto ever give these investigative tactics a rest?

"Cap, you do know that I'm of age to have watched the Godfathers I, II, and III," I emphasized.

"What's that supposed to mean?" he inquired, looking as dumbfounded as I just looked.

'Now we're even,' I thought to myself.

"Uh, The Code of Silence, La Cosa Nostra," I hit him with.

"Oh, I didn't know that they let neophytes in the Mafia. What are you, some kind of made baby? Get it made, man-made baby," he heckled, sending the whole cabin into an eruption of laughter. The joke was back on me.

Not to be outdone, I shot back, "You must have never heard of Baby Faced Nelson, Copper." Billy nearly dropped his iPhone, Day lost focus of the road, swerving the van, Chemistry clutched his chest, and Cap involuntarily slapped his knee so hard that we all heard his kneecap click. Everyone was roaring with laughter. *Touché,* I thought as I admired my work. They were in tears of joy. Considering the dangerous circumstances we were in, I maintained my composure.

Someone had to remain focused on the task ahead.

"Hoodie, you sure are something else, kid. I like that you have your own mind and aren't the least bit afraid to speak it. We could use more youth like you. Kid, I'm on your side. I'm not trying to flip you. I noticed that you picked up on grown folks talking street life. I wanted to know your take on what you see transpiring in your environment. When you look out that window, what do you see on these streets?" Cap asked, awaiting my answer.

"You mean literally?" I inquired.

"Yes, literally what do you see? What do ya'll see?" he asked.

"People hanging around idly," Billy offered, intentionally beating me to the punch.

"A liquor store, some hustlers, and littered streets," I three-pieced him.

"Squad car, squad car, squad car, and don't forget that crack house," Billy sang.

In my mind, I thought, *'He's a dry snitch. Not only is he volunteering information, but he's also implying that I knew about the red-brick crack house. Now I've heard of criminals having accomplices to commit crimes, but I've never heard of snitches having accomplices to drop dimes. I think Cap read my astonished facial expression because his next remark resonated with me.'*

"That's correct. You both pointed to the things that are wrong with too many of the streets in our neighborhoods, but now I want to see if you can identify them in an affluent neighborhood," he informed us, adjusting in the passenger seat to face us as if he were truly interested in what we had to say. Cap wasn't pulling wool over my eyes. Chemistry taught me all about good listening skills and the importance of eye contact. I knew he was attempting to gain our trust or build a rapport. The next thing I knew, Cap was on the radio directing the convoy to an upscale-predominantly-White neighborhood.

In about twenty minutes, we were cruising down boulevards that made me feel like the Fresh Prince of Bellaire. We sailed by a sea of freshly manicured lawns. The beauty of each house seemed to make the property value of the house next to it increase. The air smelled different. No trash blew in the air, no loiterers aligned the blocks, and the living spaces weren't piled one on top of the other. This must be what my first-period teacher meant by a residential area. Something in the way that she said the compound word made me suspicious. Her words were specific and oddly made me feel excluded. From then on, I always wondered whether I lived in a residential area. Was I a resident? Now I was certain I did not, I was not, and we were not. We lived in the hood, making us hood in my teacher's eyes and the eyes of what Chemistry referred to as White America. I never understood that because I was under the impression that there was only one America. I mean, Chemistry didn't believe that Whites owned America, so why pander to a false ideology? Why not say in the eyes of some White Americans, because not all Whites saw the same. Some Whites wore glasses, some wore coke bottle glasses, and some others wore contacts. Just like Blacks, Whites saw through different lenses. I also didn't understand why people blamed problems on the system when it was actually certain White people who made decisions in that system. Systems didn't make decisions; people made decisions, or rather policies that negatively affect Black lives.

At that very moment, I didn't want any part of Cap's game. I'd rather play punch buggy, a game where the only consequence was a bruised arm rather than a bruised ego. I sat there and listened as Billy foolishly played on, gambling with his own insecurities, and the sad part was that he either didn't realize it or didn't care to realize it. I guess he was too busy being a kid. Apparently, Cap intended to teach us a valuable lesson about the haves and the have-nots. I knew I was from the bottom, but I also knew that my life story was just getting started.

"I see nice houses, green trees, newly painted streets, and new street signs. Oh, there goes a nice bar. There's a pool room and a shopping center with a spacious parking lot." Those were all of the things that Billy highlighted as we drove down the wide avenue. There wasn't a bum in sight, no winos or hustlers, and there definitely weren't any pimps like the ones who flooded our streets. While I saw a pharmacy, there wasn't a single hood pharmacist posted on any corner pretending to own the entire block. Nice fences surrounded their yards with happy dogs bouncing around on plush-green grass, while circulating sprinklers showered the ground with sparkling water, minus the Flint-lead tent. It was quiet, no traffic, and amazingly, an occupying police presence was absent.

"Hey Hoodie, you're mighty quiet back there. I thought that you would have excelled at this past time," Cap poked at me, snapping me out of my bemusement.

"If that's what you want to call this expedition," I said, brushing him off.

"Well, what would you call it?" he persisted.

"For starters, it's easy to see that you wanted us to know how the other side lives in comparison to our low quality of life. Then my guess is once we are brought into this display of excessive luxuries that we don't have access to, you would provide us with the ladder to achieve upward economic mobility. Is that how you say it, Chemistry?" I asked for confirmation. He just gives me a nod of approval. I was gassed up now, so I continued, "Let me guess, next you were going to tell us about how crucial obtaining a good education is towards decreasing the ever-widening wealth gap between Whites and Blacks, or how people with college degrees make over a million dollars more over a lifetime than people without college degrees."

For a moment, Cap sat there silent. I couldn't tell if he wanted to applaud me or if he was at a loss for words. My little oration certainly had Day squirming in his seat. For once, it seemed like I had Billy's full attention. He was on the edge of his seat, looking from Cap to me, then back to Cap. Cap cleared his throat and started speaking slowly and methodically, choosing his words like a fox, "Chemistry, let me ask you a question. Have you ever known me to go for low-hanging fruit?" he asked.

"No, sir," Chemistry curtly replied.

"While I have to give it to you, kid, you did highlight an important issue that we all know too well. We all know it so well that systemic racism is no longer a complex topic. We realize that, whether it's restrictive covenants, redlining, or flat-out segregation, a duck is a duck. However, I actually wanted you to identify similar elements in this affluent neighborhood that those in power choose not to criminalize in the way that they criminalize similar, if not the same, activities in your neighborhood," he enlightened me. I had the Arnold from Different Strokes, "What you talking bout Willis" look on my face, or as adults might say, the poop face. Billy gleefully chuckled at my know-it-all attitude, revealing the real reason behind his excitement. All along, he looked from Cap back to me, anticipating my downfall. '*What a bud,*' I was thinking to myself. He was no better than the teachers who had low expectations of us. In truth, I was more frustrated with myself for fulfilling preventable prophesies.

Seeing that I was humbled, Cap went on, "The nice bar as Billy described it is simply a more respectable rendition of a liquor store, instead of cop-n-go, it's cop-a-squat. However, there will never be one on every corner. On what they refer to as gentlemen's nights, you will find some of the prettiest women sporting those fancy butterfly tattoos that had your eyes twinkling."

"They did not," I abruptly cut him off.

"Can I finish now?" he asked, and I responded with a nod of approval. He jumped right to it, "Upper-class folks refer to them as call girls, even though you can't turn them into housewives either. That's neither here nor there. The point is that practically every night, barring Sundays, they come and go with stumbling male patrons, right out of that nice bar. Along with the unlimited booze, illicit drugs are exchanged in the open. This isn't the only location where drugs are exchanged in this lily-white-nice neighborhood. The pharmacy down the block distributes enough over-the-counter opioids to flood Brown Housing for weeks on end. Only these drug dealers are almost exclusively White doctors who, with no conscience, fill numerous prescriptions for quote-on-quote legal drugs, albeit for an illegal fee. And although these legal drugs kill more Americans each year than all illicit drugs combined, there is no hyper-incarceration of White doctors. Yet, America has a well-documented opioid crisis, but no one is sending in the first infantry. There will be no War on Drugs part two."

"Hoodie, the only difference is that there is no political push to end crime in affluent neighborhoods. Whether it's Stanford, Harvard, or Yale, there are plenty of drugs being sold and used on those campuses. However, stop-and-frisk is not used at any elite institution. A cruel fact remains that developmental psychologists, judges, district attorneys, and politicians know that all young people have vices. Too often, underage, affluent kids drink alcohol, abuse other mind-altering substances, drive drunk, drag race, haze, and even gamble with date rape drugs. What are the results of these decriminalized actions?" Cap asked sincerely.

This time, Billy remained quiet and waited for me to take the bait. I accepted the challenge and, like a fox, I chose my words methodically: "I think it starts with having parents who are financially able to hand over the keys of a brand-new car to an overjoyous sixteen-year-old. Then, likely, not thinking, a sixteen-year-old races a friend whose parents also purchased them a car for their birthday. One of the cars spins out of control, killing the four other joyriders who egged on the baby driver. That happens repeatedly! In our low-income neighborhoods, daddy or mommy cannot buy us cars, so people steal cars. We like joyrides too, and that's why they made the video game Grand Theft Auto. When it comes to drugs, most Black kids start selling drugs so they can buy nice sneakers, clothes, food, and even cars. Those kids don't know anything about worrying about when you're going to get a new pair of sneakers or any pair instead of the ones with your toes hanging out. They don't know about walking past Mickey Dees on your way to school without a single dime in your pocket and a stomach full of air. We're the bad guys, but you don't hear about innocent kids dying from hazing in the hood," I said with emphasis.

"Okay, that's one way to put it. All young people have the potential to make poor choices. However, certain environments limit the types of choices a youth has to choose from in the first place. In that nice neighborhood, a youth literally has to search out trouble at the sole poolroom that their parents warn them to keep their distance from. In your neighborhood, those activities take place in every other building you pass. You turn to your right there's a drug spot. You turn to your left, and you'll find two more. Different crews on every corner, wearing the latest name-brand sneakers you can't afford, eating the food you only wished someone had brought for you. The sad part is that some of those hustlers will buy you McDonald's and put some money in your pocket. They will even tell you to stay in school and away from the streets. Nevertheless, for a young mind, it's hard to hear that message while simultaneously wanting to escape the horrors of poverty. These guys will send you to the store with a twenty-dollar bill and tell you to keep the change that's left over, amounting to more than your allowance. Most poor kids never heard of an allowance until they watched The Cosby Show. The dealers look like they got it all figured out, and that's what draws most Black youth into the criminal lifestyle." Cap added.

"I remember the first time that I heard about an allowance. I thought it was so cool until I realized that only my White friends and kids of working-class parents got allowances." I chimed in, and it felt like my pants were ablaze for telling a half-truth. I felt ashamed to tell Cap or any of the other occupants in the van the real reason that I dreaded the thought of an allowance. I sat there steaming at the memory of my mother telling me how she ought to whoop my ass for asking her for an allowance, and then she told me to ask my dead father for an allowance. I should have known better than to ask her for money. She recently lost her job, and that already made me public enemy number one. Since then, she beat me as if I fired her.

"Hoodie, are you okay?" Cap asked, noticing that I'd drifted off in my thoughts.

"I'm fine," I replied, feeling the temperature of my trousers increase about twenty degrees and hearing my interlocutor singing the familiar children's anthem *"liar, liar, your pants on fire."*

"What's going on up ahead?" I heard Cap asking as our convoy came to a halt. I peered through the front window and noticed that two unmarked vehicles appeared to be blocking us off. My head swung around to find two more vehicles resting parallel behind our convoy's last two vehicles. I saw enough action movies to realize that they had us boxed in. But something about Cap's poise made me feel safe. At that very moment, Cap turned to me and asked me if I had a cellphone on me. I slowly nodded yes. I knew this part of the movie too well. It always led to the character in my position giving up his cellphone because it was being used to track that character's every move. Lynch must have used Marisol's call to obtain my phone number. He must have contacted the NSA, you know, the National Security Agency, I thought to myself as my mind raced for answers. I grudgingly handed over my phone, realizing that Cap sat there with his hand extended.

In response to some chatter over the radio, Cap stepped out of the vehicle and walked towards a group of White men. I could clearly see that one of them was Detective Lynch. Although I couldn't hear what they were saying, I could tell from their body language that things were a bit tense. Cap stood his ground, and his men in the first two vehicles had their guns drawn at the ready. It didn't take me long to realize that Lynch didn't like one word Cap had to say as the men parted their separate ways. Lynch looked like he was trying to peer right through the tented windows. It made me feel uneasy. I felt myself sliding down in my seat out of his view. He knew I was in the back seat. I suddenly felt like a nonconforming snitch under witness protection.

What if someone else saw me in this van? I found myself questioning. I didn't think things through when I just willingly went along with Chemistry's plan. I didn't have any agency in any of these charades. Maybe the Davises were right and Chemistry was wrong. Look at this nincompoop playing Dragon Ball Z on his iPhone. He doesn't have a care in the world. Suddenly, my attention shifted back to Cap as he reentered the van. I noticed that he no longer had my phone. I immediately deduced that Cap passed it off to his men in one of the other vehicles. Once Cap settled in, our convoy started moving again, and the vehicles that had once boxed us in had completely vanished.

Cap started giving us the rundown and debunked my theory about the NSA. However, he confirmed my suspicions that Lynch believed that I was in the convoy. According to Cap, without authorization, Lynch used Marisol's iPhone to pull up the tracking app that we were linked to. He was shrewd. On a detective's hunch, he had her call me, figuring that we had the app installed on our phones. Why I hadn't thought of that is beyond my comprehension. It must be my affinity for conspiracy theories and the like. It was never simple with me. Chemistry taught me to go deeper, looking beneath the surface. As I was sure Cap would encourage, I avoided the low-hanging fruit. Lynch thought I was low-hanging fruit, an easy target. He had me pegged all wrong. I wasn't anybody's soft target. I'm a hard target, and I guess he will find out the hard way.

If I have any say in the matter, before it's all said and done, he will be charged with high crimes and misdemeanors, I thought to myself. Cap kept on rambling, and I tuned in on his reference to the detectives telling him to tell me to relax. They dropped Marisol off at her unhappy parents' home.

The detectives told Marisol's parents that I was a person of interest in a homicide, and of course, they told her parents that they should contact them if they saw me. Well, they gave me a heads up. I knew to scratch Marisol off my underground railroad. It didn't make sense. Why would they help me out, I wondered to myself. Then I came to the realization of what they were really attempting to accomplish. They were controlling the narrative, making me the usual suspect. They were the good old boys that never did any wrong. False transparency is what I call it. When people in power want to convince you that they are doing the right thing, they give you false updates or, as Number Forty-Five might say, "fake news."

I'm sure Cap knew what they were doing as well, and he was cool as a fan. I took my cues from him, Chemistry, Day, and even Billy. Billy had responsible adults around him all his life, so he had one up on me in the area of trust. I was learning on the fly, but I was learning fast.

The other vehicle pulled off our convoy and sent our so-called hunters on a wild goose chase. Cap's move brought us time to get out of dodge and to the safe house. I looked through the panoramic sunroof to make sure Lynch didn't have eyes in the sky. Okay, maybe he didn't have a chopper at his disposal, but he could have had a surveillance drone. The police department's military budget costs more than the annual budget for inner-city schools. It's no wonder we had worn books in the classroom, and as my favorite TV show host would ask: "Hey, what we doing in the classroom?" I remember the first time I saw the classroom segment on Wild'n Out, it sparked all kinds of questions in my young mind. Sure, they were having fun, but something about that question rang true. I asked my teacher why we didn't have nice books in our classroom like I'm sure her kids had at their White schools. As a result, she made me write 'I'm sorry for asking stupid questions' one hundred times on the blackboard, while the whole class laughed at me.

I'm sure if you know me by now, you know that it didn't end well for her.

After the seventh sentence, I felt stupid. I told her that I know the reason why White people hate us so much is that we were made in the image of God. As planned, she sent me straight to detention, thinking, "Hey, what are we doing in the classroom?" I remembered hearing my mother's clear voice answering, "Not writing that dumb shit ninety-three more times."

Low-Hanging Fruit

Reports said that fruit flies formed a sort of Hansel and Gretel bread trail, swarming down the corridors after a pungent order that clung to the air. As if led by a conductor, they flew in harmony to a low-deep-pounding rhythm. Although their numbers reached that of an orchestra, something about their movement resembled a band. The bugs flew with purpose like a Southern-style marching band, marking a holiday. Trumpets, horns, saxophones, and drums guided their sounds of joy and pain. The bugs flew elated as they searched for a fruit that, by the smell of things, seemed to sit at the bottommost parts of Mount Everest. Apparently, the scent was becoming stronger, sending the bugs into a frenzy. Something about the odor made them crazy and wild, turning them loose, freeing them, and freeing their souls. Suddenly, the buzzing tune became reckless, even immoral. Sin filled the air.

The headlines read, "A Mental Health Crisis Takes the City by Storm." Everyone assumed that something was wrong with the city dwellers. No one ever questioned if something was wrong with the city. No one questioned the civil service workers entrusted with the keys to the city. The so-called gatekeepers went unquestioned. They remained blameless, and the multitude of their victims remained nameless. No one spoke their names. They were just people who were lost to the system, swallowed up in a vicious torrent. Someone flushed them down the drain into a never-ending cyclone. It reminded me of the movie Alligator. In the beginning, someone found fun in flushing a helpless baby alligator down a toilet bowl. No mercy was shown to the helpless creature, as it squirmed against the person who decided its life didn't matter.

And down it went into the sewer system to begin life as the alligator that lived underground. Until one day that alligator grew strong and repaid society for casting it out. In the end, society made the alligator the villain, not the person who created the monster in the first place, abandoning it to fend for itself in a cesspool. The way I see it, the alligator realized that no one had the right to reduce it to an unfit habitat. It had every right to enjoy life above ground. However, when it protested the despicable squalor in which it had to live, it was instantly attacked. Society attacked it for refusing to live in disgust. In other words, the alligator was wrong for acting out against a society that wronged it. Experts diagnosed the poor thing as mad and vehemently argued that the monster neither could be tamed nor domesticated. They claimed that society's ill-treatment ruined the poor creature and never would it assimilate into societal norms, so they had to put the creature down. Once the creature had that welcoming taste of human blood, it had to be exterminated or else it would threaten the dinner plates of more distinguished apex predators who'd, for centuries, feasted on human blood on both sides of the Atlantic. If my memory served me correctly, I was sure, Chemistry used the term corporate cannibals to refer to those pillagers.

Unlike the alligator, having to sift through litter, rushing muddy water, and little lighting to gather its food, the apex predators used night vision goggles and heat sensors to kill their prey. The hunted didn't stand a chance against the full-body armored equestrian men, arriving on a sea of Leviathans. There wasn't a prayer in the world that could save the alligator from the power of the gun. Although the creature never converted to the gun, it ended up dying by the gun. It would die by the gun because the society it lived in loved guns more than it loved God's creatures that didn't conform to its system of oppression. Had the alligator remained in the sewer, or rather in its place, it might still be alive, I distinctly recalled Chemistry schooling me.

I remembered thinking back when Chemistry and I had the talk, what did I know about systems of oppression or being marginalized? Why was he telling me all of this stuff? Although my ears itched for more, inside, I was screaming to leave me alone. I used to watch rated G movies. I barely ever watched PG-13 movies. I couldn't help but feel like he was placing me on a fast track to rated-R movies. Maybe I'd better duck him from here on out, or he'd have me watching triple X movies, and I'm not talking about the ones that Van Diesel stars in either. Instead of going with my first instincts, I continued to show up at Chemistry's mentoring sessions. Little by little, he indoctrinated me into the school of hard knocks. Before I knew it, I was at the top of my class, maintaining a 4.0 GPA, in grown people's affairs, that is. Just as society stole the alligator's innocence, a mad city stole my innocence. I am that baby alligator.

Social media posts read, "Another Sad Tune in the City." People posted distasteful comments like, *'hang in there, what goes up must come down, or you're jingling baby.'* Others claimed that my mother caught hell up in Harlem and tried to Harlem shake the Blues. People described her as strange and said she swung like a pendulum to a different rhythm, a guitar with a missing string. Now, she was that full-grown alligator that grew big from all the shit the city's sewer consumed, from all the shit she consumed. They claimed she was ripe and ready to be plucked from a world that held her up like a pinata, only for Lady Justice to chop her down in a crash ending to a sad, lifeless sound.

The bugs were in a frenzy again, dodging the gossiping flashing lights. I wondered, did the gossiping lights shoot her without her makeup? I wondered if they got her good side or if she still even had a good side. They claimed her bad side should have gotten her admitted. She was unstable, and authorities should have known that she wouldn't survive in a cage. Some tweeters said she was better off legally purchasing an AR-15. Certainly, that would have earned her a one-way ticket to a ward. She would have gotten her fair share of adult gummy bears and a stint in the romper room.

Story captions reported that a fly colony rested on a lone slipper, glistening in liquid gold. I remember reading the word suspension in the caption. The only other time I heard that word used is when I cut class to accept a mandatory call-out at the local poolroom. Reporters used the word to refer to my mom, who was no longer in school. Billy had sung me the words alternate definition. Activists claimed that someone should have been watching her. Where was Detective Lynch? Someone reported hearing keys and a gate ease open around midnight. Where was Lynch while my sweet mother hovered three inches above the cell floor? A river of tears streamed down my face as I imagined those nagging fruit flies holiday feasting on strange fruit.

Chemistry and Cap told me that my mother's suicide served two purposes. One was to draw us from our hiding place, and two was to tie up loose ends. The detectives were cleaning house. I hungered for our Ninja Turtle moment because we had been underground for far too long. Reports claimed that after watching Spider-Man 2, Little Dee tried to scale a thirty-foot prison wall. The tower guard alleged that Little Dee left him no choice. He had reached the bottom of the prison yard's inside wall. With marksmanship, the guard ended Little Dee's life with one bullet to the front of the skull. As if he had reached the top of the wall, his lifeless body crashed down to the floor with the brutal force of a snapping bungee cord.

Headlines read, "Elderly Couple Trapped in 4 Alarm Blaze." The fire was reported over a fire alarm box, a year before the first fire truck arrived, ill-equipped to respond. It wasn't until fire trucks two and three arrived that they were able to confront the fire. Allegedly, the operator thought it was some kids playing a prank. The fire reduced the Davises to a heap of charred remains. Some informed residents from the surrounding vacant blocks called the whole saga Benign Neglect. They remembered a time when more than one fire station existed in the district. Over the years, they recalled watching house after house and building after building burn to the ground as if it were policy. Not long before, criminals moved into the abandoned properties, and crime decimated their close-knit neighborhoods.

Ironically, when Blacks tried to escape to new neighborhoods, they witnessed a similar pattern. Even when they moved to completely different states, the pattern remained. Black neighborhoods around the country seemed to be burning at the same time, and it wasn't the rioters and looters igniting the fires. One elderly man said that it was a national problem, requiring a national response. City officials defunded fire departments that normally responded to fires in minority neighborhoods. He said it was as if the government was telling Black people, *When you play with fire, you get burned*. We burned down cities in the name of social justice, and now they would let our homes burn to the ground. "Ain't that something," the old man said, "fighting fire with fire."

Chemistry later told me that the old timer might have been on to something because the timeline matched. "It all occurred in the 1960s and 70s," he remarked. He didn't put Benign Neglect past the Irish-dominated fire departments either. He definitely didn't put it past Irish politicians such as Daniel Patrick Moynihan, who had the ear of the Oval Office. Chemistry told me that the Moynihan Report became a weapon wielded against Black families, causing him to shake his head at the thought of an informed 21st-century governor's decision to name a bridge after that man, during a summer of protest over systemic racism. Chemistry predicted that in twenty years, a new generation would be knocking down bridges instead of statues. Boy, I sure loved the car chase scene in that Super Fly movie remake, when the white Lamborghini takes out General Lee. I remember shouting out at the top of my lungs, "Message."

I also remembered telling Chemistry that maybe that was the point. I elaborated, "Think about it, if a bridge were named after a Confederate soldier, the state would prosecute to the fullest anyone who tried to destroy state infrastructure." Chemistry gave me a nod of approval, recognizing my thoughts. I further told him, "Just imagine protestors trying to take down a Christopher Columbus bridge." He had to admit that the proof was in the pudding – maybe the stage was being set. Unfortunately, the legacy of the Moynihan Report and Benign Neglect was being subsidized with Black taxpayer dollars. Now that bad policy had resurrected its ugly head and claimed the lives of a stalwart-elderly-Black couple. They were pillars of the community, and the community would miss them dearly. I wondered if anyone would build them a statue.

For the first time that I could recall, Chemistry didn't blame the system. First, he blamed himself. Second, he blamed Detective Lynch. On the night of the fire, Ms. Betty, who by the way lives in her third-floor window, reported that she saw suspicious characters, "White ones," she said, "Hanging around the Davis's first-floor window." We later came to find out that the fire and police departments both shelved the reports that recorded Ms. Betty's account. I remembered voicing aloud the saying that goes something to this effect: *if you want to hide something from Black people, put it in a book*. To that, Cap responded, "If you want to hide it from Black people, file it in a report and then use the legal system to deny them access to the report for decades, might I add illegally."

That's exactly what the authorities did at every level of the justice system. We discovered reports about my mother's illegal detainment. The dialogue between the district attorney and the court was quite disturbing. According to the reports, Judge McCormick called all parties to the bench, and the following conversation took place:

"Your honor, Ms. Hoodie is an important witness in a high-profile murder case. We believe that it would be a mistake to release her on her own recognizance," the female district attorney pleaded.

"Your honor, do you know that my client hasn't committed any criminal act. She's not even under an indictment," the male public defender reasoned.

"Your honor, Ms. Hoodie's involvement in this murder case happens to be a little more concerning than defense counsel would have us believe. The shooter in this case operates out of Brown Housing, which has the highest murder rate in all of New York City. His crew not only operates directly out of Ms. Hoodie's building, but we have strong reason to believe that they are operating out of her apartment," the D.A. said with a straight face. My mother stood there shaking her head in disbelief. They were lying. Little Dee and his crew didn't even sell drugs out of our building or even on our block. When my mother tried to speak up for herself, the so-called impartial judge silenced her. I would have thought that if we had a right to remain silent, then that meant that we had a right to speak up in, of all places, the Court of Law. Chemistry once told me that, 'Silence is an admission of guilt.'

Clearly disturbed by the D.A.'s allegations, the Judge cleared his throat and asked, "Counsel, do you have anything to say about these allegations that the people just made?" The public defender was speechless. He didn't know my mother. Chemistry said that the lawyer probably simultaneously read my mother's non-existent file and spoke to her for all of two minutes. How could he possibly speak on her behalf? He couldn't. The judge had to have known, after encountering numerous defendants in similar predicaments, that my mother's best shot was speaking up for herself. I had even heard countless stories about Black defendants caving into the pressure of facing a long sentence. With the assistance of public defenders, defendants with no criminal histories take plea deals to avoid lengthy sentences even when there's no evidence against them, and to make matters worse, even in cases when they're actually innocent. Chemistry's teenage cousin, Benny, took a plea deal for possession of a deadly weapon. However, they later came to find out that the ballistics report recorded that the gun was inoperable. So not only did he have an unloaded weapon, but the weapon also didn't have a firing pin.

Although Benny was only sixteen years old and it was his first offense, the judge sentenced him as an adult. The kid weighed no more than one hundred thirty pounds soaking wet, but that didn't stop him from serving close to three years in an adult prison with stone-cold killers, doing life sentences. Benny never recovered from his experience as a teen. Defending his manhood, he'd gotten all of his front teeth knocked out. If it weren't for some conscious prisoners intervening, he would have been beaten and raped. Chemistry used to joke that they literally saved his ass! Unfortunately, for Benny, he got a curfew violation while on parole, and instead of serving more hard time upstate, he hung himself in the county lockup. He committed suicide three days before his nineteenth birthday. His mother used his employee of the month picture for the cover of his obituary because it was the last good picture taken of her only child. I don't think Chemistry ever recovered from his little cousin's untimely death either.

I don't think I would ever recover from my mother's death either. Cap and Chemistry promised that even the city wouldn't ever recover from my mom's controversial death, either. They vowed to make the whole city say her name. A Supreme Court Justice illegally sanctioned my mother's detainment. Interestingly enough, the inept public defender derided the Judge's decision to hold my mother against her will. Although the Judge accused the D.A. of using the prison system as some sort of unauthorized witness protection program, he refused to R.O.R. my mother or set bail. He remanded her to the county lockup. Black activists argued that the Judge sentenced her to death. The coroner's report determined that the cause of death was inconclusive. To add insult to injury, they never did find that indictment number. And if it weren't for Cap, they would have swept my mother's case under the already lumpy rug.

It turns out that the Judge, D.A., detectives Maloney and Lynch had a history of collaborating on murder cases. They obtained far too many of their convictions with the testimony of one witness. In some instances, these so-called paid informants testified in more than one murder case. I recalled Cap challenging, "What are the odds of the same witness being present at the time of several unconnected murders?" It didn't add up, but no one cared to listen to a prisoner professing his or her innocence. Routinely, judges, district attorneys, and even lawyers dismissed those claims with the all too familiar "everybody's innocent" retort. They double down with comments like, "There aren't any guilty people in jail." Even after hundreds of Black men have been exonerated for crimes they didn't commit, the everybody's innocent rhetoric hasn't changed. Even after uncovering corrupt DNA experts who sent innocent people to jail based on false DNA matches, people working in the criminal justice system continue to scoff at those who plead innocent. They scoffed at my mother and didn't take any of her claims seriously.

My mother cried her innocence to the bailiff, the prison guards, the counselors, and the medical staff. Each one of them dismissed her pleas. No one so much as picked up a pen and recorded the fact that she was professing her innocence. No one was responsible for looking into her claim. No one batted an eyelash at the unreasonableness of her detainment without an indictment or even a felony complaint. Cap said that confirmed the reality of normal procedures, or rather practices. No one batted an eyelash because they all expected to violate my mother's rights. As far as they were concerned, neither my mother nor any of the other minorities had any rights that a white system of oppression needed to respect. I kept hearing the words, *'Plessey V. Ferguson'* repeatedly played in my head. Although times had changed, systemic racism was alive and well. Chemistry said that until Black folk banded together politically, we could expect unjust things to continue to happen to us instead of just things happening for us. Even as a young man, his words resonated with me. From that day forward, I vowed to remain engaged in the Black struggle for equality in America.

My generation witnessed the First Black family in the White House. Unlike the lies told by Number Forty-five, in school, we fought for the privilege to learn from diverse teachers who taught a progressive curriculum that refused to shy away from uncomfortable topics like slavery. Our school was forced to embrace the 1619 Project because it taught about America's real history, not the whitewashed version of George Washington never telling a lie. Never in my wildest dreams could I have imagined that my mother's legacy would include changing school curricula, police reform, criminal justice reform, affordable housing, equal employment, and voting rights!

Cap and Chemistry turned out to be the men of their word. They turned the city upside down, ridding the city of all the rotten apple trees. Of course, they didn't do this all on their own. They benefited from my assistance, but I have to admit that I had stakes involved. I wasn't going to let Lynch get away with what he did to my mom. I certainly wasn't going to stand by while the city remained blameless. No. Chemistry had taught me better than that, and besides, I owed it to Mr. and Mrs. Davis. No matter how much I remained ambivalent about our relationship, I owed it to my mother. We owed it to my father and to the countless Little Dees and Bennies living an American Nightmare.

Grass Roots

One day, I got a frantic call from Marisol, claiming that she thought someone was following her ever since that day at McDonald's. Cap warned that it might not be the last time that the detectives would involve Marisol. He reasoned that too many people witnessed them snatching her the first time. There was no way to know if someone got the department-issued vehicle's license plate number. Not to mention the various street cameras that held footage of the incident, moreover, he was certain that the detectives realized that she was in the parking lot of America's most popular food chain, like McDonald's had cameras. Cap remained convinced that they weren't after her. They were after me. I was the last loose end that they needed to tie up, with a toe tag that is. They underestimated the wrong kid. I knew I lived in a bad city that swallowed Black boys alive. I knew that my life didn't mean any more to these particular White racists than it meant to the White racists who killed Emmett Louis Till. My mother told me that to a bigoted racist, my life didn't matter more than Trayvon's, Tamir's, or Michael's young Black lives.

Marisol's life didn't matter to a bigoted racist either, but her life definitely mattered to me and all the people who appreciated her Black excellence. She was amazing, and she always had my back, too. There was no way that I wouldn't have her back. I hadn't checked back with her after the cops grabbed her, and I never did mention the videotape to Chemistry or Cap. At the time, I was still in the process of vetting Cap. Although I trusted Chemistry, I didn't know Cap from a hole in the wall. He checked out, and now I had to bring all parties up to speed. My friend's life depended on it. Repeatedly, the detectives demonstrated that they were willing to send messages sealed with the kiss of death.

Mr. and Mrs. Davis's murders weren't so much about tying up loose ends as they were about intimidating us. We needed to stay in our place even when a lynching was taking place. Imagine that! This was the 21st century! I thought to myself, as I walked up to Cap, Day, and Chemistry busy in what I called the war room. The room was littered with computers, big projection screens like those found in the NBA replay room, and the office chairs were all fitted with roller blades. It seemed like we were on an episode of the TV show CSI Miami because the heat was on. However, we were standing our ground in the kitchen.

I copped a squat in my favorite chair, planted my feet firmly on the floor, then launched off, scooting across the floor, and then twirling the chair around to face them. They weren't the least bit amazed because they'd seen me pull this number many times. Normally, I'd go about my business, shooting back across the floor where I came from, but today was a new day. Today, I would take over the war room and commence a debriefing about highly classified information. It was my time to shine, and I wouldn't blow it. Everyone except me had provided valuable intel up to this point. Billy even came through in a big way, confirming my suspicions about Marisol. Although I thought I was mature, I hadn't made my mark. Cap continually tried to convince me that I was the most important piece to the puzzle and that I would be responsible for getting us across the finish line. I know he was just trying to cheer me up, but I'm not content with being anybody's slouch.

Clearing my throat, I spoke loudly, demanding everyone's attention in the room: "I have some important information that may help us crack the case. Well, you see, uh, my friend Marisol thinks that the detectives are following her. She kind of gave me a video of the Little Dee shooting that wasn't really Little Dee shooting the gun. I sat on it until I could do some further investigations on the matter." Before I could get another word in, I heard a resounding, "WHAT!"

Cap sounded off first, then Day admonished me, and finally Chemistry chimed in, chastising me. I don't know how many times I heard the words "What were you thinking?" or "Are you crazy?" come out of one of their mouths. Even Billy mumbled under his breath that I must have been losing my mind. They called me everything under the sun except for a "Little stupid mother, you know what!" that was reserved for my dead mother. I could swear that I heard her voice from six million feet under. Her vocal cords were still intact, and she was definitely looking up at me.

Taking a deep breath, then exhaling, Cap said, "Hoodie, you really should have given us this video as soon as you got it. You could have really endangered your friend. Now I understand that you didn't know me or Day, and that obviously caused you to feel some valid reservations about divulging sensitive information to us. Nevertheless, you took a big risk by holding on to something of this magnitude. Do you have the video?" He ended with a question. I didn't want to make Billy look like my accomplice, but I didn't want to prolong things any longer. I was caught between a rock in a hard place. Cap left me no choice.

"Hey, Billy, come here for a second and bring your phone," I demanded.

"Bring my phone. Bring my phone for what?" he asked suspiciously. He heard everything that was going on, and he genuinely wanted to know what his phone had to do with anything.

"I need to see it because I stored something in it," I responded.

He came charging into the room with the phone in hand and demanded, "What did you install in my phone? You'd better get it out of there right now!" I could see by the look on his face that he meant business. I think Cap even realized that Billy didn't know anything about what I had done. I had to admit that I felt bad about duping my own friend. I figured if the bad guys ever got their claws on us, the less that he knew, the better off he would be. I opened the storage app and entered the password, releasing the file. I then handed the iPhone over to Cap. Cap's eyes nearly popped out of his head at the sight of the video. The video was clear. It showed everything from start to finish. The girl happened to be taking a selfie at the exact moment that the murder transpired.

"Hey, load this video into the server, file a copy, and download a hard copy onto this USB plug," Cap ordered, handing the phone and the USB plug to Day. Day immediately went to work storing the footage. Cap plopped down in his seat with a stunned look on his face. Clearly, he was searching for answers. His mind was at work. Chemistry and Billy walked over to get a better look at the video playing on the large projection screen. Their eyes became as wide as Cap's whose eyes hadn't adjusted back to normal. I was stunned by the sharp clarity of the video. No one could have possibly mistaken Little Dee for the shooter. It was obvious that he emphatically wasn't the shooter.

"Day pause right there, now zoom in on the shooter's face," Cap requested. With a couple of mouse movements and a click here and there, Day enlarged the shooter's face to life-size detail. "Can any one of you identify the shooter in the picture?" Cap asked. It hadn't even been a full second before Billy jumped at the opportunity to be a Huggie Bear.

"White Boy, shooting people in the head like that. They should put him under the jail," Billy offered with frustration written all over his face. By his tone, everyone could tell that he was disgusted with the violent act. He didn't care about being considered a snitch. He cared about the community. Later, he told me that he hated the way White Boy violated our playground. In tears, he complained that it was supposed to be a safe space. He said that he never felt safe in our neighborhood, and he worried that one day someone might shoot him in the head if the cops didn't do it first. All along, I thought Billy was carefree. I was completely wrong. In many ways, just as a psychotic society stole my innocence, the mad city robbed his innocence as well. That day, I realized that the concerned citizen who Day schooled me about was Billy. He wasn't anybody's snitch!

"That's definitely White Boy," Chemistry added.

"Yeah, I know this guy. His profile should be in the system. I'm going to run a facial recognition check through the database," Day said.

"We need to get to him soon. Maybe he can answer some questions for us," Cap voiced more aloud to himself than to anyone else in the room.

"Got him, White Boy also known as Damon Smith, he's listed as residing at 222 Bank St., Apt. 3A. He's also known for carrying loaded firearms. Confidential Informants have identified him as one of Little Dee's henchmen. He has fifteen prior arrests, everything from stolen cars to jewelry heists. It appears that Mr. Smith beat a couple of homicides, too. One last note, he's listed on the department's armed and dangerous list. Any apprehension of this suspect must be pursued with caution because a violent confrontation is probable," Day warned.

As if he didn't hear Day's emphatic caveat, Cap bluntly said, "I say we snatch him."

"What do you mean snatch him... snatch him... like the Body Snatcher, snatch him?" I foolishly inquired.

Chemistry instinctually spun in my direction and demanded, "Hoodie, you and Billy go to your room." Of all people, I had to be the one to blow the spot up. I knew damn well that we had no business in the room at that time, and they would normally have kicked us out. Billy looked at me and shook his head. Boy, how fast the tables turned, and ain't that a role reversal, I thought to myself.

Attempting to save face, I said, "Hey, I made a mistake," as we made our way out of the War Room. There was no way that I was returning to our room. I provided valuable intel, so I had a right to see things through. Apparently, Billy held the same sentiments, as he copped a squat next to me right outside the doorway. Almost as if they wanted us to hear them, we could hear everything that they were saying loud and extremely clear. We really were going to kidnap White Boy. That's when I realized that they couldn't completely cut me out of the loop. Chemistry didn't know where White Boy hung out, nor did Billy. Shoot, Billy barely ever came outdoors. Marisol and I would always joke that he grounded himself, staying with his grandparents. Ain't that something, now I know the real reason that Billy didn't go out much. He feared striking his last pose for my not-so-favorite artist. I couldn't blame him one bit. Billy gave me a slight nudge, forcing me out of my head. The point was that they needed me, especially when they found out that 222 Bank St. was a fake address.

"What are you so jovial about?" Billy asked. He must have spoken too loudly because he gave up our position. I could see a huge shadow hovering over us, blocking the light that once protruded from the doorway. Yep, Cap busted us.

"You two again, all right, get up and follow me," Cap ordered with a hint of fabricated excitement in his voice. I couldn't believe that of all people, Cap would try to feign annoyance with me. His unconscious smirk gave him away every time. Anyway, we complied and followed him back into the very War Room from which they just gave us the boot. I knew something was up, and I liked it.

Cap continued, "Since you want to snoop around so much, can either of you tell us anything about White Boy's whereabouts?" he genuinely asked.

I have to admit, I wanted in, and by that point, I'd made a conscious decision to commit myself to being an engaged junior citizen. I didn't want any association with the likes of White Boy. He was a stone-cold murderer, and as Billy candidly pointed out, White Boy didn't give a damn about my safety or Breonna's, for that matter. After having human confetti mess up her pigtails, I didn't believe she would ever wear them again.

"Okay, this is the thing: you have to take me, Billy, and Marisol, along with you. I need my team with me," I negotiated.

"What? Your team, no. It's too dangerous to bring you along," Chemistry chimed in, rejecting my position.

"Cap, there's no place safer for us to be while all this is going on. We will be inside of a fully armored vehicle that can stop armor-piercing rounds, it has bulletproofed re-inflatable tires, a bomb-resistant plate installed on the undercarriage, and three-hundred sixty-degree surveillance cameras," I argued.

"How does he know all of this stuff?" Cap asked, amazed at my body of knowledge.

"I read, read, and read," I responded.

"Yeah, he reads a lot," Chemistry confirmed.

"He reads, but not more than I do," Billy threw in, being a show off.

"Yeah, well, whatever I don't read in books I make up the difference with the Internet," I shoot back. Billy knew that he didn't have anything on me when it came to the Internet. He remained afraid of the Internet and social media. His grandparents convinced him that social media was the gateway to hell. It didn't help that every time you turned around, there was a story about cyberbullying leading to some poor kid's suicide. Me, myself, and I knew that the Internet placed all sorts of information at the tip of my finger. I simply looked up the model of the vehicle and punched in a few key terms that led me to the exact department-issued vehicle. And, I found out that it's only issued to special police units, making Cap a squad commander of a tactical unit.

"So, I'm not a part of your team now?" Chemistry asked.

"You're a part of my adult team, not my junior reinforcement team. What, you never heard of Florida Congress members having youth cabinets or heard about junior civics?" I boastfully asked.

"Actually, I haven't. Maybe when this is all over, you can tell me all about those topics," he responded.

"Okay, enough with the charades. Let's just say I take you up on your offer, can you guarantee that we'll at least know White Boy's most frequented location?" he investigated.

"Absolutely, Cap," I responded with confidence.

Looking at Chemistry, Cap acknowledged that I had a valid point about safety. The confines of the sleeping giant that they drove in heightened to a level that was on par with presidential protection. We would literally be riding inside a vehicle that was tantamount to a special-ops vehicle used on foreign soil. Cap also had to consider Marisol's safety, and he knew that as things heated up, people would become desperate to protect what they enjoyed most, their freedom. Especially law enforcement agents, they had an underlying belief that they were above the law, and that somehow the law didn't apply to them, and that they, specifically white officers, could get away with murdering, who too many Americans treated as second-class citizens.

Two hours later, we all piled into the van and headed to Marisol's apartment. I called her ahead of time to give her an idea about what was taking place. 'Boy, it's a good thing that we developed a coded language,' I thought to myself. In the event that anyone was listening, they would think we were talking about something that took place in the past, and they would think that I was one of her girlfriends. I disguised my voice pretty well. Anyhow, Marisol jumped in the van without anyone noticing her. It was great to see my friend, whom I hadn't seen in some time. The three of us exchanged hugs, and then we group-hugged. Billy was overexcited to see Marisol as well. He did give me my props for demanding that our whole team be included in the operation. He went on and on about how I stood my ground and made such a convincing argument that he couldn't believe that I'm not on our school's debate team. We finally settled down, putting our heads together to focus on the mission at hand.

Just as I promised Cap, we had White Boy in the crosshairs. Dressed like an addict, Day inconspicuously crept up on White Boy. It seemed a bit odd to me that White Boy didn't so much as put up a fight, and he was packing blue steel. White Boy's nonchalant demeanor even troubled Cap. It was as if White Boy knew something that we didn't know, like the laws had changed overnight and ex-felons could become licensed carriers. We all knew that would never happen, so maybe Number Forty-Five signed a purge bill into law. We all agreed that it was more believable. *'I mean, let's face it, the man actually considered nuking a hurricane. I could see the Purge movies inspiring him to give it a world. I really could, though —I mean, I really could.'*

Come to find out, White Boy believed that he was untouchable. Now the only way a trap star believes he was untouchable is if he has lots of cash and a good lawyer – late Johnnie Cochran good. However, when an ex-felon is apprehended with a loaded firearm, that confidence is exponentially diminished. Those of us who knew better knew that his confidence stemmed from the man himself. You see, White Boy was Lynch's confidential informant, or as Cap would say, CI slash made criminal. Like the mafia has made men, law enforcement has made criminals.

These people inform on other criminals with real and false information. They do whatever they're called on to do. Raising their right hands and swearing under oath is what they're good at. It's really not surprising because they have some of the best coaches. In return, CI's slash made criminals receive limitless get out of jail free cards, continuing to live the criminal lifestyle and most egregiously continuing to commit crimes.

Until Cap showed White Boy the video, he didn't want to hear poop Cap had to say. Once Cap zoomed in on White Boy's face, the tattoo on his shooting hand, and the three rings Chat adorned the same hand, which by the way he happened to be wearing, he staffed singing a tune more to Cap's taste. He ratted big time! *But don't take my word for it.*

"I swear, man. I didn't want to kill Pop-man. Detective Lynch coaxed me into making Little Dee think that Pop-man was opening up his own drug spot on the playground. Little Dee didn't allow any drugs to be sold on the playgrounds or near the schools. Somehow, the detectives found out about his motto and used it against him. He didn't tell me to shoot Pop-man. Lynch told me that if I shot Pop-man it wouldn't raise any suspicions because I could always remind Little Dee of his motto, so that's what I did. Lynch told me that Little Dee would take the fall for the murder, and that Lynch would hand me the keys to the projects. He assured me that he would supply me with an endless supply of drugs to get me started and then introduce me to his connect. He put a hundred thousand cash in my hand and told me that from here on out, we were partners, fifty-fifty. He promised to keep the man off of me. He didn't live up to his end of the bargain, and I'm not going down for his murders." White Boy confessed.

"Listen, if you want my help, you're going to have to tell me everything that you know. You just said murders. That's plural with an s," Cap interrogated. Realizing that he slipped up, White Boy just let it all out. It became clear to me that at that point, he was plotting another get-out-of-jail-free card.

"I didn't want anything to do with killing no old defenseless people," White Boy began, and Chemistry's eyebrows practically merged. Sensing the tension, White Boy chose his words calmly and said, "I told the detectives that I'd get back to them. I made up some baloney about some business I had to handle out of town. The next thing I know, I see on the front page of the paper that an elderly couple burned to death in a fire. I knew it was them, man. They said, or rather, the fat one said it was an old stubborn couple—some meddlesome old Folks that didn't know their place. Now I'm not stupid, that was coded slave language for the types of Black folk that have Nat Turner's blood coursing through their veins. I also noticed Lynch's disapproval with the fat detective telling me who they wanted me to knock off."

"By any chance, did you hear Lynch ever call the fat detective Maloney?" Cap inquired.

"Yeah, that's his name. It rhymes with the baloney he was trying to sell me that day." He responded.

"I need something more specific to be certain that they were talking about the elderly couple that was in the papers." Cap requested.

"It's specific enough!" Chemistry blurted out, obviously losing his composure. Who could blame him? White Boy was confirming everything that we believed. Cap gestured for him to be patient.

"Nah, man, he's right. It is specific enough, but to add to your point, they suggested that I make it look like an accident. The fat one's exact words were 'like a fire or something, yeah, something like that.' Then he looked to the silver-haired detective for approval and said, 'Right Lynch, what are the chances the fire department even does a proper investigation in this police? He said that there are many sleepless nights, therapy sessions, and enough moments of doubt to go around." He finished with a categorical, 'Woe to the Black Klan's Man.'

See No Evil

It hadn't occurred to me how much time had flown by as I sat there staring at the computer screen in the War Room. Closed was the sole word displayed on the screen, boxed in capital letters. I spun around in my chair to focus on the other screens that looked identical. I stole a brief smile from ear to ear and swirled back around, planting my index finger down on the button to log off my computer. At once, the entire assortment of computer screens shut down. My smile grew bigger at the thought of Hoodie Sr. finally resting in peace. No sooner than I was about to shut the lights off and call it a night, the phone rang. For a moment, I thought about letting it ring out. I took a quick peek and instantly recognized the caller's number. I immediately answered the call.

"Mr. Hoodie, have you taken a look at the evening news yet?" the caller asked. I could hear the excitement in her voice, so I knew it had to be something good.

"No, I haven't, but I bet you're going to fill me in on the scoop," I responded.

"I'd better if I want to keep my title for late breaking news," she said, and I could hear the smile that spread across her beautiful face.

"Let me hear it," I encouraged her.

Like a little kid, Marisol exploded with detail after detail about Cap leading in the polls. She said that over seventy percent of the precincts had reported. It looked like it was going to be a landslide. I sure hope so. I mean, a grassroots movement fueled Cap's campaign, and he stuck to the issues that he promised to run on. Marisol bragged about how he stood by his base and vehemently rejected playing both sides of the aisle. She said that people were tired of middle-of-the-road candidates who placated moderates and conservatives. Times had changed, and progressive candidates were winning up and down the ballot. Marisol insisted that there was no way that we would turn back now. She reminded me of Mrs. Davis's favorite line, "We've come too far by faith."

"Hoodie, I think we're going to unseat the incumbent president of these United States! Just in, statewide, eighty-nine percent of the precincts have reported. The country is turning blue for Cap. Oh my God!" she exclaimed, overjoyed with triumph. I could feel the tears welling up in my eyelids until I couldn't hold them back anymore. I didn't want to hold them back either. I had been waiting over twenty years to shed these tears of joy. Just as I commenced wiping my tears away, Billy entered the Domestic Terrorism Tactical Unit's War Room with a big smile and a tear-streaming face. He had heard the good news as well.

"Hey, Cap, we did it!" he said and rushed over to embrace me in a hug.

"I told you to stop calling me that. There's only one Cap, and that man is our Commander in Chief," I said with pride-filled emotion. I don't know if Billy was shaking, I was shaking, or we both were shaking with victory. It felt like the Holy Ghost had taken hold of us because I was certain that the Davises were looking down on us. Even my mother was looking after us from only God knows where. Before the night was over, we had learned that Cap had won the popular vote and the Electoral College vote. The American people had spoken, and this was truly a referendum on the incumbent president.

We won on a platform that pushed for national voting standards with teeth. The American people wanted voting rights and the means to penalize state and local governments that failed to honor those rights. We won on universal health care and forced Big Pharma to create fair prices. Yet our biggest win came from a long, hard battle to nationalize the educational system. Of course, that bill would be funded by the increase in funds that would result from raising the taxes on the wealthiest Americans, who continually failed to pay their fair share. Cap vowed that they would now because our president knew that the US military's ballooning budget was a direct result of protecting American capitalists and their foreign ventures.

Cap complained that from the railroads to the internet, the government invests to start these global economic platforms, and then the corporations take the lion's share of the profits and use every loophole under the sun to rob the American people of tax dollars that should go to basic social needs. He argued that because the American government sponsored so many of the advances to make America great, the government shouldn't stand for corporate sharks getting over like fat rats. He emphasized how, before corporations hijacked the Amendment of the United States Constitution that was meant to grant freed slaves' equality, rather than granting equal rights to inanimate corporations, corporate CEOs had to gain permission from the citizens to do business in their communities.

Cap told me that in those days, corporations practiced corporate responsibility and helped with building the roads, bridges, and structures that kept the communities functioning in the municipalities or towns from which corporations made their profits. He suggested that I think about it this way: there's something seriously wrong with the wealthiest Americans wanting to keep tax codes that were written before the idea existed of an individual multi-millionaire, let alone a billionaire. He promised to go back to the days of holding corporations accountable, minimizing corporate lobbyists on Capitol Hill, and slamming the revolving door shut once and for good on those money-driven politicians who were corporate lobbyists one day and congress members/regulators the next day. He told his constituents and all Americans that the fourth branch of government had the White House now – the people had the White House!

I must admit, there were plenty of local gains as well. Just last week, Governor Jackson announced a ten-point plan to address police reform. I think that the most promising changes had to do with removing the forty-eight-hour window that allowed police union representatives to prep officers after officer-involved shootings. He implemented a policy to have those same officers' statements immediately taken, and they had to submit to a breathalyzer test to make sure that they weren't under the influence when they fired their weapons. Not to mention the strict measures put in place to address officers who disabled their body cameras. That was grounds for immediate termination.

Former police officer and now Governor Jackson understood crime. He touted the true meaning of defunding the police and reallocated funds to make sure that every single officer in the field had a body camera. He made sure that every police cruiser patrolling New York State was fitted with dash cameras. The footage was automatically uploaded to the cloud so that an independent agency could have equal access to the footage. Governor Jackson vowed to work with the President to replicate that model around the country. Most importantly, he saw record increases in African Americans joining the police and fire departments to help build up their communities.

Furthermore, Governor Jackson led a campaign to change the common narrative that told Americans that they could believe their own eyes when camera footage caught the usual suspects committing crimes, but they couldn't believe their own eyes when camera footage caught some perceived respectable citizens committing crimes. Chemistry's footage from the Little Dee incident, Shi-Shi's cousin's footage, and White Boy's testimony combined weren't enough for certain Americans when it came to convicting New York's Finest of breaking the law. He promised that with changing the narrative, a loud and thunderous public opinion, on the side of social justice, would dismantle even a deafened wall.

Although we didn't win the battle with the Davises' murder, the case brought national attention to police corruption. My mother didn't die in vain either. After several prison guards alleged that Detective Maloney got an unusual clearance to visit my mother the night of her suicide, the News ran the story and pulled up footage to show the American public a snapshot of an overly aggressive Maloney visiting my mother at the hospital. Once information was released pertaining to his disturbing record of civilian complaints, he committed suicide. Even the city's Mayor said that he didn't understand how Maloney remained on the force with over one hundred use-of-force complaints against mainly minorities, but he even knocked quite a few Whites upside the head, too. The city settled in over ten cases, making the Mayor one of his enablers. While the month of December marked Maloney's death, no holiday tune complemented his demise. There wasn't a cord in the world that could hold up his weight, so he chose a self-inflicted firing squad—suicide by cop, ironically, Black cops were the first responders.

For the rest of the homicide squad, with the exception of Jackson, Tori, and Lynch, well they were all tried and convicted on federal charges for money laundering, racketeering, and extortion. Until this day, no one knows how Lynch wiggled his way out of a conviction. Some say that he created a buffer between himself and his squad, making him completely isolated. Others say that he became a Huggie Bear. While I might like the latter version, I believe it was a combination of the latter, buoyed by the former. Lynch covered his tracks so well that the IA, DEA, and the Feds had to deal on his terms, which, without question, made his involvement fall in the highly classified category that only a president could get access to without causing a shit storm. My interlocutor and I were just pondering that last thought before Billy rudely interrupted us out of our subconscious. He shook me to draw my attention to the television screen hanging on the wall in the corner.

"This is Marisol Combs reporting live for Channel Six News. We are here in the Hamptons staring at the charred remains of a beautiful home that once stood. The home is believed to be owned by a quiet elderly couple. Neighbors say they don't know if the couple was home when the four-alarm blaze tore through the home like a raging bull. Many folks of this upscale community are blaming the Fire Department for their slow response to the fire. Many questions remain unanswered, back to you at the station, Chemistry."

"Thank you, Marisol. Hopefully, Fire Chief Day can answer some of those questions because credible sources are claiming that a power outage occurred around the time of the fire, coupled with an unusual caravan-traffic jam on the Patrick Moynihan bridge, disrupting response times. It will take some old-school investigative techniques to find the underlying cause of this tragedy. It appears that there will be no eye in the sky to assist with this one. This is Chemistry Davis for Channel Six Evening News signing off."

TO BE CONTINUED